American Rap Star

Thank you for taking time to read 'American Rap Star'. I worked extremely hard on it and I hope you enjoy!

Please leave a review on Amazon after reading and also check out my other titles 'American Boy' 'American Maniac', and 'Us vs. Them.

-Kevin Brown

Intro

"Come on, tighten up, focus. You can do this," Sharly Green spoke as she raised her perfectly rolled joint to her lips. After lighting, she closed her eyes, reclined back in the seat of her BMW and took a well needed drag. "You can do anything," she said, as she exhaled the smoke from her lungs.

In approximately 15 minutes she's set to partake in an interview that will undoubtedly take her career in journalism to a level in which she'd dreamed about for as long as she could remember. Not at all a stranger to hard work, in moments such as this she's usually focused, eyes on the prize. But today was different. A lot different.

The oldest of five girls, there was never a family matter or any matter at all that could be withheld from her. Of course her younger siblings weren't too fond of having their older more mature sister in every bit of their business. It's just that it was impossible not to. Secrets were sorta like a myth around their household. Sharly could sniff out any inkling of info from a mile away.

She just had a special knack for it. Sorta like a trained detective. But a gorgeous one. The worst kind, the kind with the ability to scrape out a juicy scoop by simply batting her eyes and asking. This tactic would work extremely well in the future in regards to men but that's a whole other story. We're talking about her sisters right now. The same sisters who couldn't so much as fail a math test, let alone sneak a boy into the house without Sergeant Sharly finding out before it even happened.

With any piece of information obtained she always had the power to analyze and blossom it into to a full blown story. It was her God given talent. A talent in which she fully embraced. Some people can go through their entire life not realizing their true calling, so for Sharly to obtain hers before puberty was a blessing.

At least that's what Nana always said. She was the first to notice her eldest granddaughter's talent. To this date she'd been not only Sharly's, but the entire family's backbone. With her age came great wisdom. Wisdom in which she cleverly dished out while never once seeming preachy or judgmental. Every word she spoke came off genuine, her tongue was filled with love. Actually everything about her was. Beautiful inside and out, not a person in the world could come across her and feel as though she hadn't touched them in some way. She was truly sent from above.

This was never more evident than the day Tamika, Sharly's mother passed away from cancer. With no Father around Nana recieved full custody of the girls. Never once complaining. She took on her responsibility with honor and dignity. Immediately rearranging her life, she put the girls in front of anything she personally desired. Without question Nana was a natural born leader who made it her duty to make sure her Grandkids walked her same path.

Selling her Beachfront Malibu Condo, she instead purchased a family home in the sunny hills of Los Angeles. As you can tell Nana wasn't your typical Grandma, she was a go-getter. Not only was she rich in spirit, she was rich in terms of materials also, allowing her to raise her Granddaughters in the lap of luxury.

Not only did she spoil them with illustrious gifts and trips, she gave them something far better. She made sure each of them had a purpose in life. With Sharly's gift of searching for the detail of the detail and being able to express them in her writing, she encouraged her to become a journalist. While also affording her every opportunity she needed to be successful.

And no, Nana never, ever showed favoritism. All five girls were sent to the most prestigious 'Mary Brown Prep', one of the finest private schools in the entire country. There, Sharly could focus on her writing.

Deshara, who was counting to 100 by the age of 2 was taught by the most knowledgeable mathematicians around as Breona aka speedy was able to expand on her athleticism, excelling in basketball, tennis and swimming.

While Tamara, studied under some to the greatest artiste of the era. And Khana, well Khana didn't necessarily have any visible talents but like always Nana somehow still managed to make the best of it, allowing her to sorta explore different aspects of learning, resulting in her growing up to be a free spirit, but not just any ol free spirit, a happy free spirit.

Nana always taught that happiness was the key to life, with happiness nothing else mattered. Not money, not clothes, spouse, nothing, because with happiness, all of that can and may be included. But with materials, happiness wasn't always a part of the deal.

Throughout their upbringing Nana also managed to keep the girls so occupied that although nothing could mask the pain of losing a parent they were still some of the most joyous young lady's one could ever encounter. Polite, courteous, loyal, basically a walking, talking reflection of Nana.

That's the reason Nana's mental state at the moment is so hard for Sharly to cope with. Two years ago, she was diagnosed with Alzheimer's. The same woman who refused to let life ever get the best of her was being defeated mercilessly. Now equipped with a murderers stare, Sharly sometimes wondered was her Grandmother possessed.

As a tear drop formed and slowly slid down Sharly's beautiful yet stress riddled face she sucked in her joint once more before stating, "You know how important this is. Get yourself together."

She then took one last deep breath, gaining her composure before stepping out into the world with a smile. Nana always said, 'never let them see you sweat'. So as she strutted, shoulders back, head high towards the front door of Nana's house, she smiled at Mrs. Monroe, Nana's next door neighbor as if everything in life was peaches and cream.

"Hey Sharly. How's everything?" asked Mrs. Monroe. Her frail body sat firm in her rocking chair, swinging away as the spring breeze blew through her shoulder length salt and pepper locks.

"Everything's great. How are you? I love what you've done with your hair."

"I'm just enjoying life. Thanks," said Mrs. Monroe with a smile.

"No problem," replied, Sharly, hoping the conversation would soon be over.

"Is your Grandmother doing ok? Haven't seen her come outside in a bit," she asked curiously.

"Yeah, she's actually doing a lot better."

Sharly always lied to people anytime they ever questioned Nana's condition. Fuck that. She knew her Grandmother didn't have too much time left. Therefore she made it her duty to ensure that every memory people had of her would be positive.

"That's great. Tell her I said hey, will ya."

"Will do." Sharly said, annoyed.

Bearing a faux smile she thought to herself, 'Doesn't her old ass know what Alzheimer's is? Nana doesn't even remember her own Grandkids. She damn sure don't remember you.' "Lord give me the strength," Sharly said to herself as she opened the front Door of Nana's house.

"Get the fuck off me bitch. Ugly Motherfucker," screamed Nana as she viciously swung her aging arms towards Deshara. Being that Deshara was substantially bigger in size it really wasn't the fact that she couldnt defend herself, it was more of her trying not to hurt Nana.

"Nana. Stop. You need to go back in your room," screamed Deshara.

"Fuck you," yelled Nana as she backed away.

Rushing over. Sharly attempted to save the day. "Oh my God what's going on?"

"I leave her alone for five minutes. Come back and she walked out the damn room and fell on the floor. I pick her up and try to take her back in the room and she goes crazy."

"I don't need no damn help Bitch," shot, Nana defensively.

"Nana, just come in the room. I'm going to turn on Family Feud and get you a snack," said Sharly, attempting to diffuse the situation. Often times Family Feud was the only thing that was able to keep her composed.

"I can get my own fuckin snack," bolted Nana.

"OK. Ok. Don't you remember you already have a snack in your room," followed Sharly.

Nana looks over confused, not saying a word.

"Yeah, Nana, You already got some apple sauce," agrees Deshara.

"Why the fuck you aint been say that then?" Nana asked, finally letting Deshara assist her into the room as Sharly ran to the refrigerator to grab the applesauce.

"Where the hell is my apple sauce?" blurted Nana as she entered the room.

"Right here Nana," replied Sharly as she rushed in. "Here you go," she said, handing over the goods as Nana snatched the apple sauce cup before plopping down into her rocking chair, staring a piercing hole through the television.

Drained, Deshara and Sharly drag their way to the doorway of the bedroom. "Girl I thought you would never make it," said Deshara.

"I'm sorry. I had to brace myself. Try to get my mind right. You know I'm interviewing Coach today," replied Sharly.

"I know girl. And you know I would cover for you but I can't miss another day of work."

"Girl it is ok. I can handle her. I'm just going to give her whatever she needs and take care of my business. I'm a pro. You know I gets the job done."

"I know girl," said Deshara before giving Sharly a hug. "Good luck big sis. I know this interview is going to take you out of this world. I'm so proud of you."

"Thanks little sis," replies Sharly as Deshara rapidly gathers her belongings before darting out of the door.

"See ya later," Deshara says as she closes the door behind her, leaving Sharly all alone. In silence, she stood observing her new surroundings. In the recent months she'd left her comfy loft in Manhattan where she'd resided since her college days. A place where everything she'd grown to love as an adult dwelled.

Not that it had hurt her career. Being a freelance writer afforded her the ability to travel as she pleased. Not to mention L.A. wasn't exactly a far stretch from New York. It was more of the fact that things didn't feel like home anymore. All of her childhood friends had either moved away or started families of their own. And of course the one person who comforted her in Los Angeles wasn't exactly all there anymore.

Ironically that alone was enough to make the move all the more worth it. There was no way possible Sharly could miss out on the final moments of her Grandmothers life. Allowing her to wither away, alone under the care of some stranger was unfathomable. After everything Nana had sacrificed for the family, relocation was something minimal. Soon, Sharly along with her sisters concocted a schedule in which they would alternate the days that they watched over her.

Like Nana always said Karma was real and for her good deeds Sharly was blessed with an opportunity of a lifetime. For years everyone in the business had tried relentlessly to get a one on one interview with the man, the myth, the Legend, hip hop Icon, Coach Coach. After a career comparable to no other, he had gone into seclusion for the past 10 years after the tragic death of his wife and son.

No interviews, pictures, nothing. Leaving millions of fans religiously dissecting old music, videos, and interviews. Over the years he had slowly morphed into what most would call a Rap God. Soon classes emerged analyzing the many roots of his lyrics, murals painted and countless unauthorized biography were published. After a career so stellar he managed to leave the world in great suspense.

Through his timeless music he had offered so much, often times baring his soul on some of Hip Hops most notable tracks. However he seemed to shy away from verbally expressing himself in the countless interviews he'd participated in over the years. This resulted in fans and historians alike both desperately attempting to somehow figure out the inner details of one of the world's most fascinating beings.

As the days and months flew by it seemed as if Coach was a lost cause. Still Sharly never lost faith. She was raised to believe only the strong survived. Blessed with a gift a consistency and patience she sent Coach a handwritten letter once a week for five years straight, praising his many accolades and pin pointing just why his story like many of America's Hero's needed to be told.

To the world Sharly's method seemed to be crazy, surely she was wasting her time. To her, she had nothing to lose. If he never responded than at least in her heart she knew she'd done all she could. However if he did respond, her life would be forever altered.

So when the day came in which she received a hand written letter from Coach she was overwhelmed. Far from prepared she nearly fainted as she read the words written out to her. Initially she wasn't even too sure of the authenticity of the letter. After all, it could be some asshole reporter playing a dirty prank.

There was only one way to find out though. In the letter he simply gave her a number to call exactly a week from the day. Dedicated and focused on the task at hand, Sharly trained like a fighter, eating, breathing and sleeping Coach Coach. She had to ensure without a shadow of a doubt she asked every question that needed to be answered. Thoughts of the letter being a phony had to be destroyed. After all, Nana always preached to always think positive.

Even as Sharly discovered she had Nana duty on the day of the supposed interview she chose to look at the bright side. She hoped maybe her Grandmother would sorta serve as a good luck charm, ultimately confirming her blessing to not only be true but to be monumental.

As the clock dwindled down and the minutes turned into seconds, the time was quickly approaching to make the call. Trembling, Sharly studied herself in the bathroom mirror. Her light brown skin sparkled as her insides tingled. "You got this," she said to herself, before walking back into Nana's room, grabbing her notebook filled with questions and notes from her backpack and copping a squat at the doorway to Nana's room. "I love you Nana. Thank you for making me who I am," she whispered to herself as she looked over to Nana who continued watching television.

Notepad in hand, phone on record. It was ShowTime. She dialed.

"Hello," said a deep, strong voice on the other end of the phone.

"Hello, is this Mr. Coach Coach," asked Sharly, nervously, clearing her throat.

"Who else would it be? I told you to call didn't I," Coach bolted, shockingly, still sounding as young and as vibrant as he did 40 years prior.

"Yes Sir. I was just was making sure," she said, after taking a deep breath, searching for her confidence.

"Alright yeah whatever. I'ma tell you how we gon do this. I'm gon talk. You gon listen. I don't want you asking me no questions. Everything you need to know will be spoken. And if it aint spoken. Well then you obviously don't need to know. But what I'm about to tell you is some shit that I aint hardly told a soul. Some real deal shit."

"Ok," said Sharly, as she dropped her notepad onto the floor as her heart thumped. "I'm ready whenever you are."

"Ok. Well you better strap up I'm about to take you on one hell of a ride."

Game

Fuck all the bullshit, I'm starting this motherfucker off in the 6th grade. Why? Because aint shit before that matter. I guess I had the life of the stereotypical rapper. Born in a little small ass town Norview, VA, Section 8 housing, teen-age mom, roaches, food stamps, no daddy. Shit, no family at all to keep it real. Well, unless you count my crazy ass Mama. Not too sure if I can even really even call her a Mama, considering the fact I can probably count on one hand how many Motherly things she actually did for a nigga. Bitch never even kept a job for more than a month. And they was all fast food joints at that.

But oh yeah I had a Grandma too, her ass lived with us for a minute before she died. Mean as a mother fucker. Don't really remember shit from her but ass whippings. She beat my ass like clockwork. Before breakfast lunch and dinner. That's how I knew it was time to eat most of the time. I guess when she got hungry, she got angry. Shit I don't really know. I just know her old ass aint take not once ounce bullshit.

But other than ass whippings she was good at one other thing. Grandma could motherfuckin throw down. I swear she made the best food I've ever eaten. See, back then the first of the month was like a national holiday to us. That's when we'd get our food stamps. 12:00a.m. on the dot me Grandma and my mama would walk down to Be-Lo the local grocery store and rack up. For the life of me I can't figure out how we always seemed to run out of food after the first two weeks of the month but I gotta say, it was worth it. During them first two weeks we used to eat like the rich folks. And outta everything, all the soul food, deserts, my favorite had to be her God damn hot dogs with chili, chips on the side and a glass of lemonade. That shit used to hit. Too bad she aint live a little longer though, after she died I was forced on a strict Ramen Noodle and syrup sandwich diet.

My crazy ass Mama aint cook a damn thing. Yeah she mite have kept a clean house but no cooking. No bullshit, I don't even think I would trust her cooking. I'm telling you the bitch was a lunatic. And yeah, I called my Mama a bitch, fuck it, it is what it is, that what she was, a crazy ass bitch. And I aint talking no ol everyday crazy Mama, like yelling at you when you don't take out the trash. Hell naw, I wish, I'm talking about just plan ol fuckin crazy. Like just bust out laughing for no damn reason crazy, the type crazy that just walk through the house naked smoking a cigarette humming Sam Cooke's 'A Change Gon come' while your homies sitting in the living room crazy. You feel what I'm saying? The kinda crazy you don't even get mad at cause you know she can't help it type crazy. That's what type of crazy my Mama was.

But yeah, like I was saying aint shit in my life matter before 6th grade. My little dirty ass was finally in middle school. I had enough of that elementary bullshit. I had already dropped out in the first grade so I was a year behind. And yeah I said dropped out. That woulda been the end of my school career if I could have had it my way. Dumb ass state got in the way and told my mama she would get locked up if I aint stay in school till I was 18. I found out later they was lying but that scared her straight for years. But yeah, fuck school, shit was straight up torture from the very moment I stepped foot in Ms. Stephenson's kindergarten class.

Foreal foreal, I aint even gonna lie I can't blame them kids for not rocking with me. I was dingy asa motherfucker, didn't know not one of them cartoons they used to be babbling about, couldn't tie my shoe, nose stayed on leak and my whole top grill was silver. Wont my fault though, I aint know no better. I had never even been around other kids before. Like I told you, the only people I knew was my Grandma and my Mama. I can't remember foreal but a nigga was probably feminine. Shit, again, if I was, it won't my fault. Aint like I had no damn male role models or something.

Unless you count them old ass nasty ass men who used to come through to have unnecessarily loud sex with my Mama. And it aint like they was really talking to me, them niggas was more so talking at me. Usually telling me to go to bed or something.

So, yeah, I was definitely a damn misfit. Foreal foreal, if I won't me I probably wouldn't have liked me either. Not to mention I was bigger than all of the other kids. Everybody knows aint shit worse than a big ol stanking ass nigga.

Life damn sure aint get no better as elementary rolled along. After kindergarten I barely even tried to fit in. Ate lunch by myself, sat on the bus by myself, even played by myself at recess. Fuck them niggas.

But middle, yeah middle school was gonna be different. A nigga aint have no bed time and my Mama always kept a nigga who did some bootleg cable so sometimes when she would fall asleep I'd have the T.V. all to myself. And on Saturday nights after about 3 a.m. T.V. would just switch over to some Gospel shit. And it if it's one thing I picked up from them niggas was that if you pray. Shit changes.

So that whole 5th grade summer I prayed my little ass off. I just had to get out of that misfit stage I was stuck in. I aint know how I was gonna do it. I just knew I needed to pray. It was two other elementary schools who was joining us in middle school. Them niggas aint know my reputation. I had a chance to start the fuck over. I had already learned to take baths and brush my teeth. I handn't had a haircut in I don't know how long so I aint have to worry about that. Luckily by then knotty afro's had become kinda popular so I thought I had a chance. I had stolen a pick from a nigga in 5th grade, so I was good. Oh yeah and we wore uniforms that the local church had donated to me so I aint have to worry about niggas being flyer than me.

Only problem man, was my fuckin kicks. My Mama aint give no fuck about no damn back to school shoes. She spent her little first of the month checks on weed and cigarettes and by the middle of the month she was always broke, hitting the local plasma bank just to get by. So it won't no way I could ask her for shit.

Her crazy ass probally would have just went off on me and started crying or venting about some off the wall shit that I aint even have no clue of what the hell she was even talking about. But I knew this shoe shit was serious. I aint know what to do though. I knew how to steal candy and dollars from out of kid's book bags and shit but I aint know how to steal no shoes. That shit seemed damn near impossible. And that right there is the main reason I know meeting my nigga Dock was written.

When the first day 6th grade finally hit I made sure I walked to school before everybody. I had to make sure I was the first nigga in class. I found a seat in the back and watched, jealous as a bitch as my other classmates strolled in fresh as hell, new shoes and haircuts. I aint gon lie I was hating. Hating hard as hell. Fuck it though, everybody hate sometimes. I don't care what you say. And that day right there was my day to hate. I would've smacked the taste out of each and every one of them niggas if I had a chance. Shit, bitches too, fresh perms and braids, baby hair all jelled up. Fuck all of them. Cause in my head I was thinking, Elementary school all over again.

That was until Dock strolled in. He didn't have on no fresh kicks either. But he aint look like he gave a fuck. Nigga was intriguing from the second I looked at him. From the first glance you'd think he was a pretty boy. No bullshit, the nigga had to be the prettiest nigga I ever seen. The nigga was so pretty it aint even gay to call him pretty. That's just what the fuck it is. He looked mixed, you could tell he was black, but you knew that nigga was dipped in something. I aint know if it was Dominican, Mexican, Hawaiian, Chinese, I aint have no idea. But I knew regular black people aint come out the pussy looking like that. He had long ass hair. But it was straight like some shit females would pay top dollar for. He aint even comb it or nothing, it was just in a ponytail, wild as hell. Hazel ass eyes, the nigga looked like he shoulda modeled for Gap kids or something.

Still he walked with an edge. You gotta remember this is before my days as a gangster. I was a punk, a pussy.

My first emotion was fear as he g-strolled towards me. Even though I was twice his size his demeanor intimidated me more than any one I'd ever encountered and with each step, my heart took 30 pumps.

Then it happened, the moment that would change my life forever. He through his body down in a seat next to me, no pen, no paper, slouched down and looked over.

"What sup phew?" he asked. Not only was his demeanor like a gangster, this nigga voice was too. Damn sure won't like nothing I'd heard in elementary school.

"What sup," I followed.

"You aint never seen me before?"

"No."

"Nigga don't you stay on 'The Loo'?" he asked.

"The what? Huh?"

"I said nigga don't you stay on Ivaloo St. We call it 'The Loo'. Your Mama the one who be walking down the street in her pink robe and shit."

"Yeah," I replied.

"Yeah I knew that was you. I stay on 'The Loo' too. I'm Dock."

"I'm Skylar."

"Skylar," he said shocked. "Nigga aint that a girl name?" asked Dock.

"No," I shot back.

"Nigga. Yes the fuck it is. Fuck that. I'm about to give yo ass a damn nick name. Aint no nigga from my block gon be named no damn Skylar. Hell naw." he said looking around. "I got it. I got it," he said as he glanced at his schedule that sat on his desk. "Your name Coach."

"Coach?"

"Yep. Coach."

"Ok," I agreed. I never figured out why he said Coach. I didn't even think to ask that day. Later on he always joked and said it was because the first thing he looked at was some girl who had on a pair of women's coach shoes. He said me and the girl had one thing in common. We were both bitches. I don't know if it was true or not but the name stuck so fuck it.

"Now we gotta go get us some more got damn shoes. We can't be walking around school with these busted shits on," he said looking down to his own kicks. To tell the truth I would have killed for his kicks. Yeah they may have been dirty but atleast them shits was Nike. Everybody know they was a million times better than the bo bo's on my feet.

"Huh?" I asked.

"Yeah you heard me. We gonna get us some new shoes next period. I got you. No funny shit. I failed. I was in 6th grade last year. Just follow me after the bell ring, bro. I'ma show you some real shit," he said as the teacher began to talk. "You from my block. Niggas on my block gotta be fresh."

"Ok."

And just like that I met the best friend I'd ever have. And from that moment I knew 6th grade would be different. No bullshit, I think that may have been the day I really knew it was a God. Prayer was real. Dude came through in the clutch. I was siked. Even though what Dock was gonna have me doing for the kicks won't Godly at all. I aint give two fucks. I woulda smoked a nigga if I had too. Shit, foreal foreal, I probally would have smoked my own Mama. Shit anybody Mama for that matter.

After the teacher finally finished rambling on about some bullshit, the bell rang. Dock ran down the plan as we walked the crowded hallways. He schooled me on how all the 7th and 8th graders already were prepared for P.E., meaning they bought extra shoes and were going to put their clean shoes in the gym locker. Only thing was, a lot of them weren't going to have a combination lock for their shit yet. And since the locker room door was going to be locked they really didn't have to worry about any one being able to steal shit. But Dock had found a way around that.

"Come on," he waved to me as we entered the Gym locker room, filled with little niggas lying about how great they summer was. Well at least I though they was lying. Come to think of it, they probably wont, I probably was just so much of a hater by then, I just assumed nobody life could be that good. But anyway we smoothly made our way to the showers and hid behind the curtain. "We gonna wait in here until everybody leaves," said Dock.

"Ok." I whispered.

In my head I'm doing backflips. Do ya hear me? That must have been how regular kids felt the night before Christmas or something.

"What the hell you smiling for?" Dock whispered as he smiled back.

"I don't know?"

"Come on," he said, shaking his head as we finally heard the silence we awaited. We slowly crept out before going off into our separate ways.

I opened every locker, carefully looking over each shoe, I had to make sure I made the right selection. Can't front, it was hard, it was like being at footlocker or something. For a minute I couldn't choose, but then I saw them. As I opened the locker a florescent bright light flashed and the Angel's hummed as I reached in, gently grabbing them. A dead fresh Pair of Air Jordan's 4's. This was the first time I had felt any. They was everything I imagined. Everything I dreamed. Strong, sturdy, nothing like the bo bo's I was used to. I obviously was mesmerized for a little too long cause soon Dock screamed over to me "Hurry up nigga," snapping me out of my zone.

"Ok." I said throwing them on and tossing my old ones in the trash before making my way to 2nd period. Dock and I had separate classes so we split up. Since it was the first day, tons of kids were late, which was good because we didn't draw any extra attention to ourselves.

I walked into class like a brand new man. Winked to the few former elementary classmates who were already seated and strutted to my seat like the boss I wanted to be. Yeah nigga, fresh jays, how the fuck you like me now bitch.

I aint hear a word the teacher said the entire class. I was too busy gawking over my kicks, that shit felt good.

There was no way I was ever going back to the way things were. If I would've known that Jordan's made niggas feel that good I would've found a way to steal them years before that.

Every class was the same. I was the man in my head. I was getting up to sharpen my pencil for no reason, throwing shit in the trash. Anything, to catch niggas attention. I had even adopted Docks swag. You couldn't tell me shit. Things was smooth as a bitch, all the way till lunch time.

"Ay nigga aint they my shoes?" some kid, rocking flip flops pointed as I walked into the cafeteria.

"No," I said. I aint gonna lie I was scared. I had been so siked to have the kicks on my feet I aint even stop to think about getting caught. Shit, I was only in 6th grade a nigga wont no professional thief or nothing.

"Yeah they is. I'm the only one around with blue laces in mine," he said, storming over to me. "Boy, I'm bouta beat your ass," he said as fire shot through his eyes and he got closer.

Little did he know fighting was my specialty. The one thing in life I was good at. Yeah I said I was a misfit and all that shit. But I aint never say shit about a nigga beating my ass. Hell naw. Real shit, they might not have liked me in elementary but them niggas knew not to try me. With all the built up anger I had inside me, I lived for times like that.

So as he stepped into my circle. I looked him square in the eyes and beat his ass up and down the motherfuckin lunch room like he was the one who stole from me or something. Man I whipped his ass so bad, his friend had to jump in. Big mistake. Out of nowhere in the blink of an eye Dock came flying with a Bruce Lee kick, knocking him to the ground before pouncing on top of him beating his face in. Security soon came and yanked us both off, but it was too late.

As I was dragged away. I discovered the entire cafeteria staring at me in Awe. I was a champion. And damn near all of Norview middle knew it. What a fucking feeling. This was the best day of my life. I was geeked up. This was the closest thing to love I'd ever felt. I'd be chasing that feeling for the rest of my life. That was the Day Coach was born. Sept ,1 2000. A day that I will never forget. The beginning of something legendary. Dock and Coach, Norview's finest. No one did it better. And no one ever will.

Street Nigga

After the fight they hit a nigga with a ol petty ass five day suspension. Let's be serious though. You think I gave a fuck? Exactly. I was in the hood kicking it like a fool. Come to find out my block was the most poppin street in the whole town. Dock had only lived there for a year and couldn't believe I hadn't been outside before. I mean yeah technically I'd been outside. But back then I was so embarrassed to be walking with my Mama I used to stare straight ahead blocking out anything around me.

Dock bought me into a whole new world. He even taught me a whole nother language. For instance, 'Jank'; when he first said it I aint know what the fuck it meant. Come to find out it could mean anything; a girl, a date, a dog, my dick. Before long he even had me saying the shit. Not only that but 'foreal foreal' 'No funny shit' and I even found myself calling everybody I came in contact with, 'Bro' or 'Phew'. Oh yeah I can't forget, 'snatch', that means to lie. Later I'd incorporate all that shit into my raps and have the whole world talking like us.

But yeah, my nigga showed me a life full of ghetto adventures. And he made sure I experienced every single one of them to the fullest. See, My Mama was the type to sleep all damn day and with her being the only role model I had, I did the same thing on days when I won't in school. Wont shit else to do. But naw Dock won't having that shit. Every day he woke me up at 9:00 on the dot banging on the door, dragging me to the corner store 'Super 10'. They sold everything for less than $10. Whatever you needed they had it. White tee's, candy, old ass DVD's, CD player, you name it, it was there. It was like the poor man's Wall mart.

Still no matter how cheap the shit was our main objective was to steal as much as we could. Back then our favorite past time is what we called 'stealing contests'. Whoever stole the most shit got to punch the other one in the gut. Safe to say I got the wind knocked out of me damn near every day.

Shit won't fair though. Dude was a pro. But now that I think about it he kinda cheated. He had an unfair advantage. Somehow the nigga always seemed to have some loose change. That way he wouldn't look too suspicious just walking in and not buying nothing.

He always wore these big ass sweatpants and I swear he use to fit the whole damn store in them bitches before walking up to the counter and buying a stick of gum. It was always some old ass church lady with glasses at the register who didn't know what the fuck was going on.

While he was in line I was always able to get a few things but it never amounted to what he had. Over the years though, I stepped my skills up. I couldn't even begin to imagine how much I boosted off of them.

Dock also introduced to me to another neighborhood activity. This one grew to be one of my all-time favorites. It involved Monica, yeah the bitch left eye was a little on the lazy side but other than that, for a 11 year old she was bad, pretty skin, long wavy hair, with a body that looked at least 16; booty, titties everything. She was by far the most appealing person in her family. Everybody else looked like something you'd see on the sci-fi channel or some shit. It won't no way Monica had the same Daddy as them. Everybody in that bitch had some type of malfunction.

TJ, her younger brother was a midget with one ear bigger than the other. Harmony her little sister was severely cross-eyed and teeth like a razor. Jerome, the youngest, well besides just being a ugly ass nigga, he aint really have no visible defects. He was just one of them stupid ass niggas. He'd do anything we told him too. Later in life he'd come in handy but I'll get to that shit later.

Back to they dumb ass family. Won't no way you could blame the kids for none of they misfortunes. Oh naw, they Mama, Ms. Eta hands down had to be one of the top 10 most vicious alcoholics to walk the earth. No bullshit, and she looked just like she smelt, pure shit. Bitch aint give two fucks about nothing but a bottle. Her drink of choice was Old English. Every morning she'd be up at 6 making her way to Be-lo. Ten minutes later you'd see her funky ass with one beer to her lips and another in hand. Throughout the day she'd make about 10 more trips. I gotta give her credit though. I never seen her pass out or nothing. She was strong. Yeah she might've pissed on herself and fell down a few times. But ol Eta always got up and made it to Crib.

Speaking of the crib. Shit was everything you're already expecting. Probably worse though. Them niggas used to have rats fighting on the roof and whenever you walked past the crib it always had this stale, stinky feet smell to it. Even if you was in a whip riding past with your windows rolled up you still could smell it. Just nasty.

Guess I was just as nasty though. Cause no matter how dirty and funky the shit was it aint stop me and Dock from entering that yard to do a little freaking. Yep, freaking was the pass time I was talking about. Freaking was a beautiful thing. And before I go any further, freaking is not fucking. No, no, no it's basically just touching, kissing and dry humping. But to most kids our age it was the closest thing we had to the real thing. And since Monica did everything Dock told her to do, getting our freak on with her was as easy as it's gonna get. So when Dock told her to stay home from school with us on the last day of our suspension she was 100 percent with it.

Her Mom was home but we aint give a fuck and neither did she. This was another Day in which Dock changed my life.

"Look what I got," said Dock as the three of us sat on Monica's porch.

I looked over as Dock held out what looked like a small tree stem.

"What's that?" I asked.

"Oooh," followed Monica, excitedly. She always talked like her mouth was full and needed to spit.

"Nigga this is weed," added Dock.

"What the fuck is weed?" I asked.

"Shit that get you high."

"What you mean high?" I was green as a motherfucker.

Yeah I know I said my Mama used to spend all her money on it but she always smoked joints and truth be told I aint even know the difference between joints and ciggs. I knew one had a different smell than the other but I just figured it was a different brand or something. Shit, how was I supposed to know?

"You'll see. Come on. Let's go in the shed," he said motioning for us to follow him to Monica's rusty garage unattached to the house in the back.

"Ok," said Monica as we followed Dock.

Soon as we stepped in, Dock put the flames to it. The smell instantly let me know that this was definitely what my Mama had been smoking all them years. That alone made me feel more at ease about smoking. Shit, my Mama got high, my grandma used to get hi, most likely my Daddy even got high. Give me one reason why can't I get high?

Dock hit it and past it to me before showing me how to inhale. I hit it, coughed and smiled. I was in love with it from then on out. A nigga felt free. Before I knew it we was zooted, laughing like hell, loud as a bitch, joking about every damn thing.

"Y'all like that shit don't you?" asked Dock.

"Nigga I smoked weed before," replied Monica.

I damn sure hadn't. I aint know what to do with myself. After I finally was able to stop laughing I won't feeling the shit at all no more. My little ass started getting paranoid as hell. Scratching, kicking, and twitching, thinking rats attacking me and shit. I was tryna stay as calm as I could. I didn't want Monica and Dock to see how bad I was tripping. But I couldn't contain myself foreal. The drugs was taking over my body, kicking my ass. No funny shit I was tripping hard. Thought I was doing a good job at hiding it until I looked up and Dock was in front of me shaking me up and down. "Bruh, chill aint no damn rats in here. No funny shit. I aint smoking with your crazy ass no more. You trippin phew."

"Ok, Ok," I said attempting to remain calm. Still I wasn't. I just sat stiff as hell with my eyes closed. I could still hear Monica and Dock though.

"Come here," he said as I heard her move closer to him. I could hear them kissing loud as hell. Smacking and sucking, I had to take a peek at the action. Them niggas was getting it in. Man you should have seen em. Dude was basically fucking her with his tongue. Both hands full, one down her paints while the other was up her shirt.

Nigga damn sure knew how to multi-task cause somehow he still noticed me staring. "Come get some nigga," he said taking a break from the action. Monica turned around too. Eyes low as hell, smiling.

I didn't know what to say. "What?" I asked, stalling.

"Man tell this nigga to come freak on you," said Dock to Monica.

"Come on. What you scared or something?" she said.

"No," I said slowly standing up.

"Come on then nigga feel on her," said Dock motioning for me to come over.

"Ok." I said as I inched over to feel on her butt.

"Nigga that aint how you do it. Put your hands in her paints."

I did as I was told. I started rubbing and pinching as they got back to kissing. I was feeling things I aint even know existed.

Boy oh boy at that moment I truly discovered the art of freakin. No funny shit. Before than I had seen kids in my class touch girl's butts and run. But my nigga Dock took that shit to a whole nother level. He was the freak God. My boy should've held a class called freakanomics or some shit.

We was having a ball. And Monica was having one literally as she reached into Docks paints and as the minutes quickly sped by we damn near had her little ass butt ass naked. That's when suddenly the shed door burst open and along with the bright light of the sun we seen a towering figure.

"What the fuck y'all doing in here?" belted Big Jerome, the Dad.

Damn, how the hell could I forget to mention that nigga? Out of all the weird ass mo'fuckers in his crib. He was the only normal one. To this day I don't even know how he got trapped in that family. I don't see how any normal self-respecting nigga could go to sleep next to Ms. Eta every night. Only thing I can think of is that he was some sorta sick freak or something. If not I just can't explain it. I been trying to for years now. Like what the fuck was up with dude?

He took care of the whole house. The nigga was the only one who worked. That's why it was so crazy that he bust in on us. With all them bums he was taking care of, how the hell he find time to miss a couple hours of work?

We all stood stuck like a deer caught in head lights as he rushed over to us, grabbing us by our collars tossing our little asses outside. "Get the fuck out of here," he yelled.

"Nigga, Fuck you," screamed Dock as he rushed back over to him fist balled up. Ignoring the fact that Dock was only 13, Big Jerome smacked his ass to the ground, hard asa motherfucker. Maybe I should have helped. But I aint even gonna lie. I was too high plus this nigga was a grown ass man, with grown ass muscles and shit. Come on now, aint too many kids would've took that risk. Yeah Dock did but he won't normal. I was still working on being a G, I won't quite there yet.

Furious. Dock yelled in anger. "I'ma be back."

I followed behind Dock as he speed raced his way to his crib. He burst inside the house and let his family know some grown ass man had put his hands on him.

Now I told you Dock was some ol pretty ass nigga. But truth is, he never knew who the fuck his Daddy was. And with his Mama being blind, to be honest she might not even have known what race he was her damn self. She damn sure knew what his big brothers Demetries and Donnell was though. Them motherfuckers was straight up niggas. No if ands or buts about it. Ol gangsta ass, wife-beater, du rag rocking, gold teeth ass niggas. They aint give a fuck about shit but making money and fucking hoes.

But most importantly respect. And touching they little brother was the ultimate form of disrespect. Yeah, they fucked him up on the regular. Even made me and Dock fight at times. But if you touched they little bro without permission, you was dead. No funny shit, them times when they made us fight, I probably could've beat Dock ass foreal but I aint gonna lie them niggas was too crazy. They carried they pistol like a I.D. and stayed coked up. Wont no way I was gonna cross them and make them mad. Fuck that.

Jerome had barked up the wrong tree and he aint have no idea what he had got himself into.

"Fuck nigga, you touched my little brother?" asked Donnell the smaller of the brothers to Big Jerome as he stood confident in the door way of Big Jerome's home.

"Yeah I--," Jerome attempted to speak before Demetries speared him into his own living room as Donnell rushed in standing over top of them with the gun drawn as Demetries proceeded to beat his ass as the kids and drunk ass Eta screamed in horror.

"Shut your bitch ass up," Donnell yelled as he pointed the gun to the family.

They all listened as Demetries hopped up from their bloody father as Donnell dropped to the ground slamming the gun into Jerome's mouth.

"What you wanna die, motherfucker?" Demetries asked as Jerome quickly shook his head in fear of his life.

"Don't ever touch my God Damn little bro nigga. I'll smoke this whole damn retarded ass family. I swear to God. We don't give a fuck." said Donnell.

"Don't give a fuck," repeated Demetries as his chest pumped out back and forth.

"You see them little niggas right there," he said pointing back to us as we stood in the doorway.

Jerome didn't speak fast enough. Donnell smacked him with his left hand. "You see them," he screamed as Jerome nodded. "They can do whatever the fuck they want. You understand me?"

Jerome nodded again. Thanks to Demetries and Donnell, from that day forward Monica was free to get freaked on daily.

Turn Around

As far as Norview Middle school was concerned, I was that mothefucking nigga. Straight up. Won't nobody fucking with me. Hanging with Dock had my confidence through the roof. I walked in school and my new found popularity was as clear as day. Suddenly a nigga was the shit and I loved every second of it. Niggas giving me dap. Bitties giving me hugs. In my head I'm thinking 'I don't even know you' but fuck it 'What sup'. Even the kids from elementary had a new attitude. Them niggas acted like they forgot who I used to be. Shit, I was fine with that. Fuck it, I'll forget too.

It was obvious me and Dock had been the topic of conversation around that bitch and the whispers only continued as I strolled down them long hallways. The reason being, I still sported them motherfucking Jordan's. Yeah nigga, I aint give a fuck. But shit, I had full permission too. After never doing shit for a nigga, my Mama finally did me a solid. When administrators told her what I had been accused of she looked them Crackers square in the eyes and told the greatest lie I'd ever heard up until that point. "Bitch, I bought my son these motherfucking Jordan's. That boy's a God Damn lie."

Tears nearly shot out my eyes. For the first time I wanted to hug her. Maybe she did really love me, shit I don't know, truthfully I aint even care why the hell she did it. I was just siked that she did.

With that being said, something inside me couldn't' wait to see the nigga who I'd fought. What was his bitch ass gonna do now? Huh? Huh? Nothing. That's what. He wont gon do a God Damn thing. He aint want to get that ass beat again. He knew what time it was with me. Too bad I never saw him that first day back. Or maybe I did, and just didn't notice, I don't know, with all the love that was showered on me I couldn't really tell.

Everybody was in my damn face. Some even complementing my kicks. Girls playing with my hair. Telling me they liked the scar on my cheek. Liked the scar on my cheek? I couldn't believe that shit. I had always been so ashamed of the shit. Niggas in elementary always had some slick shit to say about it. To this day I still think it's ugly as hell. How I get it? Shit who knows. I can't remember a time when I didn't. Aint like I got baby pictures or anything. But fuck it I'm just glad whatever it was happened the way it did. Two more inches up and I probably wouldn't have a left eye. I guess it worked out for the best. After a while, I just started using it as a conversation piece. I can't tell you all the lies I made up about it.

Sometimes I said I was hopping a gate and my face got caught on one of the wires. Other times I said I was fighting the Police and one of the Cops got so mad that he scratched me. I just used to make up shit. I was young, I aint know no better. Fuck it.

Again like the first day, I sat in class and aint learn a damn thing. I was too busy using my skills Dock had taught me the prior week. I was stealing my ass off, shit I was even taking shit off the teacher's desk for no reason. Just wilding.

But stealing aint even compare to the amount of freaking I was doing. Boy, Boy, Boy, I was freaking my little ass off. I must've felt 100 different booties that day. And I don't know how I got in it but somehow I got placed in chorus class. That shit was like booty heaven or some shit. For some reason niggas aint like to sing so that left the class uneven as hell, 20 girls and about three boys. Shit was a all-out freakfest. Naw, naw, naw, I know what you thinking. Probably thinking, yeah this is where my love for music came. Hell naw, I aint do shit but fall more in love with bitches.

Growing up a wack dude had really fucked my head up. I guess I hadn't really been looking at girls foreal because in my head I knew I couldn't get them. But in 6th grade I noticed everything about they ass. I loved the way they talked, smelled and walked. And it was so many to choose from in chorus class. Ghetto ones, fat ones, short ones, freaky ones, boy that shit was off the damn chain. Real talk. Damn!

But like every other thing in life, its always one that's your favorite. And my favorite girl was Alex. Alexandra Parker to be exact. Her little fine ass wont in none of my classes or nothing. She didn't even go to elementary school with me. All I knew was she'd just moved into this big ass house on the corner of my street. I knew she was special just from that house alone. All the rest of the cribs on the block was run down but they had just built hers. For the life of me I can't figure out why the fuck her parents moved on our raggedy ass street but I'm damn sure glad they did.

Man Alex was so God Damn fine I don't even really know how to describe her. You know what I'm saying? You ever just look at someone and it just give you a little feeling? Like a feeling you don't know the words for. But you just know it's a good feeling. I lie to you not when I looked at her it's like I looked at Heaven or something. Like she was everything I wanted. And I aint bullshitting. I'm talking about from the first second I seen her. And it won't never on no shit like, I wanted to go freak on her. It was some shit where I just wanted to know everything about her. I wanted to lay on the beach and draw hearts in the sand or sit on her roof, holding hands watching the stars or some shit. And look, don't think I'm no soft ass nigga. But I swear that's just what she did to me. I'm just being honest.

I'm telling you, she had to be the prettiest 11 year old on earth at the time. I'm talking better than movie stars and everything. Man just talking about her give me that same feeling from when I first seen her. She was just everything good in life wrapped in one. Like she just had a halo hanging over top of her or something.

And then her smile, ah man, don't let me get to talking about her smile. Shit was hypnotizing. And she had the cutest little gap in her teeth that appeared every time she laughed. Damn. Her whole face would light up and she had the most beautiful skin. Not a blemish in site. And her eyes, just big and bright. Oh my God. I can't even talk about that no more.

Oh shit I aint even tell you how I even met her. I remember it like it was an hour ago. Friday night game of 'Nigga Knock'. One of the first times I'd ever chilled with the kids in the neighborhood. Shit was popping. Everybody having a ball. But at the same time I'm trying to figure out just how to get close to her.

Before I go any further, if you don't know, 'Nigga Knock' is, it's sorta like the equivalent to 'Ding Dong Ditch; or something. We banged on doors and ran. Shit used to be fun as hell. Dock always made sure we played games that made it easy for us to freak off on the girls and shit.

But yeah, it won't no freakin on Alex. I realized she was different right off the bat. She aint even seem like she even liked niggas foreal. I mean it was 6th grade, even though most girls did, it still was a few who didn't give a damn about us. But foreal they was few and far between. Especially living on 'The Loo', everybody knew them bitches was some little freaks.

Like I said though, Alex aint play that shit. I told you she won't from 'The Loo" and I knew that night that wherever the fuck she was from they aint like niggas like Dock. Learned that the moment he smacked her on the butt as we ran down the street after knocking on someone's door.

The smile she had, those sparkles I was talking about, vanished. Gone. She transformed to the Devil in 1.5 seconds. Steam shot from her head and fangs sprouted from her mouth followed by thick ass drool as her eyes focused, smacking the taste from that nigga Docks mouth. I'm talking bout hard as hell too.

For a second he looked like he was going to hit her back, he laughed it off though. I can't even tell you why. Never seen him do nothing like that before. Probably knew she was special. Either way that was my first and last time seeing anybody, male or female lay hands on that nigga and get away with it.

Still though, five minutes later Alex was back, the beautiful girl that I had fell in love with. Looking good asa bitch. Her Mama light as hell damn near white so you already know her hair was long as shit. But it was that dark thick shit and it was always on point. Especially that day. Shit was all shiny, flowing in the wind, baby hair laying down just right as she ran bowlegged down the street.

Can't even snatch. She aint have no body, she was skinny as a twig. But that shit aint even matter. Alex was perfect. I can talk about her forever. I was gone.

The whole night I eased dropped on every word she said. I made sure I was close to her at all times. She aint even look my way one time foreal so I knew she aint notice me. But I aint care. I still heard everything she said. I made it my mission to know anything it was to know about her.

I ended up telling Dock later that night how she had me feeling. That nigga was hating though. He laughed at the shit. He figured if he aint have no chance than nobody did. In his head, she had to be gay or retarded or something. But the way my life had made such a drastic change. I knew I had to strike while it was hot. You know what I'm saying? I was on a roll and might as well keep it going.

I might not have had as much hands on experience as Dock but I'd sat in the house watching so many damn lifetime movies with my Mama over the years that I knew a little something something about women. And anytime one of them crazy ass white boy's wanted to win a girl over, they always found out what the bitch was into, and made sure they got it for them. So after eaves dropping that night I already knew what I had to do when I got back to school from suspension.

So that first day back, I searched high and low for her and after having no luck for the first half of the day, I finally spotted her sitting with a gang of her friends in lunch. In my head it was now or never. Without saying a word to Dock or Ugly ass Chris and Weak ass Chris, who were two of my new homeboys who stayed on my block, I sprung from my seat, back pack in hand, sweat dripping down my body, legs trembling. Fuck it though, yeah I can't lie my brain was spitting out hundreds of reasons why that shit wont gonna work. But I was a soldier, I fought that shit and kept trucking. Yeah, I almost turned around a few times. But I didn't. I walked up behind her and as her sweet fragrance attacked my nose I said, "Hey Alex."

Every girl including her turned around smiling. "Hey," she said.

Her smile was so bright damn near blinded me. No bullshit, I squinted and said. "I got you something," before reaching in my back pack pulling out a bag of Flaming Hot Cheetos, a hot pickle, and a pack of Watermelon Sour Patch Kids I had bucked from Super 10 the day before. I had heard her saying how she could eat those three things every day for the rest of her life.

"Awww," every girl at the table said damn near causing the entire lunch room to look over to me again. Only this time I won't beating a niggas ass.

"Thank you," she said grabbing her gifts.

I didn't know what to do after that so I hauled ass back to my seat.

"What the hell you just do?" asked Dock. "You got her number or something?" I hadn't told him my plan. I didn't know how he would feel about getting a girl a gift.

"Naw, I just gave her some candy," I replied.

"Some Candy? And you didn't get her number? What the hell kinda shit is that phew?"

"I would've had to get her number," said Weak Ass Chris.

"Yeah me too," added Ugly ass Chris.

For some 6th graders these niggas sure used to talk like they knew what the fuck they was talking about. I didn't even reply back to them niggas though. In my head. I was trying to figure out what my next move would be cause I damn sure wont done.

So far the only thought I had was to write her a note and slip it into her locker. Thank God the stars had aligned perfectly for me. None of that won't even necessary. Five minutes after walking over, I endured yet another life changing event.

"Alex said call her today, but don't call after 7:30," said Tiara, Alex's best friend as she stood behind me, passing me Alex's number on a small napkin.

"OK," I said, looking over to the girls table while Alex and the rest of her crew stared over to me giggling and waving as Tiara walked away.

"Yeeed," screamed all my homies as they congratulated me.

Life couldn't get no better. Real shit. I could've died right there and I wouldn't have gave a damn.

Beat it Up

Man the school year was moving along smooth as hell. I can't even snatch, everything was going just how a nigga wanted. After a couple nice talks on the phone and shit Alex had become my bitch. Damn, excuse me I don't even like calling her that, I mean my girl. You already know a nigga was happy then a motherfucker. She was letting me copy her homework. Braiding my hair. She was the shit. Foreal foreal.

We was the couple everybody wanted to be. I was walking her to class, giving her hugs and kisses in front of everybody, nothing too major though. Yeah we might throw in some tongue from time to time but we aint never get too X-rated. Alex won't that type of girl.

Can't lie though. I aint gon sit up here and act like a nigga was all faithful and shit. Yeah I had a few hoes around school that I used to freak down and what not but they aint mean shit. I was just doing what niggas do. On some real shit, I think I was just doing the shit to be cool. Won't like touching butts and shit was really doing much for a nigga. Don't get it twisted I aint saying I was gay or nothing like that, I liked girls and shit. It's just that I was young, and as far as that sexual feeling that niggas have was concerned. I hadn't really got there yet.

The Wayans Bros. 'Don't Be a Menace 2 South Central While Drinking Your Juice in the Hood' changed all that though. I don't know if you ever seen it but it's this scene where Ashtray is telling his Pops about losing his virginity to some bad ass bitch. Now, in the movie it was supposed to been funny but it was way more than just funny to me. As Ashtray's girl hopped on top of him a sensation shot through my entire body and landed in my ball sack. I aint know what the fuck was goin on. It was like something was stuck inside my dick and needed to be set free. First I thought maybe I had to take a piss, but naw this was different. Dick felt like it had a pulse or some shit.

A young nigga aint know what to do, so I grabbed it, I swear it was rock hard. Something told me to yank it. I did, but then remembered how all the niggas in school used to talk about jacking off like it was the Devil or some shit. The way they spoke down on it won't no way I was doing no shit like that. Hell naw.

That thought lasted about 10 seconds. Fuck that. This was a feeling I couldn't fight. I won't nowhere near strong enough. Shit I aint even wanna fight it to be honest. Besides wont no way nobody was gonna find out. It was going to be my very own little secret and if niggas ever joked about it than I woulda just lied like them niggas was probably doing anyway. Fuck it.

So I hopped up, grabbed some lotion from the closet and stepped into the bathroom. Dropped my pants and draws down to my ankles and looked down at my little man. No funny shit, I was proud, I hadn't never seen it look like that before, all strong, sturdy and attentive. It was only right I flexed in the mirror one good time. I was a man. A horny man and I couldn't take it one more second.

I squeezed the warm lotion into my right hand and slapped it on to my dick. "Damn," I said to myself as I slowly began to massage it. My lips quivered as I experienced by far the greatest feeling I'd ever came across.

I'm picturing every girl I ever been attracted to, naked, getting dicked down by me. Within two minutes I had damn near fucked half of Norview and just about every actress or female celebrity I could think of. What the fuck was wrong with niggas joking people who beat off? Them niggas must've been retarted or just ignorant to what the fuck they was missing.

As I mentally slid my dick into Michelle Freeman, a girl from my 3rd period science class, something happened. It was unexpected. At the time I didn't' know what the fuck was going on but as my knees gave out and my dick erupted I felt an out of this world feeling that I will never forget. I stood speechless for what seemed like forever as I attempted to comprehend what the fuck has just happened.

At the time I thought the lotion had gotten caught up inside my pee whole and contaminated my piss or some shit. A nigga started panicking. It was white gunky shit everywhere. "Aw Shit," I said. Man I really thought I had broke my dick. I prayed to God I didn't though. After what I'd just experienced, shit, if it was broke I was damn sure gonna find a way to fix it. Fuck that. I'll be damned if I won't gon get the feeling again.

I stood there, thinking, thinking hard as a bitch as my dick slowly shrunk back to its regular every day size, when suddenly the door burst open. My dumbass was so damn horny I had forgot to lock the bitch.

"Get out, I gotta use the bathroom," my Mom said barging in before laughing hysterically as I stood stuck.

"Ma. What are you doing?" I screamed finally moving, dick still in my hand.

"Look at you beating your little dick. Gotta little dick just like your daddy," she said laughing even harder.

"Ma," I screamed as I quickly pulled up my pants.

Ok, so I aint know too much about big dicks and little dicks. Yeah, I heard jokes about niggas having little dicks and what not but I aint never give it to much thought. So her saying that really aint mean shit to me. I was more focused on one word. Daddy. Daddy? Her crazy ass said my 'Daddy'. In all my years I'd been on earth she'd never referenced the nigga. Of course I wanted to know about him. I used to think about the nigga all the time. But you already know her crazy ass wont the one to be asking questions and shit. I figured if she aint bring it up, it must be a reason. Plus it was just easier seeing cool niggas and just hoping they was my Daddy. I can't even count all the different Pops I had in my head. A lot of them famous but some was just regular ass niggas like the school basketball coach or some parent of one of my classmates who would bring cupcakes to class or something. A nigga just had to learn to use my imagination.

But yeah, man life crazy as hell. It's funny the only time I had some sort of lead way into asking about the nigga, my dick was in my hand and ass was out. So I guess you already know I aint mention his ass.

"Hurry up. Go beat your meat in your room. I gotta take a shit," she followed with her cigarette dangling out her mouth. "You know I like to shit with my Newport and this my last one. Get out."

Uncomfortable, I quickly forgot about my Dad and shot over to my room. Out of nowhere my dick was fixed again and standing at full attention. So I did exactly what she'd just told me to do. Hopped in my bed and picked up right where I had left off before the explosion. I imaginarily fucked so many bitches that night. Shit was crazy. I hit a couple teachers. Experimented with some midget hoes, even an old Grandma. I was fast stroking, slow stroking, killing shit.

After I came about 5 times I finally got bored with my hand and stuck my dick between the box spring and the mattress. That shit burned like a bitch though, so I just went back to the regular way. Eventually I fell asleep pants to my ankles dick in hand. Besides fighting I'd found my other secret talent; busting nuts. A talent that I would cherish till this very day.

Mr. and Mrs. Perfect

"So is you gonna let me and Coach come over tomorrow?" asked Dock.

"I already told you, yeah nigga," answered Tiara, Alex's best friend.

Growing up, if either me or Dock bagged a girl it was required for the other one to get her best friend. Tag Teaming was one of our favorite past times. We liked to consider ourselves the Greatest Tag Team Duo in the world, together we were certified in bringing out the best in any girls. They loved us together. It's like we would feed off of one another or something and before you know it we had them in the palm of our hands. There was no way possible a bitch could resist the charm of both of us together.

In later years we would eventually start double dating, taking bitches to the movies, out to eat and shit like that. But before all that, it was 4 way calling. That's when someone would call you and then you call another and that person calls another. This was way before everybody had cell phones. Yeah cell phones were invented and shit but aint none of us had one. So our main source of communication was the house phone. Depending on how lucky we were we could talk on the jank all night but usually at least one of us had to get off the phone for somebody else in the crib.

"Ok so what are we gonna do once everyone's at Tiara's house?" asked Alex.

"What you think? Fuck." Dock blurted. I cringed when he said it. Even though I thought about it all day every day I still hadn't mentioned the shit to Alex. I aint know how. I was waiting for her to bring it up but she never did. So I guess in a way I was happy Dock had said something about it. That was one of the reasons I loved Tag Teaming. Truth be told, I benefited way more from Dock than he did me. Foreal foreal, he could've did everything all on his own. That nigga aint need me for shit. "Yo. Y'all acting like some virgins or something. What's up with y'all?" he asked.

"Nigga I aint no virgin," blurted Alex.

Aint no virgin? What? That was damn sure news to me. Found out later she was lying her ass off. In actuality everybody on the phone was a virgin except Dock. But in the 6th grade claiming to be a virgin was like a sin. Don't ask me why. That's just how shit was back then. I aint make the rules I just followed them shits.

"Well stop acting like one. Yo Coach you still there?" Dock asked. "You hear your girl acting like she scared of the dick?"

"Yeah," I replied, nervously.

"Dock shut your ass up. Matter fact both of y'all can shut up. I'm just asking a simple question," Alex shot back. "Tiara you better get your little boyfriend."

"Tiara can't do nothing to me. I run this shit. I'm the man."

"Nigga please," blurted Tiara. "You know what time it is."

"Alright, you aint gonna be saying that when I got your legs behind your head tomorrow, while yo ass screaming my name."

I'm telling you this nigga always had some fly shit to say. Aint no way I would've thought of no shit like that.

"Boy get off this phone. I got people to call," My Mama said interrupting us from the phone in her room.

"Man. Ok," I said.

"Hey Ms. Grant," said Alex.

"Who the hell is this?" my Mom asked.

"Ma that's Alex," I answered, annoyed.

"Oh," she followed. "Hey. Now come on boy, hurry up."

"Ok."

"Hey Ms. Grant," said Tiara.

"What sup Ms. Grant," followed Dock.

"What the fuck," my Mom exclaimed. "Oh hell naw. Hell yall got going on round here? I tell you one thing. It better not run my damn phone bill up."

"Ma. Chill," I said. "Alright yall I'm out," I said before hanging up.

I laid back on my bed thinking of how the hell I was gonna pull that shit off. I knew the real thing was gonna be a hell of a lot different than my hand. Hell yeah I wanted to do it. Wanted to do it bad as a motherfucker. But with Alex saying she won't no virgin and all, I aint want to look like no damn amateur.

I aint think she would, but what if she told people. You could never be too sure about shit. With my new found popularity I couldn't be known as a virgin. It aint match my swag. A nigga was stressing like a motherfucker. Its crazy the type of shit you worry about when you young. Not knowing that life would be getting a whole lot harder in the future.

I aint know what to do with myself though. So I did what I always did around that time when I had shit on my brain. I picked up the lotion and beat my meat till I dosed off.

Before I knew it the time had come. We all sat in Tiara's living room. Just chilling. Her Mama wont home so we had the spot to ourselves. We'd been over there for a couple hours. Everything was cool. Me and Dock had smoked a blunt so my nerves was a little at ease and shit. We was watching T.V., eating snacks, joking, freaking, laughing and what not. Just having a good ol time. Then shit got real.

"Let's go in the room," Dock said as hopped off the couch we'd all been sitting on and reached out for Tiara's hand. Without saying a word she grabbed it before making their way into her bedroom. They both looked back smiling before they closed the door. I was stuck. My high was blown and I knew it probably won't gon be no way around that shit.

Everything was different now. I dropped my head. The tension in the room was thick enough to cut with a knife. I aint even know what to say. I was just there. My body soaking, mouth dry. I tried to lift my head up to watch T.V. but for some reason my shit was heavy than a motherfucker. No matter what it just kept dropping back down. I couldn't focus for shit. I just kept thinking about how as soon as Dock and Tiara came out that room it was gonna be our turn. I couldn't even look at Alex. Sweat shot down my forehead as I took a gulp of my spit.

"What you wanna watch?" I asked, head to the floor, after several minutes of silence.

"I don't care," she followed.

Slowly lifting my head, I turned to BET. You gotta remember this was back when they still played videos. Princess Deja Video for 'Freaks Over Here' was on. If you know anything about Princess Deja than you already know her video's was always freaked out. Bitch was twerking, grinding, humping. Thinking back I should've used this to try to break the awkwardness. But naw I aint say a damn thing. Neither one of us did. Our corny asses just sat there looking everywhere but the T.V., like some wack dudes.

Next, Grown Man's 'Throw that Booty Round' came on. Man that video was even freakier. You ever seen one? Man they was damn near fucking. I don't even know how BET was allowed to play that shit in the daytime. I was sweating even more now. I had to turn the channel. I couldn't take it.

So I turned to MTV, I knew that was a better choice. Around that time they was always playing some Boy Bands or something, this was during the Pop Era. They won't playing a Boy Band but it was close enough. 'Tiffany Leads' video was on. She was this teenage white girl who couldn't really sing but she could dance like a black girl. All the little bitches in school use to fuck with her and shit.

"You think you can dance like Tiffany?" I asked still attempting to break the silence.

"I can dance better than her," Alex followed smiling, looking over to the TV.

I still aint know what to say next. My mind was still on what the fuck was about to go down. I knew time wont on my side and Dock and Tiara would be walking out that room any second.

We continued the silence until 'White Boy's' video 'Breakdance' came on. This was my first time seeing him. I had heard him on the radio. But I didn't know he was white. Yeah, I know that sound crazy considering his name and shit. But I hadn't heard a white boy spit like that. Again you probably thinking this when I knew I would be a rapper. But again you wrong. I'ma get to that in due time. Only thing I realized at that moment was that white boys could rap too.

After the video went off a commercial came on and we still sat not saying nothing. I was too busy trying to figure out where the fuck I was supposed to stick it. I hadn't seen a real vagina yet. Playboy Magazines and shit aint never show the actual hole. Yeah I know I'm about to sound dumb as hell but I thought the pussy hole was gonna be in the same place as my dick was. How was I supposed to know you had to go between the thighs?

I was cursing myself in my head. Why the fuck hadn't I just kept it real with Dock and let his ass know I was a virgin. He could've schooled me. Now that I think of it. Why the fuck didn't he just know. Common sense should have told him I was a virgin. He knew I was lost before I met him. But I guess I can't be too mad. He probably figured since he aint lie to me, that I wouldn't lie to him. Guess that was what the fuck I deserved for hiding shit.

"Yall going in there?" asked Dock as he and Tiara shot out the bedroom adjusting their clothes.

I looked over to Alex slowly awaiting her response. Her ass looked like she was waiting for me to say something first though. Instead we both nodded and stood to our feet, dragging our way into the room slowly as Dock and Tiara took our spots on the couch.

I walked in observing my surrounding. Typical little girl room, posters on the wall, teddy bears and shit like that. But what really caught my attention was the dint in the middle of the bed. Obviously that's where Dock and Tiara had been. I looked over to Alex to see if she'd seen it too but she was already sitting down on the corner of the head of the bed twiddling her thumbs.

"What you doing?" I asked looking over to her as I sat down at the foot of the bed.

"Nothing," she said looking over to me, timidly. "I'm waiting to see what you doing," she followed.

"I'm waiting for you," I said.

"You the one who wanna do it," she said.

"No. You the one who wanna do it," I shot back.

"So you don't want to?" she asked.

"I didn't say that. Do you?"

"It don't matter," she followed, looking away, shrugging her shoulders.

"Ok," I said, taking a deep breath. "Well come on."

"Come on," said Alex, still never moving.

I stood up, slowly walking over to her as she looked down to her shoes. I paused in front of her a second before I finally spoke. "Aint you supposed to take your paints off or something?"

"You do it first," she said.

"Why I gotta go first?"

"Cause."

"Cause what?" I asked. "How about we do it at the same time." I suggested.

"Ok. I guess," she reluctantly said before standing up, still never looking up to me.

Together, we both looked in opposite directions as we unbuttoned our pants. I dropped mine as she slid hers off. My first time seeing a pussy in real life. I stared searching for the hole but nothing. Figured I couldn't see it because of all that damn hair down there. It won't nothing like I expected. I thought it was gonna be all pretty and shit. I still was kinda jealous foreal foreal. How the hell she get hair down there before me. I was bald as a door knob. I still remember the first words she said when she finally got the courage to look over to my naked body.

"That's it?" she asked looking at my poked out penis.

"Yeah," I shouted. "What do you mean that's it?" I followed looking down at my Mans. He was standing at about a good four inches.

"It's all little and ugly," she replied, with her face screwed up, like it stunk or something.

"My shit aint little," I whispered, hoping Dock couldn't hear what was said. I was getting tired of that shit. How big they think your shit was supposed to be at 12?

"I guess."

Regaining my focus, I asked. "So. You ready?"

"Yeah," she said, sounding unsure.

"Ok," I replied as we both climbed to the middle of the bed. It was now time to put in work and I still aint know the first step. On top of that my dick was now shrinking back, looking like a pig in the blanket. I took a deep breath trying to get right but I aint know what the hell to do. The more I thought about it I swear the smaller my dick seemed to get. Even if I did figure out where the hole was, won't no way I could stick that flimsy shit in nobody.

After some thought I said fuck it. I was about to just tell her the truth. I was gonna let it all out. Thinking, maybe then she would work with me. I aint gon lie. I aint want to but I really aint have a choice.

"We don't have any condoms. I don't wanna get pregnant," Alex said before I could confess.

"I don't want you to either," I blurted back, relieved that there was a way out.

"So what we going to do?" Alex asked as I flopped down onto the bed next to her causing the headboard to smack the back of the wall.

"We can just act like we did it," I said, after suddenly having a bright idea.

"How?"

I pushed the head board against the wall one more time.

Alex smiled. So for the next ten minutes we sat there smacking the head board against the wall as we finally felt comfortable.

We walked out, giggling buckling our jeans back up the same way Dock and Tiara had done. Dock nodded over to me, happily. We stayed for a little while longer, joking and watching T.V. but it was about to be time for Tiara's Mama to get off so we dipped out after about an hour.

As we walked down the street back to Dock's house he thrusted his right hand in my face, "Ay smell my fingers," he said.

"Move man," I said pushing them away, I can remember the smell to this day. Smelled straight like fish. Still his ass looked happy as a bitch.

"Let me smell yours," he asked, as I reluctantly put my fingers to his nose.

After taking a whiff he looked over to me from the corner of his eye. Something told me he knew my secret. But he never said shit so I don't know.

745

You know how they say an idol mind is the Devils workshop. Boy, If that aint the motherfucking truth. Man, I'd lose count if I ever tried to figure out how much dumb ass shit me and Dock did outta straight up boredom. Especially in them hours after midnight. It won't no telling what we might get into. While all the other kids in the hood our age was tucked away sleep in the crib. We was up wandering the streets, kicking over trash cans and beating up bums. Shit, it really won't no reason to go in the crib. My Mama always blasted her music all damn night so it won't like I was gonna be getting some rest.

On good nights we'd have some weed or we'd get one of the old heads to go to the store and get a thunderbird for us and we'd mix it with the grape Kool-Aid pack. Shits used to have us bodied. That wasn't too often though, most times we'd just smoke and it never fails every time we got high we would get the munchies and neither one of us never had no damn food in the crib. Super 10 and Be-lo would be already closed and the only other store in walking distance was 7-11. Sometimes Dock would be able to steal his mom's food stamp card but most of the time that shit was already empty.

7-11 won't like Super 10 though, they was hip to that stealing shit. Won't no way you was just gonna walk in that bitch and take whatever the fuck you wanted. Oh naw, I mean it was possible, maybe in the daytime when it was plenty of customers walking in and out. But at 2 in the morning, two dirty ass kids like us walking into the store instantly drew all eyes over to us. They watched us like a hawk. Guess we looked like we was up to something.

Still, don't think for a second we aint never try. You know we did. But back then they had this one crazy ass white dude who had caught us one night and chased us damn near halfway down the street over one little ass snicker bar. We aint go back in that bitch again for a while after that but that don't change the fact that we still kept having the munchies. So one night after another smoke session, Dock came up with one of his bright ideas on how to get us some munchy money.

"You know Mr. Ramone go to work over nights," Dock said looking over to me as he kicked a can down the street.

"Yeah I know," I replied, eyes bloodshot.

"You thinking what I'm thinking?" he asked, with a smirk.

"Yeah."

"You down?" Dock asked, excitedly.

"Man I was lying," I confessed. "I don't know what the hell you thinking."

"Nigga I'm thinking we need to break in that bitch. Aint no telling what he got in that jank."

"Break in there?" I asked. You gotta remember. I had just turned 13 by now. I was barely even a teen. All this shit was new to me.

"Yeah. You want to?"

"I don't care,' I said nonchalantly "How we going to get in?"

"Easy. I cut his grass one time. All we gotta do is break the window in the back yard. Unlock it and one of us climb in."

"Ok," I agreed, giving the plan no thought.

"Bet. Let's go."

We marched over side by side. We was so dumb we aint change clothes, get no gloves, nothing. We just went, no fear in our hearts. Honestly we was too dumb for fear. Real consequences weren't anything that we could really comprehend. Well let me take that back, consequences weren't something I could comprehend. I'll be a liar if I ever tried to figure out what level Dock could comprehend too. That nigga probably wanted to go to jail for all I know. Might've thought that shit would be fun or something. That nigga aint have it all.

So yeah, we hopped his gate and crept through the back yard. "Hold on, I gotta find something to break the window with," said Dock as he began to search the yard.

I instead pushed the trash can to the back window, hopped on top and attempted to open that bitch. To our surprise, the jank was unlocked. I remember feeling accomplished after I did it. Like I had really had a part in that shit instead of Dock doing all the work as usual.

"Yo Dock its open," I said turning around, seeing that he'd found a rock.

"Damn I wanted to use this shit," he replied, holding it up.

I then slid through the window, falling to the floor. I can't front, I was a little scared. The house was pitch black as I ran to the back door to let Dock in.

He barged in, eyes wide. "You go that way. I'll go this way," he said as he pointed to the living room.

"Ok, I'm about to cut on the light."

"Cut on the light? Hell no," he said. "What if somebody see's the light on from outside. We gotta be smart," he said pointing to his brain.

"Ok," I said as we split up. Back then I thought Dock was the ultimate criminal. He was so smart. Today as I tell the story I'm realizing that he was the same nigga who was about to wake the whole neighborhood up throwing a rock through his window.

But anyway as I walked I found myself in the refrigerator. Remember I told you we was high. As I searched through I discovered that he had some OREO's and a big ass pitcher of Red Kool-Aid. Forgetting what the mission was all about I sat down and had a late night snack as I heard Dock shaking the place down. Still, I aint give a fuck. Them cookies was good as a bitch and the Kool-Aid had just the right amount of sugar. I had found what I needed.

I don't know how long I was sitting down but I know it wasn't long enough. I still had plenty cookies left when Dock burst in the kitchen pointing a gun at me, "Look what I got."

"Oh shit," I yelled dropping my glass of Kool-Aid onto floor. "Yo don't point that shit at me."

Dock ignored me as he stared star struck at the pistol. "We bouta be rich."

"What? How?"

"How? Bro, we can rob everything and everybody. Come on lets go."

I stuffed a couple cookies in my pocket and we dipped out, leaving the crib nothing like we had found it.

"Yo where we going now?" I asked as we made it onto the street.

"To get some money. My palms is itching," Dock replied, looking forward.

"Get some money. From where?"

Dock didn't answer. So for what seemed like miles, we walked aimlessly as he studied the pistol while I continued eating the cookies. Back then the weed used to really get to me. My body was small and I was young. That's probably why I didn't really give a fuck about what Dock was talking about. I didn't give a damn how we was going to get some money. I was just going along for the adventure. I won't stuck in the house bored and I had a snack. I aint give a fuck about nothing else. Life was good.

After I don't know how long, Dock finally spoke again. "Got one."

"What?" I asked.

"Follow me," said Dock as I looked a little further down the street. There was some guy wearing headphones at the bus stop chilling, rapping to himself.

We hiked down the block, Dock leading the way as the guy continued rapping aloud until we approached him.

"Yeah nigga you already know what the fuck time it is. Gimme that cash nigga. No funny shit," Dock demanded, pointing the gun sideways, like in the movies.

Obviously the nigga didn't hear him or take the gun serious. "Huh? What you say?" he asked as he removed his headphones.

"Nigga, you fucking heard me. Gimme your fucking money."

"Chill little nigga, I aint got time for the bullshit I'm the wrong nigga to fuck—."

BOW.

Dock let loose as his arm flew back and the gun fell to the ground along with my cookie, and the guy's body. My boy Dock had went crazy.

"Naw nigga, I'm the wrong nigga to fuck with. Its Dock bitch." he said excitedly. "Ay bro, come help me run this bitch ass nigga pockets," he said after picking his gun up from the ground.

Man I swear I seen the bullet enter the nigga head and fly out the other side. Brains everywhere as his head steamed. A small bit of blood even splattered over to me. It felt like warm rain drops. To this day I still get the chills when rain hits my body.

No funny shit, I was in shock. Gun smoke shot through my nostrils, straight to my brain, I couldn't think straight for the life of me. I hadn't never seen a nigga get murked right in my face. I couldn't even really make out what the fuck had just happened. I aint know how to feel about it.

"Come on lets go," said Dock as he began running down the street as I quickly followed.

All in all we had smoked a nigga for 6 dollars a box of cigarette and some stinking ass Nike Air Force one's that neither of us could fit.

In no time we somehow made it back to Docks house without detection. We sat down on the porch. I didn't know what to say, didn't know a lot of things when it came to what was right and what was wrong. But I can't lie I did have a feeling that what had just happened was wrong. But to keep it all the way real, it still won't the normal feeling a person would probably have after being involved with a murder.

Like I said, I knew it was wrong and shit but I still had part of me that was kinda happy. I felt protected. I felt like as long as Dock had that pistol nothing was ever going to happen to me. Or him. Actually the more I sat there thinking about it every piece of me that was kinda thinking shit was wrong had vanished. I was proud of my nigga. He was a super hero to me.

After some time to think about what he did. Dock finally spoke again. "Bro. No funny shit. I aint even know I was gon pop dude. I planned on just robbing him," he said, looking me in my eyes. "I don't know, I guess something just came over me. I couldn't even help it. No funny shit," he confided.

"It's cool bro." I said comforting my nigga. He was a 14 year old murderer. I didn't know what was going through his head at that moment. I just knew that I was gonna be there for him.

"Here bro," he said handing me over $3. "You tryna want to walk to 7-11? We aint gotta steal shit this time," he said smiling.

"Hell yeah." I said.

We walked to the store smoking the Dead man's cigarette, so young, so stupid, we still had the murder weapon on us.

I'm A Star

Ghetto fucking superstar! That's exactly what I was by the time I stepped foot in Norview High School. Dock had helped me step my swag all the way up. I was fresh as a bitch Roca Wear down with fresh ass Bo Jackson's to match. Wont no more mo'fucking Uniforms in high school. I was sweet as a bitch, gold teeth, gold chain, I had dreads by then and them shits was hanging, boy oh boy them was the days. I aint tryna toot my own horn but I'm just being honest when I say I was a young legend.

Let me explain why. In them three years I'd spent in middle school, me and Dock had damn near done everything under the sun. So much, that Dock didn't even feel the need to even show up to High School. Shit, to the 8th grade either for that matter. When they tried to hold him back in the 7th grade that was the final straw. My nigga won't having it. I mean come on just think about it, who was they to tell a nigga like Dock that he couldn't do something. Let's just be real. Them dumbass teachers was lucky he aint give a fuck about school in the first place. Cause trust and believe if he did, the moment they said they was holding him back he would've been in the school office strapped up, pointing a pistol at everybody in that bitch, demanding he be promoted. I know he would've.

Those was the beginning stages of Dock's addiction to pistols. He could tell what kinda weapon a nigga had from three miles away. Around this time his best friend was Buster. Buster was his gun. And naw it won't that little ass deuce deuce he found in Mr. Ramone's crib. Buster was a big boy. Matter fact Buster won't no boy at all. Buster was a grown ass man.

A Glock 40, same shit police officers carry. Shit was damn near bigger than him. He aint give no fucks though, he toted that jank like it was his new born baby or something. Polished it, read it gangster bedtime stories, took him for nice long walks around the hood, and fed him with hollow tips.

To my knowledge Buster hadn't caught any bodies but if you think he wasn't put to use I got one thing to say. Think a motherfuckin-gain. Along with me we had formed a little robbing team. We aint give a fuck, we took everything we wanted, from any nigga we wanted it from.

It aint matter who the fuck you was. With our rep and the fact that Demetries and Donnell ran the older crowd when they weren't in jail, it won't shit niggas could do but respect it, or check it. And you won't checkin shit unless you had a death wish or something.

At first we was just robbing niggas barefaced, no mask, no scarf, nothing, just give me your shit or we smoking you. Simple as that. I can't front though, I aint really like that method. Rumors was being spread around school about us. Alex was questioning me and shit. But more importantly I had finally realized that there were consequences for the shit we was doing.

Seeing Demetries and Donnell constantly on the run taught me that. The way I saw it, jail had to be a fucked up place if them niggas aint never wanna go back, always running from the police, hiding and shit, going to other states and what not. I knew them niggas couldn't be running from a place that was cool. I won't the sharpest knife in the kitchen but I won't stupid. It won't like they ran or backed down from anything else. They was the hardest niggas I knew. Anything that had them scared had to be a motherfucker.

With the thoughts I was having I convinced Dock to start wearing a Ski mask. You know his ol crazy ass aint want to at first. "Fuck them niggas. Fuck they gonna do to me? If they try to go to the Police we just gon off they ass, simple as that. I want niggas to know what time it is with me. Niggas don't try niggas that set examples. Remember that," he would say.

It was hard but I just had to make him realize we couldn't kill nobody if we was already in jail. He still didn't want to do it but he eventually agreed.

Foreal though, I don't even know how effective the masks actually was. In the three years I'd been in middle school I had grown to be a damn 15 year old giant. I was standing about 6'3 and a solid 180 while Dock was about 5'4, 135. Everybody in town knew we was together all day everyday, so it won't never too hard to realize who the fuck was sticking you up. Not to mention the same deep distinctive voice that would eventually get me famous was basically the same one I had back then. Still, fuck it, we aint give a damn. Won't like niggas could prove shit and that's all that mattered to us.

But anyway, yeah niggas knew who robbed them and the fact that no one ever tried to do anything about it is why I feel we were legendary. It won't like we was robbing all little pussy ass niggas our age. Why would we? That wouldn't make any sense.

Ok Ok, let me be honest, yeah we did rob a few niggas our age but they aint never have shit foreal. Yeah maybe some Jordan's. But we learned quick not to keep wasting our time on bullshit. We preferred to rob the older niggas. Niggas who hustled or had jobs or something. That way we could always take they Jordan's and the little cash they had, shit and sometimes free drugs. Occasionally they'd even have a little middle of the mall jewelry on too.

Can't lie though we was like some fucking junkies foreal. Our main concern was getting some cash to get high. When I tell you we aint do shit sober, I aint fucking lying.

I know, I know, seems like a pretty fucked up way to make a living huh? Yeah, I can see why someone would think that but fuck it. I aint never said I was legendary for doing good things. I just said I was legendary. It's a cold world out there. We was just giving niggas the same treatment the world was gonna eventually give to them anyway. Of course that aint what we thought back then. I just came up with that rationale right now to be honest. Back then we just did it cause we wanted your shit. It won't a whole lot to it. Hey, at least I'm being honest.

Hold on, now that I'm being honest. Since I was a robber does that take away from me being a Ghetto Superstar? You think that's a stretch? I mean are Super Stars always loved for what they do?

Naw wait hold on, what am I saying, Donald Trump was damn sure a Super Star and I don't personally know one nigga that loved his ugly ass. So yeah, I was a Super Star.

Matter fact, I don't give a fuck what the fuck I was considered to be. I'll tell you one thing, everybody in the whole town knew who the fuck I was. And they knew exactly what I was about. But the best part about it was, they knew they couldn't do shit about it.

Let me take that back, the best part about it might've actually been the bitches. Females loved a nigga. I was popping. Fuck a damn jock I was way more popular than them corny ass niggas. My name was probably bought up about 100 times a day throughout the town. And like the saying goes, all publicity is good publicity. The more people talked about me the more them bitches wanted to know.

Now I aint gon say all, but throughout my experience with life, females often want to be associated with a nigga with some Power. A nigga with a name, I think it kinda makes them feel like they got a name too.

Truthfully they probably was scared of me. But fear don't mean nothing when compared to attention. And being associated with me would guarantee attention. See, a lot of niggas don't know but attention is all these females want. Aint no telling what a woman might do for attention. Not all, I said some. And I aint saying this is the Gospel or anything, just my own personal opinion, from my own personal experiences.

Now during middle school, yeah I fucked a couple of them attention seeking hoes. But it was middle school, niggas was freaking and shit but for the most part a lot of girls was scared of some real deal dick. Wont nobody fucking foreal foreal. Well, except Dock, he was hitting bitches like a full grown man in his prime. But that's whole other story.

No funny shit, I could've probably been on his level too. I had grown out of that scared of sex stage. But I was still taken. Yeah Alex had my little heart. She was still the baddest thing walking in my eyes. It won't no way I was letting her go and she felt the same damn way.

She knew them hoes was on me and she tried with all her mite to stick to me like glue. Especially that first day of High School. She knew what she was up against. These won't just little girls no more, these was basically grown ass women. But Alex won't no chump, she was always down for a challenge. My baby was a straight up gangster. One of the million reasons I loved her ass.

"I see I'ma have to fuck one of these bitches up already," said Alex as we strolled side by side down the noisy, cramped hallway. Through all the madness, we still stood out like a sore thumb.

"Huh? Hell is you talking about?" I asked. Acting as though I couldn't see the gangs of bitches staring at us as we walked through.

Naw they won't making it obvious that they were staring. I know for a fact they had all heard about how crazy Alex was but still it won't hard to tell that they were whispering about us. Every time we got close to a group of girls they all of a sudden got quiet and started looking down at their schedule or something. It was funny to me.

"Nigga you know what I'm talking about," Alex said as she looked me square in the eye. "Don't make me remind you about Freaky fucking Kesha."

I think I Love Her

Oh shit before I go any further I gotta rewind and tell you a little story that happened back in 8th grade. Shit was wild as hell.

Alright so it was a beautiful night. You know one of them spring nights when it wasn't warm enough for shorts but still not cold enough for a jacket. Just a good ass night, clear sky, nice breeze, all that good shit. So yeah, me and Dock was doing what we do. Just taking a little late night stroll looking for some shit to get into. Hoping we'd find an unlocked car or some innocent sucker walking down the street with some shit that we wanted. Basically just trying to pass the time, won't shit else to do at Midnight on a Tuesday.

"Yo who the fuck is that?" Dock asked as he nodded further down the street.

Through the darkness I could see the silhouette that looked like a coke bottle. She was walking slow, body swaying from side to side, clothes looking painted on, long braids dangling down past her shoulder. Her face was unclear but with a body like that who the fuck cared.

"Yo I don't know who the fuck that is," I finally replied to Dock as I wiped the drool from around my mouth.

"Come on bro, we gotta find out," Dock said as he began speed walking down the long street.

I followed as her face grew clearer with every step. And with every step it seemed as if she was looking better and better. I grew anxious as I found myself seeming to participate in a foot race with Dock. I wanted her. Even with the coke bottle shape, her demeanor still was one of a teen-ager and I had to have her.

We finally got close enough to make eye contact. I swear she was licking her lips at me, staring me dead in the eyes. I don't know though cause Dock told me she was doing the same to him. Maybe it was both of our imagination. Who knows. But what I do know is that bitch was fine as a motherfucker. Dark baby smooth skin and pretty white teeth. Found that out the moment we finally met up.

"What sup I'm Kesha. What yall bout to do?" she asked before we could even speak.

That shit aint only shock me, it shocked Dock too. We won't used to girls coming off so strong. Yeah I know she just asked a question but her whole body language was screaming 'Fuck Me, Fuck me'.

"We--we just chilling," Dock stuttered. "We--we aint really doing nothing," he added.

"Damn. I was looking for something to do," she stated as she seductively looked us up and down continuing to lick her lips.

"Like what was you planning on doing?" I asked taking over still trying to figure out where the hell the bitch had come from and why we hadn't seen her before.

"I don't know. Something fun," she replied staring me in my eyes.

Seeing me making moves motivated. Dock. "Well we always got something fun for you to do."

"Something fun like what?" she asked, flirtatiously.

Dock looked over to me and smiled. Next thing I know we're in the park getting it. I'm getting head, Dock getting pussy, ass getting smacked, balls getting sucked. Man if we would've had a camera we would've had a million dollar porno on our hands. No funny shit, it was going the fuck down.

After a while I got tired of getting head though. I was ready to fuck. Yeah, by then me and Alex had already been having sex but like I said earlier it won't like I was getting ass on the regular. I wanted to try as much as I possibly could. So I signaled to Dock to switch, and of course he was down. But when we made our move, that bitch said the unthinkable.

"I hope you got a condom too," she said as she stood straight up.

In my head I'm thinking, a condom? Bitch what? You out in a park at one in the morning fucking some niggas you just met an hour ago. Now you wanna scream about some damn condom. Yeah Dock was using one but he always had them on deck. Only this time he only had one.

But shit, if you think that stopped two young horny niggas like Dock and myself, you must be smoking crack. Alright, so what I'm about to tell you may seem disgusting and unbelievable but I don't give a fuck. I'm here to tell you my story and that's what the fuck I'ma do. I aint gon cut no corners. If I did something. Then I did it. I aint ashamed of shit. What we did is what any real niggas would've did in our predicament.

"Here bro," Dock said as he took his condom off and handed it over to me.

"Thanks phew," I said as I turned it inside out, sliding it on.

Ten seconds later we was right back in business. For a freak bitch I aint gon lie. She had some good ass pussy.

That next day in school the bell rung for lunch and I walked through the hallway dragging, tired as hell. After we fucked we ended up smoking with bitch in the field. I aint get in the crib till about 4 in the morning. We talked about every damn thing. She was new in town, she said she was 16 and going to Norview High. Like always I lied about my age, told her I was 16 too but told her I aint go to school. That shit was for suckers.

Turns out we was both some lying sack of shits as I wiped some of the leftover cole out of my eyes, blinked once, than blinked again I saw this bitch Freaky Kesha walking towards me. I wanted to turn around but I couldn't. It was clear we'd both seen each other.

"I thought you was in High School," I asked as we finally met up.

"I thought you aint go to school," she shot back as we both laughed, knowing that we'd been caught in our lies. "I had fun last night," she said.

"I did too," I followed.

For that bitch to have been such a hoe she was still pretty as a bitch. Her face was like a trap. Still I found my way out of it as I realized I was standing in the middle of the hall talking to a girl when Alex could walk up from anywhere any second.

"So are you gonna walk me to class? I don't have a clue where I'm going," she stated, batting her eyes.

"I can't," I replied, looking around for Alex.

"Oh I get it," she said nodding. "You don't want your little girlfriend to see you with me."

"Girlfriend?" I asked, stalling, trying to figure out my next move.

"Yep. You must got one if you don't want to walk with me."

"Yeah," I replied slowly. "I can't even lie. I do gotta girl. And she would fuck both of us up if she seen me talking to you. No funny shit," I said confessing. I figured it won't no use in lying. She was gonna find out sooner or later anyway.

"Too bad," she said with a smirk. "I aint really want to go to class."

"Huh? So where the hell was you tryna go?" I asked.

"I don't know. Yall niggas did me right last night. I can't even lie I just wanna fuck," she said giving me the same sexy look from the night before. My dick got hard as a motherfucking rock. I looked around to see who else was around. It still was only us.

"Where--where, was you trying to go?" I asked trying to get my words together.

"I don't know. Anywhere," she said shrugging her shoulders.

"We can go to the auditorium. Don't nobody ever go in there."

I knew that because the year before, Dock and I used to sneak in to smoke cigarettes sometimes.

"Ok. Let's go. You got a condom this time?" she asked.

"No. But I know somebody who does."

I rushed Kesha too the auditorium and shot to the lunchroom. I eased my way in. I couldn't let Alex see me. But I had to find Weak ass Chris and Ugly Ass Chris. I knew they had some rubbers. They always did. They was the type of little niggas who kept condoms for no damn reason even though they knew damn well they won't getting none. But since we'd grown to be cool asa bitch over the years and the fact that they was both undercover virgins. I decided to take them with me.

Once we got in there, it was on and poppin ASAP. Only this time I made sure I got mines and got the fuck out of there. I had to at least see Alex for a little while before the lunch bell rung.

Turns out I dipped right on time. Freaky Kesha, Weak Ass Chris and Ugly Ass Chris got caught red handed by some teacher and just my luck word got around that I had been in there earlier. Chris and Mike said they won't the ones who told. I never got to the bottom of it but considering things that happened later in life. I know one of them bitch ass niggas ratted on me. Dock always wanted me to beat they ass for it but I aint never do it. I fucked with them. Can't lie though the fact that Alex had found out had made me consider it.

Man, when I learned that she knew what had went on, you already know I got the fuck outta dodge. Fuck school. I already knew Alex was gon be on some bullshit the second she seen me. I ran over to Dock's crib, woke his lazy ass up and told him everything that happened.

His dumbass came up with some ol retarded ass lie. I can't even remember what the fuck it was cause I aint even never get a chance to use it. It was too late for all that. While me and Dock was scheming up a story, Alex was in school shutting shit the fuck down. Together we had made for one of the most popping days in Norview Middle History. First me and the homie's was running trains on the bitch in the Auditorium and then Alex topped it off by beating the bitch ass.

Yep, they say as soon as Alex saw Freaky Kesha getting escorted out of the building by her Mother due to the fact she'd been expelled, she pounced on that bitch like a tiger. They say she went to work on that ass. Her Mama tried to break it up. But one thing about Alex, when she get mad, all that Angelic shit go out the window. She transform into Laila Ali, man they say she fucked around and beat her Mama ass too. No funny shit. Can't snatch, I was proud as hell.

So yeah, of course she broke up with me for a few days but she eventually forgave me. She had too, it still won't no proof that I had actually did anything. She had accomplished her main goal anyway and that was to show bitches that she was crazy and that if you fucked with me, you'd end up like freaky Kesha, beat to a bloody pulp before vanishing, never to be seen or heard from again.

I'm a Star (Continued)

OK. Back to the first day of school.

"Man why you gotta always bring up Freaky Kesha?" I asked Alex.

"The same reason you fucked the nasty bitch. Because, I want to."

"Aint nobody tryna keep hearing that shit though. It's old," I replied as we continued to walk.

"Yeah, it's old to you because you the one who fucked up. Let me have pulled some shit like that. You and Dock would be ready kill somebody."

"Naw aint no ready to kill. Somebody would be dead," I said strongly.

"Ok. So isn't me keep bringing it up better than somebody being dead?"

"Shit, foreal foreal for all I know Kesha is dead."

"What you been looking for the bitch or something?" asked Alex, rolling her eyes.

"Man stop that shit."

"I'm just saying," she followed.

"I swear you crazy as hell," I said as we walked up to an open classroom door. "This your class right here?"

"Yep."

"Ok. I'll see you later," I said attempting to walk off.

"Oh that's how we doing it in High School? I know you aint about to walk away without giving me a kiss," said Alex, pausing with her right hand on her hip. "So we showing off now?"

"Hell naw," I said before turning back around, leaning in for a kiss.

"Nope," said Alex, backing away. "Forget it, I don't even want a kiss any more. Since you want to be funny."

"Shut up." I said grabbing her, pulling her in closer. "Crazy ass," I said before we kissed.

"Whatever," she said, still full of attitude.

"Love you Baby," I said, sweetly as the bell rung.

"Love you too," she said, blushing as she turned to walk into her class.

There I was, alone. As I walked down the hall I could sense the stares from inside the classrooms. Feeling myself, I began walking slow as hell, looking into each door. It was so many new bitches. See, High School was a mixture of my old middle school plus another, not to mention all the upper class hoes I had never got to talk to before. A young nigga hormones was going crazy, them bitches was looking good asa motherfucker. That nigga Dock aint know what the hell he was missing. But shit maybe it was a good thing he wasn't there. Aint no telling how shit would've been.

"OOOH girl you see him?" I heard one girl say from inside her classroom.

"Yep. That's Coach," said another.

Fuck that. I had to look inside. So I backed up. "Yeah it's me." I guess their teacher was in another room or something because I didn't see no adults inside.

"I seen you walking with your little girlfriend," said the initial girl as she rolled her eyes.

"What girlfriend?" I followed.

"Nigga don't play. I seen you. I guess yall cute or whatever," she said.

"How you know she my girlfriend though?" I asked, smiling. I knew bitches liked my smile.

"Trust me, I heard all about yall."

"What you hear?"

"A lot?"

"A lot like what?" I asked stepping closer to the entrance of the classroom, poking my head in so the bitches in the back could see me too.

"Oh it's nothing, I just know you can do better," she said as a few other girls giggled.

"Do better like who?" I asked before getting tapped on my back. "Yo," I said, as I turned around to see who it was, thinking it had to be their teacher.

"What were yall saying?"

It was fucking Alex, and if looks could kill, I would have dropped dead right then and there.

"What sup Alex," I whispered, scared for my life.

"Nigga don't 'What sup Alex Me'," she said before turning her attention to the girl in the class. "And bitch you said he can do what?"

"Chill baby," I said as I held her back from walking inside the classroom.

"Aint no fucking chill," shot back Alex, breaking away from me before swinging.

"Yo I said chill," I shouted as I dodged her blow.

"Fuck you Skylar," Alex shouted. "You can have these little groupie ass bitches. I aint got the time," she said before looking back over to the girl. "But best believe I'ma still fuck you up," she added pointing to my admirer.

"Alex," I called as she stormed down the hall as I watched her figure grow smaller. "Damn," I said before turning around only to have a teacher behind me.

"Are you lost sir?" he asked.

Man I was so damn mad I coulda punched that nigga in the face. But I didn't. I ignored his ass and made my way to class. The whole time I was thinking how I should have dropped out of school just like Dock had.

Use Me

Alex always made a nigga forget about my pain. When I was with her, the fact that I was basically out there fending for myself aint mean shit. I told you she was like a powerful drug to me. Real shit, stronger than any man made one I ever took and trust me I done dame near did them all. In a way I became addicted to her.

Anytime we ever broke up I aint never know how to handle it. It's like I would go through withdrawals or some shit. Real talk, I used to get fidgety, angry for no reason, I just aint know what the hell to do with myself. On a bad day my young ass might just burst out crying. Naw not in front of nobody, you know I was too damn cool to do some shit like that. But in my alone time, yeah.

It's like in my head I felt like I don't give a fuck what I'd done, she was never supposed to leave me. Never. I mean come on, she know a nigga needed her, like foreal, what gave her the right to just act like a nigga aint exist.

And she was so damn good at it. That whole first day of school she would just look right through me. No matter what I did or what I said. I swear I could've walked up to her and screamed in her face and she'd just turn around and walk the other fucking way.

And don't let me touch her. Oh hell naw, she'd hit me with a two piece to the chest before proceeding to ignore me like nothing ever happened. Real shit. Her ass even had her friends trained to do the same. Them bitches is the ones who really made me mad.

Now I loved Alex and I guess I knew what I did was wrong but fuck her motherfucking friends. I aint love them hoes. Hating ass bitches. Man I swear I used to want to beat the breaks off they ass. Who the fuck did they think they was playing with? Ignoring me? Me? Had me all out in the open embarrassing myself and shit. Fuck them. They knew damn well they wish they had a nigga like Coach. Truth be told I probably could've fucked each and every last one of they stupid asses. I could tell by the way they used to look at a nigga.

But yeah, by the end of the day I started acting as though I'd given up. "Cool. Fuck you then. You don't want me. I don't want you either. I don't give a fuck. You must don't know who the fuck I am."

I thought that would get the reaction I was looking for, instead all I got was "Girl did you see Jasmines make up she looked like a damn pumpkin. Shit was orange as hell. Yuck."

Dog, like they really kept ignoring me. It was like a game or something. I hated that shit. So I went on my separate way. I knew it wouldn't be shit for me to find another girl. She was tripping. Fuck it, it's her life. Girls are like busses, miss one, next fifteen one coming. I was saying all this shit in my head. But who was I fooling. I won't about to let her go that easy. Fuck that. What did she think, she was just gonna move on and get one of them lame niggas in school or some shit? Ha-ha. Yeah right. I would've caught my first body quick. Yeah they say niggas shouldn't fight over girls. But I won't fighting. I was murdering. Cold blood. Fuck that.

All day I was thinking of a way to get her ass back. I won't never gonna give up. Then it hit me, I'd came up with a plan and had a few dollars in my pocket. So after schools was out I made a few quick runs and about an hour later I was in her back yard with my Boom Box to the Sky Blasting Love Posions 'I Love You'. That was Alex's shit back then.

Yeah I know the whole boom box shit won't really original. But you gotta remember I was only 15. How romantic you expect me to be? I aint know what else to do. I aint have a car, aint like I could take her to some 5 star restaurant or something. Besides, she probably wouldn't've got in the whip with me any way. I had to do something where I came to her. To tell the truth, shit was genius if you ask me. I was just doing what the fuck I had to do. Fuck it, thugs need love too.

After about a minute of me blasting the music, singing my heart out, her and her Mom burst out the back door.

"Boy what are you doing?" Alex shouted.

"Aww," said her Mom as she stood behind, smiling with her hand over her heart. Despite everything I ever put Alex through her Mom always fucked with me. Her Step Dad, Francis on the other hand, no. But he won't never really there around that time anyway. He had like two or three other families. The nigga came and went as he pleased.

But when he was there, he on his Hitler shit. Straight Dictator, he was an ex-Marine and whatever he said was law. 8:00 bedtimes, 6:00 wake ups. He was crazy as hell. So crazy, that out of the five kids Alex's Mom had. Alex was the only one left standing. All the rest had moved far away, in other states and shit with other family members. They couldn't take his shit. I had never met any of them at the time, but his craziness had definitely rubbed off on them.

Her oldest brother tried to kill himself one day, her other brother tried to Kill Francis, her little sister tried to burn down the house and her big sister told the school that Francis had tried to rape her. She eventually took it back. But with all that going on and the fact that everyone knew that her Mom would never leave his ass. Family members from all over agreed to take all but Alex away. They knew she would never leave her Mother.

Alex and her Mom were like best friends, you couldn't have a conversation with her without her mentioning something her Mom said at some point. But on those rare days when Alex would get upset with her, she'd always tell me how she really made her feel and how stupid she was for staying with Francis.

In my head I always figured she stayed cause Francis had a lot of dough. He made that Military money look good, Alex said he used to have a lot of investments and shit. I don't know but I do know all her Mama had to do was hold down a job at Wal-Mart and she could spend her checks how she pleased, Francis payed all the bills.

In a way, her Mom was the reason that she always stayed with me. But in another way, she was the reason, she always wanted to leave. Her worse nightmare was ending up a sucker just like her.

But anyway let me get back to the story.

"Ma don't 'Aww' him. He aint shit."

"Alex, watch your mouth," said Mrs. Parker.

"I'm sorry Mom but it's the truth," replied Alex, staring down at me.

"Alex just talk to me. I'm sorry," I pleaded over the music as I sat the radio down. "I got something for you," I said pointing behind me. I had set up mini pic-nic, equipped with flowers, a card, a blanket I'd took from the crib and a basket of food. "Please Alex," I begged.

"Alex just go talk to him. He's so sweet," her Mom said.

"Ok," Alex said after taking a deep breath. "You got three minutes," she followed, pointing over to me, seriously. "But I swear that's it. Don't even know why the hell I'm doing it anyway."

I smiled as Mrs. Parker through me a wink before heading back in the crib. As Alex made it over to me I attempted to grab her by the hand to escort her to my home made date. She wont having it though, of course she snatched it back, "Move nigga," she said.

Still trying to be apologetic I hurried over to the sheet and picked up the Roses I'd just bought from super 10. I mean flowers, I'm pretty sure they won't real Roses or nothing but shit that's all they had. I was just being resourceful. Her ass must've really wanted roses or some shit cause as I handed them over to her she smacked them bitches to the ground the second they touched her. "Nigga I don't want that fake ass shit."

"Come on Alex. I said I was sorry," I replied.

"Boy do you know how many times you've said sorry? You embarrassed me for the last fucking time. Got bitches out here talking behind my back and shit. Fuck you."

"Baby I'm sorry. I don't even know why I do what I do," I said. "Well I guess I do. But no funny shit it's like I can't even really explain it."

"Nigga whatever," Alex replied, arms crossed. "You can't explain it cause you don't have a reason. You're just stupid as hell. And I aint got time for no stupid ass nigga. I'm abouta get me a smart nigga. Someone with some common sense, who appreciates me. Watch."

"What?" I blurted before containing myself. I knew she was mad. I had to make it better even though the thought of her with any other nigga had just almost killed me.

"Yeah nigga you won't the only one getting attention today. You're trippin if you think I'm about to sit around here playing dumb. Boy, you must don't know," she said, shaking her head.

"Man Alex I'm sorry. I can't lose you though. No funny shit."

"Boy whatever. I'm done. I heard all of this shit before," she said as she spoke using her neck. "I'm too young and too bomb to be wasting my time. You said what you got to say. Now I'm going in the house. Pick up all this shit before you leave," she said turning around.

"No. No," I said before grabbing her by the arm. "You all I got foreal Alex. And you probably gonna be the best I'm ever going to get. I don't really know how to do this love shit. Aint nobody never loved me before. See, you can go in the house and leave me and you know for a fact your Mama love you more than anything in this world. I don't got nobody to love me. You the only one. You leave me and I'm alone out here. Dolo. No funny shit."

"Ok," she said, as she turned to look me in the eyes. "So if you love me so much. Why do you keep hurting me?"

"I--I don't know," I stuttered. "I guess I'm still getting used to all the attention. Man before I met you aint no girls ever liked me. Bitches treated me like I won't shit. Matter fact everybody did. I swear sometimes I think my life a dream right now. You don't know how it feel to just want to be dead every day you wake up. Not even knowing why God even made you. Then for shit to just change all of a sudden and people acting like they fuck with me. That shit fucked me up a little. I don't even know how to handle the shit foreal. I know I'm stupid but I don't mean it. I swear. I love you man. I love you more than anything. I promise," I said quoting the lyrics from the song that was still playing.

"Man, Sky I love you too. I just can't keep getting played. Like foreal. Do you see how my Mama let a Man come in here and rip our whole family apart," she said as she pointed over to her house. "I love you to death. But I'll be damned if I lose myself over a nigga."

"I know. And I'm sorry. Just give me another shot. There aint no me without you. You're my everything. Fuck them bitches. I'd die for you," I said.

"Boy stop lying. No you wouldn't," Alex said blushing.

"I would," I said noticing that I was winning her over. "But more importantly I'd kill for you."

"What?"

"Yep. So even if you don't take me back. I'm going to kill your next boyfriend. So if you don't want that on your conscience you might as well sit down and eat," I said jokingly, pointing over to the pic nic basket.

"You're crazy," she said smiling.

"Yeah crazy about your ass. Come on think about it. You think I would go through all this trouble if I won't sorry. I made a fucking pic-nic. A fucking pic-nic Alex. I'ma gangsta. Gangsta don't do pic-nic's. Shit don't even sound cool. But I did it for you. I'd do anything for you, " I said sincerely.

"I hate you," she said smiling. "What you got in there anyway?"

I reached down to the basket. "I got your favorite. Popeye's Spicy Chicken with double fries and a sweet tea, lemonade mix," I said as I opened up the basket, exposing the food.

"Oh my God," she said smiling. "Hold on, did you remember my hot sause and barbeque sause?"

"Of course," I said as I reached down pulling a few packets out.

And just like that. I won my girl back. Shit, if that wouldn't have worked I would have been back every day with a new idea. Real shit, when it came down to Alex, giving up won't even an option.

That evening was everything I could've ask for. The sun was setting and the air was just right. We talked for hours. No question that was the night we really truly fell in love. Yeah we loved each other before. But that was just that ol young little kid love. Shit had elevated. Even though we was still only teens, I swear our love was real. Sitting out there with her was like sitting high on a cloud, floating away. Sometimes we didn't even have to speak, just being there with her, I knew she understood me and I know she knew I understood her.

I been around for a long time and after years and years of trying, I still aint found the perfect words to illustrate the feeling of being with someone you feel completely comfortable with. Money, drugs, sex, nothing, can compare to Love man. I swear. Shits priceless.

"Baby. I got to go do my homework," she said as she stood to her feet.

"Homework?" I asked. "On the first day?" I added, as I stood along with her.

"Yeah boy. I'm sure you have some to do yourself."

"Fuck that," I followed.

"I'm serious. You don't eever think about your future do you?"

"Baby you is my future," I said grabbing her pulling her closer to me. We stood chest to chest, arms wrapped around one another.

"Baby I'm serious," Alex said looking up to me. "You do know you're not going to be a fifteen forever. One day you're going to have to get a job or something. You can't be out here doing whatever the hell you and Dock do to get money for the rest of your life."

I paused, thinking. I had never gave my future too much thought. "Yeah. I guess you right. What you going to do?" I asked.

"I'm going to be a famous Hairdresser," Alex said looking up to the sky, as her eyes sparkled.

"You like doing hair that much?" I asked.

"Yep. It's like I feel like I got the power when I'm doing it. It's like art to me. You start off with something ugly and you transform it into something beautiful," she said, now looking into my eyes.

"You think you can get rich like that?"

"Hell yeah. I'm going to travel, do hair for the stars, open me up some hair salons. Trust me I got it all planned out. I aint gonna need a nigga for nothing."

"What?"

"Just cause I say I don't need one doesn't mean I don't want one," she said as she gave me a kiss. "But trust and believe I aint gon have no broke ass husband. So I'ma need for you to get up off your ass and make some something shake. Do you hear me?"

"Man, I don't even have no talents. Aint shit good about me."

"What? Boy are you crazy? You better just look at everything you got that others don't."

"Like what?" I asked, curious.

"First of all you got the power to influence people. You got everybody in the whole damn town scared of you."

"So what the fuck is that? What I'ma be a WWE wrestler or something?"

"I don't know, maybe. You know you can fight your ass off."

"Whatever," I said as we both laughed.

"I'm serious Sky. Do you know how beautiful you are?"

"Beautiful?"

"Yeah boy. Beautiful. Your hair, your face, teeth. Everything," she replied as she admired me. "You're just beautiful all the way around. The way you walk. Your personality. The way you speak just makes me want to keep listening. You're special. I'm telling you, I see something in you that you can't see. Why do you think I keep taking your stupid ass back," she finished as she playfully punched my shoulder.

"Man you just saying that."

"Whatever. I'm serious. I'm going to stay on your ass," she said pulling me tighter. "Tomorrow you better go to all your classes."

"I am. I promise," I said.

"Ok. Give me a kiss." We kissed and at that second I really believed in my heart that I wasn't going to cheat on her anymore.

I left all the pic nic shit at her crib. She said she wanted to keep it there so that we could have another one. I walked home whistling love songs and shit, thinking about what the fuck I was gonna do with my life. My mind was blank as hell. I couldn't believe she had already had them types of thoughts. Made me feel like I was behind or something. You feel me? I knew I had to catch up though. Fuck that. She said she wont gon have no broke ass husband and I knew she meant it.

Damn she was the shit. I mean what other kids thought like her? She knew she aint like the situation her Mom was in. But instead of complaining she just thought of a way to overcome it and be a boss. Damn. I knew it was a must I keep her in my life.

And I still couldn't believe she said I was 'Special'. Me? I'd heard I was Special before but that usually came with an 'ED' after that. Boy I swear I was thinking hard as hell about career choices and shit. What could I do? I was wrecking my brain until I was interrupted by a voice coming from further down the street.

"Get that nigga Coach," it was Dock. Some young junky looking white boy was running away from him towards me. Without thinking twice or knowing what the fuck was going on I stopped him in his tracks. Clocked his ass, knocking him clean to the ground as Dock caught up too us. Together we stomped that nigga flat as he screamed for help. "Nigga didn't I tell your bitch ass the next time you come around this motherfucker to have my Goddamn money."

"I'm sorry Dock," cried the Pluck.

See, Dock was always a hustler. In middle school we used to steal candy from Super 10 and sell the shit in school. By this time he was a little more advanced though. Demetries and Donnell had put him on to the crack game, even had set him up with a couple plucks. That white boy that we fucked up was one of them. He had owed Dock some money and tried to get away without paying. He must aint know who the fuck Dock was though. Outta all the streets in Norview what in the fuck possessed him to walk past Docks house. Lucky he aint get shot.

"Aint no sorry, "continued Dock, angrily. "What you think Ima hoe or something?"

"No--no Dock, I don't think you're a hoe," he said as Dock pulled Buster from his waist.

"Naw nigga. Yes the fuck you do," he said pointing the gun at him. "You must think I'm a hoe. Run his shits, Coach," Dock demanded as I reached inside his holy pockets, pulling out nothing but lint.

"Man this nigga broke as hell," I said as Dock gave him another kick to the dome, still pointing the pistol to him.

"I'm sorry Dock. I'm sorry," the Junky continued to plead, as blood slid from his mouth.

"Fuck that," Dock said as he dropped down to the ground shoving the pistol closer to his head.

WOOP WOOP, the fucking cops. Aint it crazy how the Police just come from nowhere. When you need them niggas they aint nowhere to be found.

Well maybe I shouldn't say that, because the white boy did kinda need them. But man you get what I'm saying. Like why out of all times they had to just be pulling around the corner, catching us right in the fucking act? Like, what the fuck kinda luck is that.

Safe to say we got the fuck out of there. Back then we knew every possible short cut on our block. Hopped a couple fences, cut through a few yards and we was home free. But naw it was far from over. That would have been just too easy.

Swing My Door

"I can't wait till we finally get to the Goddamn Park," said Dock excitedly as he sat in the passenger seat of his Brother Donnell's Nissan Maxima rolling a blunt.

"Hold on. Fuck we going to the Park for?" I asked from the backseat. "I aint even in the mood to be playing. No funny shit."

Dock and Donnell both laugh. "Nigga the Park aint no Park foreal. You trippin," replied Donnell as he drove.

"Yeah, you can tell you aint from Norfolk," followed Dock.

"Ok. So what the fuck is the Park?" I asked, curiously.

"Nigga that's what we call the Projects. The hood," said his bro.

"We got like Five Parks in Norfolk. We from the hardest one, Wellington Park," followed Dock.

"Yeah, it's real out that bitch. Shit go down," added Donnell.

"Don't be scared though. You gonna love that shit. Bitches every Goddamn where. No funny shit," said Dock.

"Hell yeah," follows Donnell as he and Dock gave each other dap.

No funny shit, shit had really went the fuck down. Man after all the dirt me and Dock did in the street, everything had finally caught up to our little dumbasses. Life was crazy. My first time on T.V. should've been on BET, instead, it was the news, forcing us to live life on the fucking run.

Man not only did the Police catch us in the act, the fucking white boy who ass we beat had a damn fake eye. I guess with all the stomping and kickin we was doing we must've shattered that bitch or something. I don't know, I just heard that when the ambulance showed up he was laying on the ground with blood leaking out his eye socket. No funny shit.

So you already know with him being a white boy and shit, the news media blew it up. They had Police with Dogs searching everywhere for our young asses. Crackers made it seem like we had killed a president or something.

At first we hid out at one of Donnell's bitches crib but Norview was getting too hot. Police was knocking on any and every body's door who had ever spoken to us. I can't even stunt, that shit had a nigga nervous as a son bitch. I lie to you not, anytime I even heard a car drive by the crib I was peeking out the blinds. Real shit.

Of course Dock's crazy ass won't acting like he gave a fuck. The moment he seen the story on the news he got mad as a bitch. And naw, not mad cause they was looking for us. But mad because the Police hadn't shown our faces due to the fact we was Juveniles.

"Man what the fuck kinda shit is this?" he shouted, pointing at the TV. "I want niggas to know what the fuck happen when you fuck with my money."

"Nigga the whole town know we did it," I told him.

"Yeah, I guess you right," he said smiling over to me.

I swear, that nigga was a real live lunatic. But yeah like I was saying we knew we couldn't stay round that bitch house much longer. It was only a matter of time until the boys found us. And even if they didn't, we would've eventually got caught anyway. As you can already tell, Dock won't exactly the type a nigga you could just keep caged up in a crib. My boy was the true definition of a 'Street Nigga'. He was gonna make it out that door one way or another and that's a fact.

Thank God his Aunt Kim had said we could crash at her spot for a minute. She lived all the way in Norfolk. It was about an hour away from Norview. That's where Dock and his family was from, he'd lived out there his whole life before moving to Norview.

The whole ride over, I'm mentally fucked up. So fucked up, I was feeling sick. Not really cause we was on the run. I mean I guess I was a little nervous about that. But to tell the truth, not so much. Looking back, it's kinda crazy how the mind of a 15 year old works. Fuck the Police and the fact that I was facing serious charges and didn't really know for sure how I was gonna eat or survive.

It was only one thing on my mind. Well not thing; person. And no it wasn't my fucking Mama like most kids my age. Not saying I had never thought about her. After all the looney bitch was still my Mama at the end of the day. In a crazy dysfunctional way I loved her ass. I guess. But yeah anyway, she was far from the person who had invaded thoughts. Of course that person who I'm talking about is motherfucking Alex.

Just my luck right after we had that long ass talk, I'd get in some shit like that. I mean damn, life went from sugar to shit fast as hell. But that was only an indication of how my life would be for years to come. Unpredictable. I would grow to get used to it but back then, I aint really know how to handle it.

But back to Alex, I was fucked up yo, real shit, all I wanted to do was hug her. I knew she was the only person who had the power to make me feel better about the situation I was in. What made shit even worse was the fact that I hadn't even talked to her since the shit had went down. Donnell's bitch aint have no house phone so I aint even have no way of contacting her. Not knowing when the next time I would see or talk to her shook my whole damn world up.

Yo I swear to God without that bitch I had a feeling of nothingness living inside of me. Her ass was all I had. A nigga emotions was all fucked up. I wouldn't go as far as to say I wanted to smoke myself. But what I will say is that it aint matter to me if I was on earth or not. In all honesty I was confused as a motherfucker. Only thing I knew was that I wanted the pain to go away, I just aint have no idea on how to go about doing it. Shit was crazy.

Ok I'm done with all that soft ass shit. I just had to keep it real for a second. Fuck it, but anyway back to the story. Where was I at? Ok Ok, I remember. But yeah this nigga Dock kept saying we could be on the run until we was 18. He said that's when the charges would be dropped and we would be home free. Now first of all I aint even know if that shit was true. Seemed kinda fishy to me. Secondly, I was only fucking 15. To me, 18 was decades away.

A part of me wanted to just turn my ass in. But again. I say, a part of me. Fuck that shit. I won't that sad. I told you my thoughts on being locked up already. I won't scared but if Demetries and Donnell aint wanna go then it damn sure won't nowhere I wanted to be. So I had no choice but to say hello to my new home. Norfolk.

"Yo what the fuck is this?" I asked as we seemed to be driving into a black hole.

"What you mean what the fuck is this?" asked Dock.

"Exactly what I said. What the fuck is this," I repeated, continuing to look around. "What are we in right now?"

"We in the tunnel phew," said Dock.

"Fuck is a damn tunnel?" I asked as we continued to drive.

"A fucking tunnel nigga," followed Dock.

"Bro you still aint telling me what a damn tunnel is."

"Oh yeah damn, my bad I forgot they aint got no tunnel in Norview," said Dock," as he passed Donnell the blunt he'd just rolled.

"Oh yeah. I forgot about that too," said Donnell.

"Yo Norview wack as hell," Said Dock. "I'm mad we even moved to that shit bruh."

"Got some nice hoes though," said Donnell.

"Yeah I can't lie them hoes is nice," added Dock, smiling.

"And easy as hell." Donnell said as he dapped up Dock, as they chuckled.

"Yo," I yelled, breaking up their brotherly bonding moment. "Is yall gonna tell me what the fuck a tunnel is or not?" I asked as Donnell passed the blunt back to me.

"Oh shit my bad" said Dock.

"Man we under water," answered Donnell.

"What the fuck you mean we under water?" I replied, completely lost.

"We fucking driving under water," Donnell shot back.

"How the fuck they build some shit under water. What they was in scuba gear or something?"

"Nigga hell naw," fired back Donnell as he and Dock both laughed once again. "Matter fact I don't even know to tell the truth," said Donnell.

"Yeah nigga you asking too many damn questions just pass me the damn blunt. You always want to learn and discover some shit when you get high," said Dock.

It didn't take long for us to get out that spooky ass tunnel and when we did I remember my eyes lighting the fuck up. No funny shit, my little ass was in awe as we passed by what seemed like hundreds of big ass office buildings and five star hotels. The way I was staring you would've thought we was passing the Eiffel Tower or some shit. I hadn't never seen no shit like it. Of course, later on in life, after traveling the world I realized Norfolk really won't nothing special as far as the buildings and shit, but at that moment, a young nigga was mesmerized.

By the time we finally pulled up out Wellington Park it was the same feeling. I had never seen project apartment buildings. We aint have that type of shit in Norview. Yeah we had based on income housing and shit, I had grew up in one. But that Norfolk shit was different. A lot different. It was like a thousand tiny identical brick apartments bunched up together. Riding through the neighborhood seemed as big as the whole Norview to me.

"I'ma catch yall boys later," said Donnell as we pulled up to Docks Aunts Crib.

"Alright bro," said Dock as he hopped out with his two book bags.

"Alright my nigga." I followed, looking around at my new surroundings.

First thing that came to my mind was, 'Where the fuck is the grass at?' Out of all the lawns out there it was probably about four patches. No bullshit. I mean damn I thought we lived rough back home but that shit was different. Them motherfuckers out the Park aint give a damn. They was living raw as hell. And that won't even the half.

Next door to Docks Aunt house was a yard full of fucking big ass baby diapers. Did you hear me? Fucking Diapers. Dirty ass, stinking ass, doo-doo diapers. A yard full of them.

"Yo what the fuck is going on round here?" I asked Dock as I pointed over to them.

"Oh that's just Sasha crib," he said nonchalantly. "Her ass got bout 10 kids. She too lazy to go throw the pampers in the trash in the middle of the night so she just throw them bitches out the window."

No funny shit, hearing that gave me a little more respect for my own crazy ass Mama. Lord Knows she was fucked up in the head but I doubt she ever did some ol nasty ass shit like that. Of course you gotta take in consideration I really don't know because I was a baby but I'm just hoping she didn't. I'm sorry but throwing dirty ass diapers into your own front yard is a different kinda crazy. Straight trifling.

Shit really had me thinking. Who knows, maybe if my Mama lived around people like Sasha I wouldn't have looked at her so crazy. Kinda made me miss her. Well I don't really know if miss her is the right words but it made me think about if she was thinking of me. Had me wondering if she even gave a fuck that I was gone.

But never mind all that. As we walked into Docks Aunt house I just through all my problems to the back of my head, I couldn't be focused on that shit.

"Yo," yelled Dock after we walked into the unlocked apartment.

"Who that?" Docks Aunt screamed from upstairs.

"Lil Dock," Dock screamed back as I looked around at all the club pictures placed alongside the concrete walls.

"Oh hey bookie," she said as she was heard coming down the steps.

"Hey Aunt Kim."

"Hey baby," she said as I got my first glimpse of her.

Dock had always told me how cool she was. And from the looks of her I could instantly tell he won't lying. She was a little short ass lady, no bigger than 5'1 but her whole aura was just as big and bright as her gold tooth smile.

"This my stickman, Coach," he said pointing over to me. "He gonna be staying here too,"

"Now hold on Motherfucker," she said looking over to me. "You aint tell me shit about nobody coming with you."

"My bad Aunt Kim. He cool though. This my right hand man."

"He better be," she said as she began looking me up and down slowly. "Hey I'm Aunt Kim."

"Hey," I said.

"Dock will tell you I'm cool as a motherfucker. You aint gon have no problems with me. But its two things that I absolutely don't tolerate people bringing over here. The motherfucking police and bed bugs," she said sternly. "If you can keep them away from here, you're fine with me."

"OK," I answered as the door burst open and I turned around startled.

"AYYY bitch," said two niggas our age as they barged into the house.

It was crazy, no funny shit, from the moment I seen them they reminded me so much of Dock. Their whole mannerisms were identical to his. Of course they aint look shit like him, one was tall and just a naturally big muscular black ass nigga, and the other was just a regular heighted nigga who was kinda muscular too. Both had knotty ass cornrows in they head and sagged they pants to they knees with gold teeth.

"What sup bitch?" Dock screamed excitedly as they embarked in a mini reunion, dapping and hugging one another.

"Hold on, Hold on. What I tell yall motherfuckers about bursting in my Goddamn house like yall aint got no motherfucking sense. I'ma start beating yall ass," Aunt Kim shouted over the noise.

"My bad Ms. Kim. We just knew Dock was in here," said the shorter one.

"I don't give a damn if Jesus was in this motherfucker. Yall don't know what I could be doing in here. Me and my man fuck everywhere in this motherfucker," she said as she pointed in various spots.

"Come on Aunt Kim chill, aint nobody tryna here all that," followed Dock.

"I don't give a damn what yall wanna here. I'm just being real. That's all I know how to be. What's that shit yall say? Keeping it 100? Well yeah that's me. That's all I know how to do motherfucker. Keep shit 100," said Aunt Kim as she walked to the kitchen.

"Yeah I guess we can't be mad at that," added the taller one. "We just seen Donnell and he said Dock was down here. Had to holla at his lil Mexican bean pie head ass."

"Fuck you bitch, your Goddamn Holliday Heart face ass," added Dock as the three burst into more laughter.

"Hell you doing here itch-bay," asked the shorter one, as I tried to decipher what the fuck he'd just said. Later I'd find out it was Pig Latin. That's when you take the first letter from something and put it to the end of the world added with an 'ay'. Only you couldn't do it if the word started with a vowel. For example, my name is 'Oach-Cay or Dock's name is OCK-Day' It's really pretty simple.

"Fuck you nigga. I am the Park," boasts Dock.

"Hell naw nigga, you a ol country ass Norview nigga now," said the taller one. .

"Fuck you. Ima Wellington original, you got me fucked up," Dock said before forgetting that he'd yet to introduce me. "Oh yeah this my nigga Coach."

"What up nigga," the taller one said as he extended his hand for some Dap. "I'm Jah."

"I'm Mank but you can call me ank-May," said the other.

"What sup," I said as we all dapped up.

"What yall niggas bouta do? Yall tryna blow?" asked Jah, pulling out a bag of weed.

"Damn right," answered Dock. "I need that shit."

"Well bring yo Aladdin face ass outside. It feel gooder than a itch-bay out here no funny shit," said Mank.

We stepped out. They talked loud as a bitch while I tried to soak as much in as I could. Man something so simple as just standing outside had me excited as hell. I felt like Christopher Columbus or one of them white niggas who came to America and seen the Indians living. I'm telling you, this was a whole new world to me. A world where old tennis shoes hung from wires, shopping carts were used as strollers and dealers hustled openly as if Police didn't exist. Dog, I couldn't even focus on just one thing going on out there. Noise was coming from all directions.

It was late September so everybody had their windows open. I could hear radios blasting, fussing, or just loud motherfuckers casually talking like Dock and his homies was doing. It was like niggas was in competition to see who could be the loudest. Shit was weird as hell to me. Little did I know in a few weeks I was gonna be doing the same damn thing.

Oh yeah and I can't forget to mention the noise from all the kids. It was midnight but you'd never guess it in a million years. It was about a thousand of them little motherfuckers playing around, cursing like grownups, running up and down the sidewalks bumping into the junkies who were outside dancing around in small groups tryna find a way to scramble up a few dollars.

Shit was unbelievable to me but as I looked over to Dock and them, them niggas was just chilling, unfazed, like the shit was just normal as hell.

"Ay yall know we beefing with them bitch ass ity-cay niggas across the street right," said Mank as he passed me a forty ounce of Steel Reserve and a fat blunt.

"Swear to God," Dock said. "What the fuck happen now?"

"Man them niggas just some hoes. Simple as that." followed Jah.

"Damn right, bitch ass niggas think they hard. I know them niggas though. They aint bout it-shay," said Mank.

"Yeah, we had to bang Manny and Tree top up the other day," followed Jah.

"Foreal? Yall beat up Tree top? That was my boy," Dock said, disappointingly.

"Fuck your boy," replied Jah.

"Well fuck em then," followed Dock, shrugging his shoulders.

"Damn right. But hold on, what the hell yall niggas doing around here?" Mank asked, looking over to me and Dock. "Don't tell me yall on the un-ray or something."

"You better bet it. Shit got real out Norview. Had to flee on them niggas," said Dock.

"Damn bro what the fuck happened?" asked Jah.

"Some bullshit," Dock followed. "It's all good though I needed a vacation anyway."

A fucking vacation. Boy, I swear them words struck me like lightning for some reason. Soon as he said it I learned to appreciate my situation. Drinking forties, smoking weed. Not a damn care in the world. Why was I complaining? The higher I got the more I started to see the advantages of being out there. No bullshit, hands down the best thing about it was the fact that I wouldn't be waking up to go to no school in the morning. Shit had me feeling like a man. Out on my own doing what the fuck I wanted. I mean yeah, you can say I did what the fuck I wanted back home. But shit was different. I aint have to answer to nobody. Can't really say you a man when you still go home to your Mama every night.

My life was fully in my hands and I was prepared to do whatever the fuck I had to do to survive. Shit, I started feeling like Norview was too small for me. I was a king amongst peasants. No disrespect to my peoples but shit the truth is the truth. I was anxious to see how niggas really got down around the world. If I could learn that much about the streets from Dock, who knew what I could soak up if I was around niggas like him all the time.

The more we got fucked up that night, the more I realized that Norfolk felt like home. For a moment I forgot about everything that was back in Norview. I still missed Alex and shit but her high had been temporarily replaced by another drug 'The Real Streets' a drug that I wouldn't be able to kick for a long time.

I'm the Shit

"Yo," yelled Jah and Mank as they burst through the door, waking Dock and I from our comfortable slumber on the couch.

"Motherfucker didn't I tell yall bout bursting in my Goddamn house," shouted Aunt Kim as she darted out of the kitchen.

"I'm sorry Ms. Kim," said Mank.

"Yeah my bad Ms. Kim," followed Jah.

"Fuck that," she yelled. "Take yall black asses back outside and try that shit again."

"Foreal?" asked Jah, as Dock and I sleepily looked over to the two.

"Hell motherfucking yeah I'm foreal," she blurted.

"Man," they complained as they walked out.

Yo Ms. Kim was the shit, cool as the other side of the motherfuckin pillow. Back then I hadn't met a woman like her before. She was like, let me see how I can put it, like a young girl trapped inside an older lady's body. But it was different though, she still carried herself in a way that made you respect her.

It's just that she knew all the latest songs, Smoked weed, drink liquor. Every weekend she had all her friends from the neighborhood come over and kicked it. They old asses would play spades and dominoes all night till they passed out drunk. Aunt Kim was all ways down for a good time. I think that's why it was so easy to treat her like someone our age. But best believe she aint have no problem putting little niggas back in they place.

I liked her style. Real O.G. She aint really have too much money but you better bet her ass stayed with a smile on her damn face. Yeah, she'll cuss your ass out in a heartbeat but still she gave off that feeling that she genuinely cared for you.

"Who is it?" Aunt Kim yelled as Mank and Jah knocked on the door.

"It's us Ms. Kim," said Jah.

"Us who?" she yelled again.

"Mank and Jah," said Mank.

"What yall want?" she said smiling over to us, playfully.

"We want to talk to Dock and Coach for a second," said Mank.

"Ok. Hold on one minute. Let me see if they're here," she says as she laughs to herself. "Ok come on in. Their available," she said as they stepped back into the apartment. "Now was that so hard?"

"No," answered Jah.

"Good. Now try that every time," she said before exiting back to the kitchen.

"What sup niggas," said Jah as he and Mank both dapped us up.

"What sup," me and Dock answered.

"Yo 'The ustler-hay's' ooting-shay a mo'fuckin video out the ity-cay later today," said Mank.

"Yep," said Jah, excitedly. "And you already know we gotta be in that jank. No funny shit. Yall niggas tryna go?"

"Hell yeah," blurted Dock with no hesitation. "But what the hell they doing shooting a video out 'The City'? Them niggas aint even from Norfolk."

"Nigga you know they can't shoot no video to 'Hustling' in the suburbs. Shit wouldn't even look right," said Jah. "Aint nobody hustling out there."

"Yeah they gotta come to the ood-hay for that."

"And niggas cool with that?" asked Dock.

"Hell yeah. Why not? Niggas finally gonna be on TV. I'm about to be in that bitch like 'Ayyee'," Mank says as he and Jah both start dancing around.

"True. Well hell yeah I'm down," Dock says, as he stands up to dance along with them. "I can't wait, I aint never been on TV before," he says before looking over to me smiling. "Well unless you count last week."

Failing to catch what Dock was saying Jah says, "My nigga. I already knew you was gonna be with it. Seem like everybody else around this bitch scared or something. Niggas got a million and one excuses for why they can't come."

"Nigga I'm strapped fuck I got to be scared of?" says Dock, tapping his waist.

Yeah, in case you're wondering, he slept with his gun. Actually after living out the Park a little longer, we all did. It became a part of our wardrobe. You wouldn't catch us without one.

"Y-may igga-nay," yelled Mank.

"You rolling too Coach?" asked Jah.

"Yeah I'll come," I replied.

Phew, I aint even gonna lie I aint really want to go to that shit. Fuck naw. Why the fuck would I? Yeah yeah I know I said I was digging the Park life and what not but fuck that. Going to a damn video shoot in a neighborhood who don't like the niggas I'm with seemed kinda dumb to me.

No, no, no, not saying I was scared of the niggas who would be out there. But must I remind you we was on the fucking run. A nigga was tryna be low-key, I wanted to take every precaution to stay my little ass out of jail. I knew if anything popped off out there then the police was going to be out that bitch ASAP and that was only if they won't out there from the beginning.

Times like that I use to wish Dock won't as wild as he was. Nigga aint have no damn chill button. I should have told his ass 'Naw Fuck that we aint going.' But you know I didn't. Like a dumb ass I just went with the mo'fuckin flow.

That day, part of that flow, was ecstasy Pills. I had heard Dock and his bro's mention them before but we aint have them in Norview so I hadn't ever seen none until Jah whipped them out.

"Yall niggas tryna pop?" he asked, pulling a bag of small blue pills from his pockets.

"Oh shit. Is those Gangsta Bitches?" asked Dock excitedly.

"You already know my nigga," replied Jah, equally as excited.

Man looking at them shits had me even more nervous about that video shoot. I already didn't wanna go but now niggas wanna do drugs I hadn't never took before. I aint even have time to think of a good excuse before Dock looked over to me. "Bro you gotta try this shit."

"Best drug ever made," said Jah.

"Makes everything in life better," Mank pitched.

"I fucked a bitch for 2 hours straight," added Jah.

"You can do anything," followed Dock.

Man that shit was crazy, it was like one of them commercial when they talking about peer pressure and the little white boy is getting asked to smoke cigarettes, but instead he walks away. Only difference was my ass aint walk away. 'Fucked a bitch for 2 hours' 'Best drug ever made', Shit, I was sold. "Gimme one," I said as Jah passed them out.

"Yo I swear to God I'm about to get so many bitches. They aint seen me in a while. Them hoes about to go crazy, watch," said Dock as we made our way to the video shoot after popping the pills and buying a bottle of water each. They all had told me that I was going to need it after the shit kicked in.

"Nigga stop saying that dumb ass shit," said Jah to Dock.

"Nigga what the hell you talking about? You know I always had all the bitches. I know they missed a nigga," shot back Dock.

"Man I don't give a fuck about them bitches. Everybody got bitches."

"So what the hell your dumb ass talking about then?"

"He talking about you saying you swear to od-Gay," butted in Mank.

"So nigga. What the fuck wrong with swearing to God?" Dock asked as we all looked over to Jah.

"Nigga it aint no fucking God," Jah exclaims.

"Boy shut your dumb ass up," Dock fired back.

"Nigga fuck you," said Jah. "I'm dead ass serious. I aint tryna hear that shit no more. We all gods. Aint no damn "Sky Daddy.""

"Yo how long this nigga been on this bullshit?" Dock asked looking over to Mank.

"Ever since his uncle came home from behind the G-Wall."

"See, its niggas like yall who make it bad for niggas like me who actually try to understand the world. I'm talking some real shit. If we was still in Africa we never would have known nothing about this Christian Bullshit. The white man beat this shit into us. We was Gods before we came here."

"Man shut your ass up," followed Dock.

"See, that's exactly what he want you to do."

"Who the fuck is he?" Dock asked.

"Nigga the white man," Jah shouts. "He been lying to us since we got here. How the fuck can you believe it was a damn Adam and Eve and all that bible shit when science say that it was niggas in Africa building pyramids and doing math way before that shit."

"Nigga shut your dumb ass up. You aint never passed science or math. You 15 still in the 6th grade," said Dock as he and Mank burst into laughter.

"Alright don't listen to me. I'm just trying to teach yall young lost asses something. Keep on thinking life a joke."

"Naw nigga we don't think life a oke-jay. We think you a oke-jay," Mank said as he and Dock continued to laugh.

The whole time them niggas was laughing and joking, I'm behind they ass about to croak. Man I felt like I was marching through mud with thousand pound weights on my toes while them niggas seemed to be speed racing to some finish line or something.

I was out that bitch sweating, getting dizzy asa bitch. Eyes so Goddamn blurry and watery I couldn't see a motherfucking thing. Real shit, all I saw was the silhouettes of people but I couldn't make out who the fuck they was.

With everything in me I wanted to tell them niggas they was lying. Best drug ever my ass. Only problem was, I couldn't fix my mouth to talk, my shit felt like a desert and by then I was feeling so fucked up that I had forgotten that I had the bottle of water in my pocket.

Then out of nowhere my stomach started feeling funny, shit was bubbling and jumping up and down. Still, I couldn't talk so I wiped my eyes real good, and seen what looked like a dumpster coming up. Using all my mite I through myself over to it.

"Oh shit. Yo boy letting ose-lay," said Mank as he looked back at me.

"You alright bro?" asked Dock as he ran over.

"Yeah bruh. I'm good," I said lifting my head smiling. Everything all of a sudden changed. No funny shit, I could see clear as day and my legs was loose, back to normal. Matter fact better than normal. Turns out, throwing up was all I needed. I can't say ex was the best drug ever like them niggas had said but as far as the drugs I'd taken up until that point. Hell yeah. No funny shit, I instantly felt a high I'd never felt before.

"Yo where your water at? Drink that shit," Dock said. "It's gonna make you feel even better," he said as he took a sip of his.

"Oh yeah. I forgot all about my water," I said retrieving it from my back pocket.

I took a big ass gulp and I swear that nigga Dock won't lying. Shit gave me a power boost or something. No funny shit. I felt charged up. I was on 100 percent. Looking Dock square in the eyes, I said, "I'm ready to turn up." No funny shit, I think I even had a little extra base in my voice or something. I was feeling too good.

"Bet. Let's go," he said turning around, noticing that Jah and Mank won't nowhere in sight.

Now that I had a clear view of everything. I looked out and seen that shit was like the million man march or something. Mo'fuckers everywhere, it won't even no use in looking for them niggas. They was good as gone. And to tell the truth. I didn't even give a fuck. That ex had me ready to move. I aint know where I wanted to go, but I knew I wanted to go.

So we slid our way through the crowd. Music blasting, everybody chilling having a good ass time. This was my type of party. Man I swear I felt like the sun was a camera or some shit. Fuck that video. I was making my own. Pill had me walking smooth as a bitch. Straight Pimpin. Aint nobody out there matter but me. I was special. My swag was new. I stared, studying bitches entire body.

And the niggas; fuck them. I swear I looked at them up and down, ready for a nigga to try me. I was prepared for anything. And you already know my nigga Dock was strapped. We was both on our wish a nigga would shit. Young and reckless. Not giving a fuck.

My adrenaline was pumping and as I sipped my water, I seemed to gain a little more power each time. As we kept strolling, I slowed down my pace. I wanted everybody to take a good look at me. I was a face they needed to remember. Norview's finest.

I looked over to Dock, I could tell he was feeling the same way. With him I felt even cooler.

"Yo did you throw it all up?" he asked.

"Huh?"

"Did all the ecstasy go out when you through up?"

"Hell naw," I said.

"So you feeling just like me then."

"Even better," I said as we posted up at our destination. Well I can't really say our destination. Cause truth be told we aint have one. But the spot we happen to land in was perfect.

"Everybody right here is about to be in the first scene. Stay right here. I repeat, stay right here, don't move." screamed some white guy holding a blow horn from behind some barricades in front of us. "I repeat stay right here."

"Oh shit. We about to be in the video," said Dock as we embraced. "I told you Norview aint have shit on Norfolk."

Dock kept talking but I was too damn high to listen. Plus, 'The Hustlers' had walked up.' Jewelry glistening, designer clothes. Real Deal Superstars in the flesh. Back then I hadn't never seen nobody famous before. No homo but I was in love. Not with them but what they represented. Success. Here they was in a hood they won't even from and they had bought everybody out to see them. Bitches screaming they name. Niggas reciting their lyrics as they smiled and gave head nods. They was like Royalty or something.

Then 'Action' the music started playing and them niggas transformed to rap stars as they spit into the camera, standing directly in front of me. No funny shit, I'm telling you they was dead in front of me. If I woulda reached my hand out I coulda touched them niggas. That close. As everyone danced around trying to get there 15 seconds of fame something took over my body. It was like a weight was lifted off my shoulders and something was propelling my soul through the sky. A nigga felt reborn as all these different words and sentences started to form in my head.

It was right then I knew. This was it. This was motherfucking it. I knew what the fuck I was gonna be. I finally knew what I was put on this earth to do. It's like I had an outer body experience or something. I couldn't've asked for anything better. I had to be a rapper. It was as clear as day. No it won't the drugs. That shit was real. It was crystal fucking clear. I'm telling you man that shit was beautiful. I had never been so sure of anything in my life. I'd found my calling. I'd fucking found my fucking calling. I blacked out after that. Can't tell you shit else about the video.

I was busy. I was getting my thoughts together. It was so hard though. Even though I knew what I needed to be in life, I was still trying to figure out what to do with the knowledge I'd just acquired. Like yeah, I knew I was supposed to be a rapper but how in the fuck was I supposed to make it happen?

Man those thoughts along with hundreds of lines and metaphors was crowding my damn head. While everybody else was reciting lines from 'The Hustlers', me on the other hand was busy making up my own shit. No disrespect, but fuck them niggas.

I aint even gonna front, I can't tell you one line I came up with that day. All I know was them shits was some fire. No bullshit. I was killing shit in my head. It's like them shits was raining down from the Heavens, I was in a zone, straight lost in a daze. One after another, rhymes just kept coming and coming, flooding my brain till it was finally time to go back out Wellington Park.

Shit was beautiful out there, the sun was just setting and motherfuckers was out there having a ball. It was like a celebration or something, everybody enjoying one another like one big ass happy family.

Well hold on maybe happy aint the word cause it was a lotta fighting and hating and gossiping that when on. But when you live that close to people and have to see them every day, that's kinda inevitable.

But fuck all that, I aint even tell you the best part. You'll never guess what the fuck niggas was out there doing. Fucking rapping! After never in my life being or even witnessing a rap cypher, the first thing I see when I get out there is one. No funny shit. I guess the vibe from the hustlers being across the street had inspired more niggas than just myself.

So me, still feeling the ex-pill, I walk away from Dock and step my little young ass in the cypher. Niggas aint know who the fuck I was and I aint know who the fuck they was. But the shit aint even matter. Completely ignoring what the fuck they was yappin about. I closed my eyes, zoned out again, and cut right cross a nigga. It was uncontrollable, I just had some shit to get off my damn chest.

Like I said I don't know if niggas was battling or not because I won't listening, but I know I aint battle, I was from Norview, I aint know shit about a damn battle. I just started rapping, letting shit spill out my god damn head.

I was just going and going. It was like I was all by myself all over again. When I finally opened my eyes and took a breath, it was like a crowd of damn near a hundred people staring at me, until about a second or two later. That's when they all rushed me, praising me and shit like I was Michael Jordan or some shit.

"Yo you the shit."

"Yo somebody sign this nigga."

"Who is this nigga?"

That's when Dock stepped in. "Yo what the fuck bro. Let me find out the Ex got you giving niggas free concerts and shit. Why the fuck you aint never tell me you could spit?" he asked." "*I wake up thinkin bout money... the next dollar I'ma get...then I start thinking pussy the next bitch that I'm gon hit...pistol underneath my pillow... case a nigga think he slick...try to catch me while I'm sleeping...I'll throw bullets like Mike Vick,*" he said reciting what I'd just spit. "Damn. You killed it. Bro why you aint tell me?"

"Bruh I aint know," I said looking around still in shock at all the attention.

"Man you should've rapped for 'The Hustlers'. Nigga we could've been rich," Dock added.

Man shit was like a movie, I looked around and besides the people on my dick showing me love, it still was

124

plenty people just chillin off in they own world. I aint never wanna go home.

No funny shit, I probably would've said Alex who? If you asked me about her. I'm sorry it's the truth though. Especially when the little bitches hopped on my dick, asking me what my name and where I was from and shit. When I tell you they was treating me like a celebrity I aint fucking lying. Only thing I was missing was people asking me for autographs.

Everything was going perfect, then all of a sudden the mood changed when Jah and Mank staggered up. Fucked up from they head to the toes, clothes ripped and all, bloody as hell.

"Yo them bitch ass City niggas jumped us," said Jah, as everyone rushed over to him.

Frowney Face

"It's the City Bitch," screamed a gang of 'City Park' niggas.

You ever seen the old footage of Martin Luther King Jr. and all them old ass niggas marching for freedom and shit down the street? Now imagine that same crowd, high and drunk as hell right after somebody killed Martin. I don't know if that's a good description. But I can't really think of one to describe what the fuck I seen that day.

But I'ma say this, them City niggas was deep as hell bouncing up and down, cracking they knuckles, ready to fuck some shit up. It was about 100 of them, I swear. No lie. Nobody over 23 years old. Straight young motherfuckers. Some on bikes, some walking, damn near everybody in all black. You woulda thought the police would have stopped them. But they didn't.

Of course I aint want them too. But shit, I can't lie and act like I wanted them City niggas to keep walking over either. It was no way I could stop that though.

As we all stood in this big ass vacant field in the heart of Wellington I looked around at Dock and all the other Wellington niggas. They was equally as deep, if not deeper but as far as the looks on they faces. I don't know man, I didn't see the same confidence that the City niggas had. I can't even lie. I aint saying they was scared. But shit, they seen the same shit I was seeing.

It was about to go down. 15 on 15 all out rumble. The City vs. Wellington. Niggas had been talking about it all day. You woulda thought it was The Bulls vs. Jazz NBA championship in 97 or something. Of course I was on the Wellington side so all I heard all day was niggas talking about how they was gonna fuck the City niggas up. I believed them; until I actually seen the City niggas.

The rumble was strictly for the 17 and younger. The old heads from each hood won't beefing. Yeah back in the day they had the same little issues as youngstas but that shit went out the window when they grew older and started getting money together. Still they respected the tradition of young niggas scrapping it out. So they organized a quick brawl. And with the death rate sky high in Norfolk back then you can't even be mad at them. In a way, if you actually think about it, they was helping the community. Them niggas was keeping niggas alive and outta the cemetery. If it won't for them; Dock, Jah, Mank and every other lil nigga from Wellington was ready to body something.

See, I won't involved in the fight. Yeah niggas had been showing me love and shit. But foreal, at that point it was really just off the strength of Dock. No question I woulda rumbled if my nigga asked me too, but he didn't. And from the looks of them niggas, I won't just about to just volunteer.

Especially with T.J. out there. Niggas had been speaking on him all day. I kept hearing how he'd been knocking niggas out since 2nd grade. Ol big ass nigga. Big black ass nigga. I knew who the fuck he was the second I saw niggas walking. He was in front, looking like a damn pit bull, eyes like blood. Big ass shoulders, with big ass arms attached to them, ready to punish something. He won't for no games. As he got closer his body grew bigger and bigger. I remember looking over to Dock, he was already nodding over to me. Without speaking he already knew I was asking, "Is that T.J.?"

Chill though, I aint never say Dock was scared. He aint have no fear in him. I could tell. He was the most focus out of every nigga on Wellington side. Even Jah and Mank. Not saying anybody was scared. It's just that niggas won't looking like my nigga Dock.

Foreal, foreal, I was probably more scared for him than he was for himself. Real shit. I aint want to see my nigga lose. Don't get me wrong, I had faith in my boy. It's just that shit just won't looking all that good. Most them City niggas was about 16 or 17. While the Wellington niggas about 14 or 15. Might not seem like much but round them ages, it was. Still my niggas was ready. As them niggas got closer. Niggas got hyper. I told you it won't no bitch in niggas.

"Yeah," screamed Dock, hopping up as the City niggas got closer.

"Damn right," said Mank as he clapped his hands while jumping up and down. "I been waiting for this it-shay."

"It's the City who with me," screamed an older guy, walking up with the City.

"We with you," yelled back the 'City's' entire crowd.

"Fuck the city," screamed Jah as the Wellington side screamed along with him.

"Shut your ass up! That's why we fucked you up yesterday," screamed back one of the City niggas.

"Yeah shut the fuck up," added another.

"Fuck yall! Ill bang all yall niggas up right now though," Jah replied attempting to run over. Only to be stopped by one of the older Wellington guys.

"Chill," yall gonna fight organized, he said as he continued to hold Jah back.

"Yeah," said one of the City old heads.

"Yall two niggas pick who yall want," said Chuck, another one of the Wellington old heads to Jah and Mank.

"I want his bitch ass," said Jah, pointing to Lil Marvin, a skinny guy from the City.

"I want him," pointed Mank to Lil Ray, another skinny little nigga.

"We bouta fuck yall up," said Lil Ray as he and Lil Marvin stepped in front of Jah and Mank as both sides stood to their feet, eyeing the competition as us bystanders watched from the sides.

"Alright yall niggas square up," said Chuck.

I swear the crowd got even larger, niggas was running up from everywhere. Hopping out of cars. No funny shit it seemed like niggas was sprouting from the grass. Still no police. At that time, with everything going on I won't even thinking about they ass though. I was locked in. This was big. Bragging rights, respect, shit, niggas life's was on the lines. I'ma loyal nigga so I was team Wellington all the way. My heart was even pounding.

I walked up close as I could to the action as Jah and Mank matched up with their opponents.

Then, shit went silent. Nothing was heard. The breeze stopped blowing and the birds stop chirping. It seemed like cars even stopped driving. That's when Lil Marvin through the first blow. "AWWWWWWWW YEEEEED," everybody screamed as Jah ducked the first hit, scooping Lil Marvin to the ground.

Boy when I tell you all hell broke loose after that, that's exactly what the fuck I mean. Niggas was going crazy. Mayhem out that bitch. Everybody coaching.

"Hit his ass."

"Slam him."

"Get your bitch ass up."

"Box that nigga."

The whole time I'm tryna keep my view. It was hard as hell though, I'm swimming through niggas, pushing. Man I can't even lie, from my view. The city was going in. Kicking ass, taking names, Wellington niggas was dropping like flies.

T.J. was going crazy. He was smiling every time he hit a nigga. "Yeah nigga, yeah," he said in with his raspy voice. No funny shit, every time he touched a nigga they fell immediately. Even Big Frank. He was 14 years old and about 280 pounds back then. When he fell, swear it was like an earthquake or something. He got right back up, but still, it was just crazy to see T.J. make somebody that big fall.

After peeping that, I had to look around for my nigga Dock. It won't long before I found him. He was like a lil pin ball machine out there. Fast as hell, punching niggas and before they could react his lil ass was already on another target. Bro was handling his. I started watching him like a hawk, fuck everybody else. Dock was true entertainment. A nigga his size going so hard. I started shouting my own self. "Yeah Dock, whip his ass," I said, cheering him on. I was getting hype as hell. No funny shit, I started shadow boxing and everything. That shit was intense.

Then it happen. My nigga came face to face with T.J.. I swear shit went black and white and switched to slow motion. I remember Dock cocking back not wasting a second, just like the fucking Gangsta I knew he was, only he missed and that's when T.J. got em. And boy oh boy, did he get him. Haymaker to the jaw sending Dock flying to the ground as shit quickly switched from black and white slow motion back to regular life.

"Oh hell naw," I said to myself.

I darted in, picking my nigga up before the big nigga looked at me. "Oh you want some too pussy nigga?" asked TJ, looking me in the eyes.

Without thinking, I swung. My dumbass messed around and missed too. That big ass nigga was quick, I knew I had fucked up. Just like he'd done bouta 100 other times in that fight. He caught me, sending my big ass to the dirt. Hands down the hardest blow I'd ever felt. No bullshit, I saw the 'Wam' when he connected.

If you don't know what the 'Wam' is, let me explain. You ever seen them old 1950's episodes of

Batman when he used to hit a nigga? The Words 'Wam' and 'Bam' would pop up. Well yeah, that's exactly what the fuck I saw, real shit. It was crazy. Usually when your adrenaline pumping you don't feel the hits. Naw not that time. He knocked the damn adrenaline out my ass. Had my shit ringing. My whole face was on fire.

Ima G though, so you know I hopped back up, gathering everything I had in me, for some revenge. Fuck that. I went in full beast mode I swear. I hadn't never been dropped to the ground before. I was mad as a bitch. I wanted to kill something, bad. Already hated them niggas but now that shit was personal.

Only problem was, after I'd finally fully regained all my senses, that nigga T.J. was long gone. I swear the nigga vanished into the air or something. But I was too mad just to walk back to the sidelines. Hell naw, I told you I was in Go mode. So I just ended up hitting the first nigga in all black I could find. I caught his ass good too. Knocked his ass out cold.

After that I went on a damn rampage. I'm surprised I aint hit a couple Wellington niggas. You gotta remember I only knew them niggas for a few days, it was kinda hard to remember who was who, when shit was moving so fast. Still, I didn't.

But yeah I'm out there punishing niggas. I'm in straight savage mode and T.J. was still on my mind. Obviously I was still on his too because as I turned around looking for another victim. Bam! That nigga came outta nowhere, rocking me in my face. This time I fell even harder.

His big ass had me hearing some loud beep inside my head and shit, leaving me confused, not knowing what the hell was going on. By the time I got back up and regained my focus, I looked over to my left and one of the wellington niggas 'Lil Man' was on the ground laid flat, motionless.

Everybody rushed over as The City niggas ran off the scene as if they had won the motherfucking Super bowl, screaming 'City Bitch'.

T.J.'s ass had to be fucking different though. In the blink of an eye he did the unthinkable. While everyone from Wellington was rushing over, crying and checking on Lil Man, T.J. crazy ass ran over pushing niggas out the way only to stomp Lil Man in the middle of his face. "It's the City Motherfucker," he said menacingly before catching back up with his crew.

Boy that shit was brutal. Dude put the icing on the cake. No funny shit, you woulda thought somebody got shot. Bitches was screaming and crying. Mamas falling out to the ground, even a few Wellington old head shed a couple tears.

As I looked around I remember seeing most of the young Wellington niggas who was fighting passed out all over, bloody, barely conscious, struggling to breathe. Shit was sad. But hey, on the bright side my niggas was straight. Jah, Mank and Dock were all right behind me, tired as hell walking over to Lil Man.

I was almost over there when I felt somebody grab my shoulder. I balled up my hand, still in go mode ready to attack. Only when I turned around it won't a City nigga. It was some old head I had never seen before.

He aint look like the other old heads though. Most of them was in they early 20's, this nigga looked at least 30 and he won't dressed in urban gear like them. He was hood but a little more professional, sporting a button up shirt and fitted jeans. Not to mention he was built like an NFL player with the Jewelry to match. "What sup Young Nigga," he said.

"What sup," I said still trying to catch my breath.

"You from around here?" he asked as he spoke with a slight stutter.

"Naw. I'm with Dock," I said pointing over to him. "I'm from Norview."

"I aint think you was. I heard yo young ass rapping the other day. You know I might be able to do something with you."

"What you mean?"

"Take your ass to the studio or something. You aint never thought about taking that rap shit serious?"

"Naw, not really," I said.

"Well your ass need to. I'm about to go out of town for a about a week or so. But be out here when I come back. We gonna get some money."

"Ok."

"By the way. What's your name?"

"I'm Coach."

"I'm Rich. Ask your homies about me. They'll tell you that when I say I'ma do something, I do it. They'll tell you."

"Ok," I said as he walked away.

"Yo what the fuck was Rich over here talking about?" asked Dock as he walked over to me.

Now considering what the fuck had just happen, it's clear that nigga Rich was important. With all of Dock's childhood homies laid out on the ground, he acted unfazed, only thing on his mind was what Rich had said to me.

"He told me he was gonna put me in the studio."

"Say word. Oh shit. We bouta be on. Nigga that's Rich. He got all the dope out here. All of it. He been running shit for years. He don't even talk to niggas if it aint bout money. Bro. No funny shit. We bouta get rich. Foreal foreal," Dock said as blood trickled from his nose."

Before I could speak, damn near 30 motherfuckers rushed over to me.

"Yo, this little nigga right here got heart," said Chuck, the Wellington old Head. "Aint even from out here and I seen him getting it in," he continued. "Anybody under 18 who didn't help and they from around here is a pussy. Straight up."

"Damn right," yelled Dock as he put his arm around me, proudly. "My nigga official."

Slumber Party

Alex, Alex, Alex, let's talk about Alex. Did I miss her? Damn right. A nigga thought about her all the time; when I was sober. Only Problem was, a nigga won't never sober. It aint like I was purposely neglecting her or nothing. I'm just saying, that Park life was time consuming. No funny shit, it was always something going on from the moment you wake up till the second you close your eyes. Niggas be fighting, shooting, joking, getting high, all types of shit that just completely take your damn concentration off the things that's important.

Life was crazy. I was doing wild shit I had never even imagined. No funny shit, I even fucked around and fucked a crack head. Now, before you go judging me and shit like I already know you are. Let me explain, it won't no ol toothless stinking ass bitch. She was phat as hell and probably kinda cute if you cleaned her up a little bit. I'm serious. It won't just me, every street nigga don fucked a fein. If you meet one that tell you he hasn't, than that man is a damn liar.

But yeah man, my life had changed so much from them boring days on 'The Loo' when me and Dock had to create some business. First of all Norfolk was 10 times bigger than Norview. So naturally it was ten times more places for us to straight terrorize. When I first got out there besides beating up feigns and bums like me and Dock used to do in Norview, we also robbed everything in sight.

Well not really everything, we aint never fuck with stores and shit. That would come in the future. At that time what I really mean is that we robbed everybody. Real shit, if you aint know us, then my nigga consider yourself a walking lick.

Naw, naw maybe I should rephrase that too. Cause we did rob a couple niggas we knew. What I really should say is if we aint like you than you was good as got. Don't get if fucked up though we won't just whipping out guns on everybody and making them get down. Naw, we was more professional than that.

To be honest, we really grew out of the whole robbin niggas thing fast. Yeah we did it from time to time but shit was always so damn complicated. We couldn't just rob any nigga out Norfolk with no consequences. Even if a nigga was a straight bitch aint no telling who his family was. Taking something from the wrong niggas could cause a damn war or something. We won't bitches or nothing, we just aint have time for all that.

That's why after a while we learned to focus more on the bitches. Bitches was easy. No disrespect. I'm just telling you how it was back then. Shit, probably still the same way. See, the bitches loved us in Norfolk just like they did in Norview. And I hope you noticing how I said bitches in Norfolk. Not just the park. I'm talking about the whole damn city.

Niggas had all types of hoes, from the park bitches, too the rich ones who stayed in this Neighborhood called Ghent. We had ugly bitches, cute bitches. You name it, we had it. Real talk.

No funny shit, at first, Norfolk bitches was weird as hell to me. I still remember them always saying 'I'm weak' after someone said a joke. At first I aint know what the fuck they was talking about. But then I found out it meant something was funny but I still didn't understand because if it was actually so funny that you were weak, why the fuck weren't you laughing. I never got that but yeah anyway.

We used to meet a new group of bitches damn near every day. Especially at the teen parties. It was a couple of them motherfuckers every weekend and we made sure we hit all of them. See, bitches loved me cause I was new, not to mention, had started rapping every damn where I went. That shit was fun to me. Especially when I seen that the bitches liked it.

Then the bitches liked Dock cause he was pretty. Nigga was like gold. He shined every time he came in a room. Bitches just stared at him automatically.

But you'll never guess the reason them bitches loved Jah and Mank. Shit even surprised me when I first seen it. Alright I already told you about Jah and Mank. Straight gangsta ass little niggas. Type of niggas old ladies clutched they purses around. The crazy thing is, the first time I go in the party with them, me and Dock both grilling niggas, staring them down, letting it be known that we was about that life.

Only thing was, Jah and Mank was standing next to us on some other shit. Soon as the beat dropped I looked over to them niggas and they both had this crazy ass smile on they face. Then next thing I know them niggas turn into fucking Dance machine or some shit. I'm talking really getting loose, on some 2003 Kid n Play type shit.

I was like "Yo Dock. What's up with your boys?"

He just shrugged, smiled and said, "Oh yeah, I forgot to tell you they do that a lot."

But shit I couldn't hate. The bitches was crowding around them more than when I rapped. They really loved that shit. Mank and Jah even had they own dance call the 'Wellington Shuffle'. All the niggas would do that while the girls from Wellington would do the 'Park Girl'. Well, obviously you probably already know that. Cause of me it got famous later in life but initially that was all them. Real shit, we was in parties for free and everything.

Sometimes they even put them niggas pictures on the flyer. Come to think about it we should've been charging for that shit. But this when we was young. We was just happy to be around all the bitches.

So yeah we had all the hoes locked down. Us four was like a super crew or something. Hold on for a second. I'm really thinking about how we missed out on so much money. That's crazy, we could've started some party promoting group and took over the party scene. Fuck it though. But ok, let me get back to the story.

With the bitches we'd learned to get exactly what we wanted out of them. They was so damn easy. We aint need no pistol or nothing. All we needed was access to their crib and it was a wrap.

Yeah, we'd play the lover boy role. Kissing and hugging, looking at movies and all that sweet shit but what we really was doing was scoping out the place. Checking for all the valuables. Making little mental notes.

Before we left, after giving them bitches a night to remember, making them fall head over heels in love with us. We'd make sure we left a door or window unlocked. The next day after finding out they parents schedule the night before, we was in that bitch having a field day. Boy we used to come off with so much shit. Little brothers play stations, Moms jewelry, big brothers shoe collection, tons of stuff.

And most them bitches never suspected us. They loved us, why would they think we would do some shit like that to them? Shit, even the ones who did think we did it, it won't nothing they could do about it. Nine times outta ten they'd snuck us in through a window or had company when they won't supposed too. Shit was too easy.

Foreal foreal most of the time after we stole the shit, we'd still be back in the bitch crib, sneaking through the window the very next week. Real shit. I'm telling you. Them hoes loved us.

No funny shit, I aint love them bitches though. I was just having fun doing what the fuck I had to do. Aint shit change. I was still was in love with Alex. As you can see, I just aint have no time for her.

But on them sober nights or them rare high nights when I was up by myself. I still thought about how I was going to get back to her. I aint have no idea on how I would do it but I knew I would.

Out of all the hoes we was running into. Not one of them compared to Alex. Not one. And I was dead sure of that shit. Dead sure. Well until Chenell got a fucking hold of me. Shit got a little fuzzy then.

See, Chenell lived out Wellington. She was an 18 year old part time stripper, part time weed salesman, part time Mom. She was young though so you really can't get mad at her. She was lost. But to me, a 15 year old boy. She was grown. And bad. And not bad as in a girl that all the girls wanted to be or look like or nothing. She was the kinda bad that only niggas could see. She was the type bitch who girls would say "I don't know how she got that nigga, her ugly ass."

Hold on though don't get it twisted. I never said the bitch was ugly. Naw I aint gon go that far. I'm just saying, that's what bitches would say.

Ok let me explain her. She was short, caramel complected, a few scratches on her face but nothing too major. Small framed, no phat ass or big titties or nothing. She aint even have a whole lotta hair. But im telling you, none of that even mattered.

Besides, she kept a fresh weave no matter what. And her smile, man, her fucking smile. Shit just did something too me. She aint do it much but when she did, it just sucked you in. That and her fucking eyes, she just had a way of looking at you that made you rock hard. Like she was undressing you with her eyes or something. It's like she just had this thing too her. This thing that attracted the fuck out of me. I had to have her. I just had to.

The bitch won't easy though, for months she aint give me no play. Every day she'd walk past me and smack her lips and roll her eyes anytime I said a word to her. "Boy if you don't get your little young ass out of my face," she would say in her classic ghetto girl tone. She talked with so much attitude, like her words was bullets or something. She made me feel what the fuck she was saying. Shit made me want her even more.

Especially knowing that she was 18. I was the last one out of the bunch who hadn't fucked a grown woman before. I felt like a failure. I was feigning to see what it was like. Them niggas was always talking about how grown bitches was so much better. I wanted some. Bad.

So yeah I was persistent. Every day, no matter what, I shot my shot. Then one day, a Tuesday, I'll never forget. It was chilly. I had on a red Roca wear Jacket and she walked her sexy ass up holding her son, he was asleep.

"You need help carrying him in the crib?" I asked as I stood on the curb smoking a cigarette.

"Boy your ass just won't stop will you," she said.

"Nope. Ima keep it real. You the shit to me," I said confidently. "Every time I see you, you just do something to me. I don't know if I'ma ever be able to stop. No funny shit."

She smiled. That same smile I loved, my knees got weak and everything. I was tryna play cool but it was hard. Her lip gloss was popping like a mo'fucker.

"Well I'm about to go put him in bed. Come to my crib in a hour or something. We can watch a movie."

"Bet," I said excited as hell.

"Don't get all happy and shit. Aint nobody say you was getting no ass. I just aint got shit else to do, that's all."

"Ok." I smiled. "That's cool. I'll take whatever I can get." I said.

She walked away. "And make sure you bring some weed," she said looking back to me. "Some good shit too. Not none of that bullshit yall little niggas be smoking."

"Bet. I got you."

Boy I damn near fell to the ground and thanked God. A nigga was happy as hell. It aint nothing like trying and trying and trying with a girl and finally getting her. I was mad as hell Dock and the homies won't there to see. But then again she probably only said yeah cause I was by myself.

I remember looking at the time on my Michael Kors gold watch I had stolen from some bitches Dad. It was about 8:00. I ran to Aunt Kim crib, hopped in the shower, brushed my Gold fronts and through on my freshest shit. Even went around the corner to the neighborhood barber, Kenny's crib and got a quick edge up. Copped some weed too, he had it all. Matter fact he even let me spray some of his Burbery cologne on when I told him what I was about to do.

Man a nigga was siked. I had been sneaking in bitches windows for so long I couldn't wait to finally walk through a front door. I knew she said I won't fucking her but shit I'd wait. I just knew the first step was done.

I smoked a blunt on the walk over, I had to get my mind right, I knew I couldn't fuck that opportunity up.

Interlude

"I gotta pee," screamed Nana

"Excuse me Coach," said Sharly.

"Excuse you?" replied Coach.

"Yes. Sorry. I love the story, it's absolutely amazing. But could you please hold on for one second. Please," Sharly said as she stood to her feet.

"I gotta pee," Nana screamed once more as Sharly quickly placed her index finger to her lips, motioning for Nana to lower her tone. Of course this only seemed to make things worse. "Fuck you. I gotta pee," Nana screamed as Sharly cringed.

"What the hell you got going on back there?" asked Coach.

"I'm so sorry," said Sharly as she assisted Nana out of her seat.

"I guess its ok. I gotta piss my own damn self. But if I get back to this phone and you aint ready to talk, I'ma tell you right now. I'm hanging up. Patience is something I lost a long time ago."

"Ok, Ok. I promise I'll be ready."

"Yeah, ok," says Coach as he's heard putting the phone down.

"Ok. Nana, let's go to the bathroom," she said as she held out her hand to assist Nana out of her seat.

"Bitch get your funky ass hand out my face I don't need any help," Nana said as she rocked back and forth attempting to lift her body from the seat.

"Nana, just let me help you please."

"No," Nana screamed still attempting to stand up on her own as Sharly took a deep breath attempting to remain calm.

After about another 45 seconds of relentlessly trying to stand, Nana finally says, "Girl is you just gonna stand there? Help me up."

"Ok Nana," Sharly said. "1,2,3," she counted as she pulled Nana to her feet and walked her to the bathroom.

As they both entered Nana looked back at Sharly. "I can go by myself," she said as she pushed Sharly back, slamming the door behind her.

Taking another deep breath, Sharly checks to see if Coach had arrived back on the phone yet. "Hello, Mr. Coach Coach are you there?"

It's silent. Relieved, Sharly reflects on all that she'd uncovered. Grateful, she looks up to the ceiling. "Thank you Lord," she says as she hears the sound of the toilet flushing. "You ok in there Nana?"

As usual Nana ignores her as she fumbles with the door knob, attempting to open it. "Stupid door," she says.

"You need me to help open it?"

"I didn't ask for no help," Nana says as she continues fumbling with the door.

"Ok," Sharly shays before gently twisting the knob, secretly assisting her.

"I told you I got it," says Nana as she walks out of the bathroom.

"I knew you could do it," says Sharly as Nana mumbles to herself on her way to her rocking chair.

"Hello," Coach says as he returns to the phone.

"Hey I'm here," says Sharly as she stands close to Nana making sure she sits down easily. Of course Nana doesn't feel like being helped. She's silent, but if looks could kill.

"Ok where was I?" asks Coach.

"You were telling me about the time you went over to Chenell's house," says Sharly as she makes her way back over to her spot by the door way.

"Oh yeah, oh yeah. I'm old, my memory aint what it used to be Charlie."

"It's actually Sharly sir."

"What?"

"My name, it's Sharly not Charlie."

"Tomatoe, Tomatoe, who gives a damn. You ready for me to keep going or what?"

"Yes."

"OK."

Slumber Party (Continued)

KNOCK KNOCK. I knocked on the door.

She opened up. Head scarf on, boxer shorts, mix matched colorful socks and a wife beater. Straight gutter. Just like a liked it.

"Why the hell you knocking so loud? My baby sleep," she stated.

"Oh shit my bad," I said walking in. The crib was identical to Aunt Kim's, actually every house out the Park was.

"Yeah, your fucking bad alright," she said as she rolled her eyes. "You bring my damn weed?" she asked as she closed the door.

"Yeah."

"You better had."

"Yo why you so mean?" I asked as I sat down on the pleather couch.

"I aint mean. I'm just real."

"Yeah, real mean."

"Boy shut up," she said as she took a seat. "Give me the weed."

"Why? I can roll it up," I said pulling it from my pocket as I removed my jacket.

"Cause I don't trust nobody rolling my weed," she followed holding her hand out.

"Whatever," I said handing it to her as I looked around at the pictures placed alongside the wall. "Who that?" I asked as I pointed to a picture of her and some guy.

"My Baby Daddy," she answered as she examined the smoke before pulling out a backwood to roll.

"Where he at?"

"Damn nigga. You nosey as hell. What you the feds or something? But if you must know, he locked up," she said as she rolled the blunt faster than anyone I'd ever seen before.

"What the hell he do?" I asked. Had to see if he was a murderer or something. Not that I woulda left. I just had to know what I was up against.

"Shit, what didn't he do. Hopefully he'll be home soon. He aint no snitch like the rest of these clowns in this city."

"Oh so yall getting back together?"

"Who the hell said we was broken up?"

"Oh I was just assuming because--."

"Didn't your Mama ever tell you not to assume?" she replied, cutting me off.

"No," I answered truthfully.

"Well she should've. But if you truly need to know. Naw we aint together. But that's my nigga though. We been through a lot together."

"True."

"So since you asking me all these questions. What sup with you? Why the hell you out here? Actually where in the hell did you even come from? Seems like you just popped up outta nowhere one day."

"I'm from Norview."

"Oh so you a little country ass boy," she said, jokingly.

"Yeah I guess you can say that. But I always heard it aint where you from its where you at."

"Yeah whatever," she said as she lit the blunt. "So let me ask you another question."

"What sup?" I asked.

"What made you want to keep hollering at me even though I kept shutting your ass down?" she asked as she took a puff.

"I told you already. I think you the shit. I needed to get to know you."

"Nigga shut your lying ass up," she said as she passed me the blunt.

"What? How you figure I'm lying?" I asked as I took a puff.

"Cause nigga. I'm not stupid. I been around niggas all my life. I got four older brothers. I know what you want. You want to fuck. It's ok, you can keep it real."

"I am keeping it real," I said hitting the blunt once more. "Of course I want to fuck. Look at you," I said staring at her figure. "Who wouldn't? But it's more to it than that. I just think you dope and I wanted to get to know you."

She smiled. "I'm weak. You think you got game don't you."

"Naw baby aint no game. I'm just telling you the truth."

"Yeah. Yeah. So how old is your little truthful ass?"

"17," I lied.

"17. Yeah right," she said as I passed the blunt over to her. "You probably lying. Probably 16."

"No funny shit, I'm 17 foreal." I said.

"Ok. Fuck all the bullshit," she said, hitting the blunt once more. "Let's cut to the motherfuckin chase. Before we go any further. Let me see that dick."

My eyes got big as shit. Young bitches I was used to aint never come at me like that. Can't even lie, I won't even ready. I aint know what to do. "Huh?" I said, trying to think.

"Nigga you heard me. Let me see your dick. I aint stutter," she said as she continued to smoke. "Life is short and I don't got no time to waste. I need to see what the fuck you working with. Let me see that dick."

Now mind you. In my head I was still thinking about all those times I had been told my shit was small. Naw, I hadn't heard it lately, in fact a couple bitches had even said it was big. But they won't grown. They hadn't even seen too many dicks at that time.

I started doing that nervous sweating shit I be doing. But I knew it won't no way I could get around it without looking like a chump, so I stood up and whipped out anyway.

I turned away as she looked at it. "Oh shit now," she said as she grabbed it. "Ok Ok. I see you," she said as I finally looked down. She had a big Kool-Aid smile on her face. That along with the fact that she had grabbed it, had my shit hard as a rock. "Yeah I can definitely work with that," she said, licking her lips as she took another hit.

"Foreal?" I asked. I aint really mean for that to come out but I was surprised.

"Let's go upstairs," she said, standing up to her feet, pressing her body up against mine.

"Ok," I said as she passed me the blunt. I put my shit back in my pants and followed her up to her room as I smoked.

Stepping in, I looked around. I could tell she was a neat person. The bed was made and all her perfumes and makeup was perfectly placed along the dresser, she didn't even have any clothes on the floor or anything. This wasn't typical of most of the bitches I was fucking with.

"We about to play a game. Take your clothes off," she said as she closed the bedroom door.

"What kinda game?" I asked.

"You'll see in a second, just take your clothes off."

"Ok." I said as I undressed.

She lit candles all throughout the room as I stood watching. Next she looked me in the eyes as she undressed until we was both standing there completely naked. I hadn't been in no situation like that before. She was looking good as a bitch. I wanted to just jump on her. But she was taking shit slow so I chilled.

"Sit on the bed," she said as I obeyed. Next to me was a small bowl with tiny pieces of paper inside of it. "Ok. Like I was saying, we're gonna play a game. Whatever piece of paper you pick is what you will have to do," she said as she laid her naked body across the bed.

"Ok," I said, still mesmerized.

"I'll go first," she said as she dipped her hand inside the bowl. Slowly reading it, she stated, "Massage your partner for 1 minute. Turn around," she said as I followed orders.

Closing my eyes, I flipped over to my stomach as she reached over to the side of her bed, retrieving a bottle of hot massage oil. After squirting a dab into her hand she then slid her fingers down my back in a way I had never felt before. Damn near had a nigga moaning. She definitely did have my toes curling though.

After the minute was over I sat up and it was my turn. I picked up my piece of paper and read, "Give your partner oral sex for 45 seconds."

No funny shit, that shit scared the fuck outta me. Ok let me explain something to you. It was a time, a long long time ago when eating pussy won't really acceptable. Well at least not for hood niggas. I'd like to say I had a part in changing that years later with my songs. But this was long before that. So with that being said. I had never actually ate no pussy. Niggas always told me that shit was nasty. Especially Dock, he always prided his self on being a master tittie sucker. But fuck them niggas, I won't bouta mess up the mood, especially as she laid back, spreading her legs revealing that fat bald pussy. Still, something in my eyes must have let her know I was an amateur.

"You aint never did it before have you?" she asked.

"I mean--."

"It's ok," she said, cutting me off. "You're going to learn everything you need tonight. Come here," she said, signaling with her index finger for me to move closer.

Let me tell you one thing. Her ass won't motherfucking lying. She taught a nigga so much that night. Damn near changed my life. Boy, that bitch turned my young ass out. I don't even think you understand what I'm saying. I went in that house a little ass boy. Came out a grown ass man. Bitch had me in that motherfucker sucking toes, massaging feet, of course eating pussy.

Matter fact she gave me a full tutorial. Sat there and told me the spots that women like. Told me don't be sucking all in the whole. Just massage that clit passionately with my tongue. Some of the most valuable info I ever got till this day.

Man I can't even snatch. Bitch even had me sucking ass. Yep. "Only do this if a bitch is fresh out the shower. Any other time it's nasty. But trust me, girls will go crazy," she said.

And when we fucked boy oh boy that pussy was biting. I lie to you not we did every position ever created.

"Fuck me like this," she'd say. She took control at first. But by the end of the night after hearing so many "Yes Daddy. Yes. Just like that. I love this dick's," I had the confidence to take control.

Oh yeah did I tell you she sucked my dick with a damn fruit roll up? Man, she bought out my inner freak, and that nigga aint went back in since.

Alex was again, the last thing on my mind. Sorry but that's the motherfuckin truth. What can I say? Chenell had me feeling like the way I'd been having sex all them years was just some childish bullshit.

Foreal foreal, it's kinda like she took my virginity. Before her, I was just playing around, pumping without a purpose. Fucking with her, I learned to make an art out of sex.

You know what they say. If the head right, I'll be there every night. And that's just what the fuck I did. I swear every night seemed to get better and better. Can't even snatch, just thinking about it got a nigga dick on hard. Damn Chenell.

Greasy

"Who the hell is that knocking on my damn door?" asked Chenell as we both were waken up. It was about 7 in the damn morning. It had been about six months since the first time I'd came over and a nigga had been there almost every fucking night.

I aint mean for shit to get that serious. At first we was just friends with benefits. I'd even lay next to her while she took her baby daddy jail calls. But after a while shit got deep.

Man, I couldn't even tell you the last time I had talked to Alex around that time. It wasn't really my fault though. It was damn near impossible. Chenell worrisome ass was always around. Bitch was like my damn shadow or something. Looking back, it's clear as day that bitch was fucking up my mojo. No funny shit, I was probably broker than I ever been in my life while I was fucking with her ass.

Foreal foreal, me and Dock both was. Yeah, he was out there hustling and shit but nothing major. Shit had kinda went a little downhill since Jah and Mank had got locked. I'ma get to that in a second though.

And yeah I was still rapping around the hood and shit but it aint like that shit was paying off. I hadn't seen a dime from it. Day after day I hoped I'd run into that nigga Rich, but day after day I was disappointed.

Shit was real. Even when I did have some change in my pocket I couldn't hold on to it if my life depended on it.

Man I blew that shit like I printed it. It's safe to say, being grown, taking care of my self was harder than I expected.

Especially considering the fact Chenell had a seed. I was basically a teenage step Daddy by then. Even had taken family pictures with matching outfits and shit. I was a cold sucker. I couldn't really help it though, I hadn't never had a family, that shit was cool to me. Can't even front, I liked that shit.

And yeah I know I said I aint really ever get a chance to talk to Alex. That don't mean a nigga forgot about her. I still thought about her lil bad ass every day. In the back of my mind I always imagined doing all the shit me and Chenell did with Alex instead. I like to say Chenell was just practice. I aint never want it to be permanent. Shit was just convenient as hell. No matter what, Alex still had my heart. No funny shit.

But yeah, somebody was banging on the door.

"I don't know who the hell it could be," I answered still lying in bed.

"Well aint you gonna go downstairs and check?" shot back Chenell.

"Why don't you go? It's your house not mine."

"Aint you here every night?"

"I'm just saying man. What if it's the police?"

"Boy shut up. If it's the police than just bring your ass back up here and I'll open up. You just being lazy and don't feel like getting outta bed. I swear I'm done messing with yall young ass niggas."

"See, why you always gotta go there. What my age got to do with any of this?"

"Boy I'm not trying to argue with you. Just go get the damn door."

"Man alright," I said as I grabbed my strap from the side of the bed and quietly crept down stairs before peeking out the window.

"It's Dock nigga. Open up," he said as we looked at one another.

"Damn bro," I said opening the door. "What the hell happened to you?" I asked as Dock barged in. His face was fucked. You could tell he'd just got in a fight. Lips swollen. Eye black. Hair fucked up.

"Niggas just banked me bro," he said angrily.

"What? Who?" I asked clutching my .38 tighter. "Fuck they at? Let's go get them niggas."

"Man some fucking plucks."

"Some fuckin feigns?" I asked.

"Yeah nigga. One of them motherfuckers called and said he needed a dub. Then soon as I go meet him, him and his dirty ass heroin homies shot the monkey to my ass and took my work."

"Aw man. What you tryna do bro?"

"It aint what I'm tryna do. It's what I'm gonna do. They lucky I forgot to bring my gun. I'ma kill them niggas soon as I see they ass. No funny shit. I swear to God."

"Kill who?" asked Chenell as she walked down the stairs in her bath robe. "Oh shit," she said as she discovered Docks face. "Who the fuck did that?"

"Some fucking dope feins," I replied as Dock steamed around the room.

"Damn Dock. You need some ice or something?" Chenell asked.

"Man fuck some ice," Dock yelled. "I'm about to put some niggas on ice. I can't believe this shit," Dock screamed. "Dumb ass niggas took everything I had."

"All of it?" I asked.

"Hell yeah! Bitch ass niggas left me out here with nothing. Fuck," Dock screamed again. "I got robbed by some fucking wops. After all the times I cut they ass deals when they brung me all that bullshit ass electronics and shit. After they done dropped to they knees crying for me to save them. They gon pull some shit like this? What the fuck kinda shit is that? I aint never been robbed in my damn life. I do the robbing."

"Damn I always knew them heroin plucks was the worse. Them the type motherfuckers who buy dope before they even buy groceries for they kids," said Chenell.

"Fuck them feigns and they kids," he shouted. "I swear soon as I view one of them niggas I'm dumpin on site. They aint seen crazy yet."

"Come on bro you gotta chill. Don't go too crazy. I don't need your ass in jail too," I said, trying to calm him down.

"Nigga fuck that. I don't give a fuck about shit. I'll die for my respect. Aint no nigga on this earth gon take shit away from me and get away with it. I don't give a fuck bout no jail."

"Ok. Ok. I understand bruh and I'm with you. Whatever you wanna do we can do it. We just gotta be smart. We can't go out like Jah and Mank. No funny shit."

Ok so about Jah and Mank. Around this time, them niggas had got locked up. And naw they won't in no little juvenile detention center, they was charged as adults and sent to 811, the big boy jail. Yeah, they was locked for some serious ass shit. So serious I never even asked them if they did it or not.

See, them niggas had went to a party without me or Dock one night. Long story short they end up getting into it with some Lindenwood niggas from across town. One thing led to another and like most of the parties we went to back then, Jah and Mank ended up shooting the shit up, only difference from past times was that when it was all said and done, one of them Lindenwood niggas was dead.

Only it was the wrong Lindenwood nigga. Instead of one of the so called gangsta niggas who Jah and Mank initially had the beef with getting smoked, some high school football nigga did. He was supposed to be the next Michael Vick or something. So you know everybody in the city went crazy. Next thing I know the Police picking up Jah and Mank two weeks later, saying they did it and shit.

"Nigga didn't I just tell you I don't give a fuck about no jail," Continued Dock. "This shit about principles. Bum ass niggas crossed the fucking line. I don't play with my money."

"Oh yeah, speaking of money," interrupts Chenell from the couch. "I met this white boy at work yesterday who was looking for some weed. Said he was from out of town. I gave him my number. He should be calling me today."

"So what you saying? We can rob him or something?" asked Dock.

"Hell yeah, you know them white boys be full up," answered Chenell.

"Yeah but then he gonna know who did it and where you work," I said.

"Do you know my name? I don't care about that job. I'll quit. I'm getting tired of that shit anyway. Customers be rude as hell," said Chenell. "Besides what's the worst that could happen. Aint like he can go to the police. We good."

"So you think he really gonna call?" asked Dock.

"Shit, I don't know," Chenell said, shrugging her shoulders. "I guess. He said he was."

So we sat down and did what we did every day; smoked. We got high as a bitch. The whole time I'm tryna keep my eyes off Dock face. Shit was hard as hell though. Even after the 'Wellington vs. City' rumble he hadn't looked like that. Dude was fucked the fuck up. Forehead humongous, knotted up. I had always heard heroin feigns was the craziest plucks and Dock face let me know the shit was fucking true. True as hell. Shit made me wanna never wanna serve a feign again. Won't like I was good at it anyways. I was too lazy to be waiting around for feigns and shit. I rather get the fast cash.

That's why I couldn't wait for that white boy to call. We needed that money, I was broke as a bitch. Man sitting here talking to you really got me thinking about what I said about me being a sucker earlier. I can make excuses about never having a family and all that bullshit. But I let that bitch Chenell bring me down.

My dumbass should've have known she aint have no sense. She was the type bitch who always was talking about how her son aint want for nothing. That would be cool and all if she won't just talking about New Jordan's. I mean foreal what the fuck kinda logic is that? Jordan's? Babies don't give a shit about no damn Jordan's. Dumb ass. Sometimes broke people can be so fucking backwards.

But yeah man I was doing perfectly fine without her ass. Getting money, fucking bitches. Soon as I settle down and be a family guy I started struggling. I aint gon say loving a bitch is wrong. But I guess when you love the wrong girl, God gon give you all the signs that she aint the one.

Only problem is, that love shit leave you blind. Have you making the dumbest decisions. My bad, I know I bought that up outta nowhere but telling my story, just gets me to thinking and shit. But anyway, back to what I was saying. We needed that lick.

We all sat quiet as hell, waiting impatiently for the white boy to call. Hours went by. Still nothing. Growing restless, we started to think he'd never hit her up. But about damn near 8 hours later. The phone rang.

"Hello, yeah this is her," said Chenell. "What sup Dillon," she says as Dock and I focus our attention over to her." Yeah he has anything you need. Hell yeah. About 5

Ok, that's cool. The address is 1300 Bancker. Ok cool," said Chenell before hanging up the phone. She sat calm for a second as Dock and I waited for her to speak. "This nigga wants to buy 3 fucking pounds of mid," she screamed. "I told his dumbass $5000."

We got hype as hell. Together we had hit plenty licks and shit but never as much as five thousand dollars at one time. "Yo when is he coming?" I asked.

"He said he's on his way. I gave him the address to the house on Bancker."

Bancker was this street right across from Wellington Park with a bunch of Abandoned homes. All I had to do was sit on the porch and act like it was my crib. Now that I think about it, Chenell wasn't all bad. She had a few smart moments. "Ok. Which one of yall going to do it?" she asked looking over to Dock and I.

"I'll do it," said Dock.

Now let me make something clear, I had never actually officially ran a play without Dock. But with that nigga over there beat the fuck up I knew I had to take control. Besides, it was about time I put in some real work. I had to learn one day. "Naw I got it," I said, standing up.

"Bro chill, it's cool I don't mind," said Dock.

"Hell naw bro. You round here looking like Martin Payne after he fought Tommy Hearn's. Aint no way I'ma let you go."

He and Chenell both laugh. "Yeah bro. He's right," followed Chenell.

After a little more convincing, I finally got Dock to agree that I was going dolo. Cant front, walking over I felt like a real gangsta. I liked that shit. I knew I had to pull that shit off. I had been in Docks shadow for way too long. It was time for me to put on my big boy drawers.

Once I got there, I posted up looking around for the police. They was my only worry. I damn sure wont scared of no white boy. If push came to shove and he tried to act tough, I had my strap, I was just gon smoke him and dip. Fuck it. I won't scared to catch a body. It seemed like I was the only one around who hadn't murked somebody anyway.

Time was moving slow as hell as I sat on the porch steps smoking a cigarette, rapping to myself.

'I treat my pistol like my son...Raise it and let it go.'

As I rocked to my imaginary beat I looked around, patiently. I would've stayed there all night waiting. I didn't give a fuck. Shit was important. Plus Dock and Chenell was depending on me.

Then finally, out of the darkness I spotted his little white head driving up. Somewhat nervous, I hit my cigarette one more time as his Malibu pulled up to the curb and he waved for me to get in.

"It's ShowTime," I said to myself as I flicked my cigarette, walked over and hopped in.

"What sup man I'm Dillon," he said. He was a wigger. Hat to the back. Listening to Rap.

"What sup bro? I'm Larry," I said.

Don't even ask what made me say Larry. Usually I was Jamal. But that was when I was bagging bitches. I hadn't ever had to come up with a robbery name before. Larry just slid off my tongue for some reason.

He pulled out the cash. "It's 5000 right?"

"Yep and it's some straight fire. I smoked some about three hours ago and I'm still high. You gonna love it," I said.

"Great. That's what sup," he replied before handing me over the cash. I couldn't believe he did that shit. He had just made my job 1000 times easier.

"Man the weed's in the house," I said pointing over to it. "I'm going to go get it. I didn't want to bring it out until I knew you weren't the police. You can never be too safe."

"Oh ok bro. No problem I understand."

"Cool I'll be right back."

I hopped out the whip. I couldn't believe shit was so fucking easy. It was unbelievable. The front door was unlocked as I walked in the vacant crib as if I lived there, dodged a couple spider webs. Opened the back door and dipped through the back yard.

After hopping a gate I started to sprint, running faster than I'd ever did in my life. Fuck that. I had to finish that shit. "Oh shit," I repeated over and over to myself. I really couldn't' believe it was that easy. Like how? But fuck it, it was what it was. I aint stop running till I burst back in Chenell's crib.

"Yo what sup?" yelled Dock as he hopped up gun in hand. "You good? Somebody chasing you?"

I stood speechless for a few seconds, bending over to catch my breath. "We rich bitch," I shouted as I reached in my pocket, throwing the cash into the air.

"AYYYE," screamed Dock, excitedly.

"AYYYE," followed Chenell.

"AYYYE," added Joel her son as he through his little arms into the air.

I flopped down onto the couch feeling like a boss. I had finally did shit on my motherfucking own. Yeah Chenell helped but I was the one who executed it. Now I really knew I was a man.

That night we copped some weed, got some pills and liquor, invited some of the Wellington Park niggas and bitches over, got fucked up and partied all night. Yep, Dock too, we was so high he forgot how fucked up his face looked. I didn't though. Joked his ass the whole damn night. We had a ball.

Nothin on Ya

After we got that damn money we split that shit three ways and with my cut I already knew what the hell I had to do. Wasting no time me and Dock got Aunt Kim to rent us a whip and we shot back out to Norview.

I told Chenell that I needed to go see my Mama but really she was the last person on my mind. Yeah, I did think about stopping through. I'll be a liar if I told you I never thought about her. But come on now you already know all I was really worried about seeing was Alex. I was feigning, I even tricked off a couple hundred on a promise ring just to let her know everything was going to be ok and that I won't going nowhere.

Driving back to Norview, Dock drove the whole way. Since moving to Norfolk we had both been practicing our driving skills on feign whips. Besides the fact that we both drove with two feet, one for the gas and one for the break, we had grown pretty good at it. So good that I didn't even pay any attention to Dock as we skated through traffic. The entire drive I sat, leaned back listening to Surf Rider, smoking weed, thinking about the first words I was gonna say to Alex when I saw her. A nigga had butterflies. I couldn't wait. And the closer we got the more nervous I got.

Man riding through had me really missing the old hood. I had been so busy in Norfolk getting high and shit, I had kinda been mentally disloyal. In my head, I was thinking as if Norfolk was my home. But as I cruised through, breathing that good old Norview air, I grew an appreciation for the place. No matter what Norview had my heart. Being there just gave me an at ease feeling. Like I was at peace or something. Complete comfort.

Before I knew it we was pulling up to Alex's crib right behind some little Toyota Camry. Instantly I sprung up from my seat. From where I was sitting it looked like two people was sitting in the car. A boy and a girl. But it couldn't be.

"Yo what the fuck is going on?" I asked as I looked over to Dock. He shook his head and shrugged. It was obvious he seen the same shit that I did.

Man I knew it was Alex but my mind aint wanna believe the shit. Yeah, I had been gone for a while but still, the thought of her with another nigga aint never even cross my mind. You know what I'm saying?

In the movies the girls always wait for the nigga no matter what. Guess I had been watching too many cause that definitely won't how real life was playing out. In complete disbelief I rubbed my eyes trying to make sure they won't playing tricks on me. "This can't be what the fuck I think it is bro," I said to Dock still never taking my eyes off of the car.

"I think it is bro," said Dock as we both continued staring. "Yep. I think it is," he repeated.

Then it was solidified. My world came crashing down, heart sunk down to my damn stomach and eyes got watery. My worst nightmare had happened right before my eyes. Them motherfuckers had the nerve to kiss.

"Oh hell naw bro," I shouted, voice cracking, before I hopped out the whip sprinting over to that bitch ass nigga's car. I opened that motherfucking driver side door and let his ass have it. "What the fuck is yall doing?" I yelled.

"Who are--," he attempted to say before I stole off on his bitch ass repeatedly in the face as he screamed like a little hoe.

"Stop," yelled Alex as she hopped out the car rushing over to pull me off. "Stop it Skylar," she screamed as I pushed her away.

"What the fuck," I said, finally turning around. "You cheating on me?" I asked as her little boy friend sped off.

"What the hell is wrong with you?" Alex screamed.

"What the hell is wrong with you?" I shot back. "Sitting out here kissing other niggas and shit."

"So."

"So? So? You my fucking girl. What do you mean so?"

"Your girl? Your girl? Since when? I aint heard from you since Christmas. It's April. What did you think, I was just going to sit around waiting for your ass?"

"Hell yeah," I shouted. "So what? So what? It's over? You don't want to be with me? Is that what you're saying?"

Alex took a deep breath. A tear shot down. "I can't believe you. It's you who doesn't want to be with me.

You're so selfish. You don't think I've been worried about your ass. You don't call. You don't send letters. You could be out there dead for all I know," she said as she shook her head in anger. "Now you wanna show back up like everything's all good. Running people away. Fuck you. I hate you," she shouted.

"You don't mean that. I know you don't hate me."

"Yes I do."

"Look me in my eyes and say it."

She looked up. "I hate you."

"No you don't. You love me. And I love you."

"Whatever Skylar," she said as she turned away from me.

"Tell me you don't love me."

"Leave me alone."

"No. Tell me you don't love me. And I will. I promise I'll leave you alone. Just tell me."

"I don't love you," she mumbled still looking away.

"Man I aint tryna hear that shit. You do and I know you do. Man what we got is special. This shit mean everything to me and I thought it meant something to you too. I love your ass more than anything and you know that."

"You love me? Love me,?" Alex said, finally looking back up at me. "How? You love so much that you don't call and check on me? Is that how you think love works?"

"I'm sorry baby. Foreal. I just got so much going on."

"Too much going on to check on me? Or even just to say hey?"

"I know. I know it aint no excuse. I'm sorry."

She huffed and puffed.

"Can I have a kiss?" I asked as she turned from me once again. "Please. I miss you," I said. "I miss everything about you," I followed up before stepping closer, pecking her on her cheeks and neck. "Give me a kiss." I continued pecking her before grabbing her face and turning it to mine. "I love you baby," I said as Alex finally looked me in the eyes, allowing me to kiss her lips.

And just like that we was back. We had to get the fuck away from her spot though. Francis was back and she knew if he caught me over there he was calling the boys ASAP. So later that night she snuck out and I got Dock to drop us off at a hotel.

"You fuck that nigga?" I asked as we laid cuddled in bed. She was half sleep. I had just showed her everything I'd learned from Chenell. But boy, doing it with Alex was like a million times better. I swear.

With Chenell it was just some good ol fucking, ass smacking, thumb in the booty freaky type shit, you know what I'm saying. With Alex though, not saying I aint get nasty, but it was slower, it was like our souls was connecting or some shit. Made me never want to leave her again. I could tell she felt the same way by the way she was holding me.

"No. Hell no," she answered. "To be honest, the only reason I was even with him was because I had to get my mind off of you. How about you?" she asked.

"How about me what?"

"Did you have sex with anybody?"

"Huh?" I said, gathering my thoughts.

"I don't even know why I asked that," she said turning to her side.

"Baby, no. No I didn't. No funny shit I'm out there stressed out. Shit crazy in Norfolk. I can't even begin to tell you what's been going on. But I can tell you one thing," I said as Alex sat silent still turned to the side. "I guess you don't care," I said.

"I do. Tell me," she said turning to look over to me.

"You know the last thing we was talking about when I was here."

"What?"

"You don't remember?"

"You talking about careers?" she asked.

"Yeah. Well I found something I'm good at."

"Really? What?" she questioned, turning around to look at me.

"Probably aint gonna believe me but I can rap. I'm gonna be a rapper."

"A rapper?"

"Yeah. Bae I'm the truth. No funny shit. Everybody in Norfolk loves me. I even met this big time nigga who's about to take me to the studio. I write songs every day."

I had to throw a little sauce on it. Aint like I was lying. Rich was supposed to take me to the studio. Yeah I hadn't heard from him since the first day we met. But shit, I still thought about him every day. And I really mean every day. How couldn't I? He was my way out. It was damn near impossible for me to forget. There was no other way for me to make it and I knew it.

And yeah maybe I won't really writing new songs every day, I was on the go too much. I aint have no time to be jotting down rhymes but I had gotten kinda good at memorizing all the good ones. For some reason they just stuck to me.

"Ok. Mr. Rapper. Let me hear something," Alex asked, smiling showing off her tiny gap that I loved so much.

"You wanna hear something?" I asked. "Ok .Ok. Hold on. I got you. I wrote something for you matter fact," I said as I cleared my throat.

"No you didn't," she said as she blushed.

"I'm dead ass serious," I said standing up. "You ready?" I asked as she nodded.

"I'm outchea tryna get it...

You know my time is limited...

I'm riding with my pistol.....

Aint riding with no bitches...

I know you don't trust niggas...

I'm nothing like them niggas...

I spit for about 3 minutes before Alex started crying.

"I love it."

"And I love you too," I said before crawling back in bed.

You know a good way to tell if you're in love? Listen to an old RnB song that you grew up on. If you don't listen with a new ear and start understanding the lyrics a little more than you used to, than you aint in love.

Safe to say I was in love. I think if we both could've just stayed locked up in that damn hotel for the rest of our lives, we would have been just fine with that. Everything was perfect. I had a hit of my favorite drug one more time and I was back hooked. It was just what I needed.

The next morning was the worst. No matter how bad I didn't want to go back to Norfolk, I knew I had too. We was living two separate lives. I remember holding her tight wishing the nightmare of me being on the run could be over. She felt the same way. She begged me to just turn myself in. I couldn't though. Not yet. The way niggas had explained it to me, they could sentence me to Juvenile Life and have me in that bitch till I was 21 or something. Trying to wait it out till I was 18 seemed to be the best option. She hated it but she understood. Plus I told her I would do whatever I had to do to see her more often and make sure I called every day. We hugged, but it didn't seem long enough. I had to force myself to let her go.

It killed me seeing her walk away when we dropped her off. Felt like everything I had was leaving me. Had a nigga feeling empty. Probably the main reason I told Dock to stop pass my Mama crib. I guess I hoped somehow she could make me feel better. Temporarily fill Alex's void or something. After all, it was my Mama.

I figured even though she was crazy as hell she still had to be wondering was I good. Showing my face was the least I could do.

We pulled up and I hopped out the whip. "Yo I'ma come say what sup too," said Dock.

"Ok," I said as he followed me inside.

We walked up to the door, no matter where I lived I always kept my Mama house key. So yeah, I opened the door. And do you know what the fuck I saw? I bet you'll never believe it.

You remember how me and Dock had Freaky Kesha? Butt naked, one of us in the front, the other in the back? Well yeah you guessed it. My Mama was butt naked in the middle of the living room, screaming and moaning, getting pounded from the back while a dick was shoved deep in her mouth. Yep. Yep. Now I'ma tell you something, growing up I can vividly remember probably hundreds of niggas coming in and out my house. So I guess it kinda goes without saying that I'd caught her doing the nasty before.

One time in particular that I can't seem to get out my head is the day I burst into her room before school. I had to be in about 2nd grade. I had left something in there, can't remember what it was, but yeah I was going to get it.

Man what I saw damn near made me throw up on myself. My Mama, the lady who'd birthed me, was getting beat from the back by our old ass next door neighbor Mr. Jenkins. It fucked me up cause dude was like 80 years old. Still, with time I got over it.

But what I seen on this particular day, was a little harder to forget. Her crazy ass had not only crossed the line but she squatted down and shitted on that motherfucker. Naw, not just because it was two niggas but because of who the two niggas was. Weak ass Chris and Ugly Ass Chris. The only two niggas I had considered my friends besides Dock in Norview.

"What the fuck," I shouted.

"Oh shit," said Weak ass Chris as he hopped up, throwing his hands in the air like we was the police or something.

"Yo. Yo. My bad," said Ugly Ass Chris as he did the same.

"Boy what the hell you doing here?" my Mom asked, still on all fours.

I looked over to Dock. I aint have to say a word. We hopped on them nigas so damn fast it would've made your head spin. I aint never think I would have to beat a nigga with his pants down but fuck it. We went to work on they ass, straight beat the dog shit outta them as my Mama sat on the side laughing.

"So is yall still gon give me that weed yall promised me?" she said to Ugly Ass Chris and Weak ass Chris as Dock and I shot out of the front door.

Stunt

"Fuck," I screamed as I walked away from a dice game. Man ever since I'd come back from Norview it seemed like I won't catching shit but losses. A Nigga couldn't win for losing. Had me bouta off myself. Stressed out like a motherfucker.

It had been two weeks since we'd robbed the white boy and I aint have shit but $100 to my name. Actually I had 0 because I had just lost that in the damn dice game. I thought about going back and sticking that bitch up but I knew that was out the question. It was too many consequences that came along with it and I aint even have time for all that shit.

What made shit even worse was the fact that Chenell was counting on me. She was gonna have a selling party the next day and was gonna use her ebt card to buy the food and my job was to use the $100 I had to buy the liquor. But with me losing all my money I had fucked the whole plan up. I aint know how I was gonna tell her that shit.

Yeah a smart nigga would've invested his money in some drug; weed, crack, dope, something. But naw I won't a smart nigga. I was a dumb nigga. Ol dumb ass broke ass nigga. I was the type of nigga who would have $200, spend $100 on some shoes, $30 on a hat another $30 on some smoke and try to win all of it back with the other fourty at the dice game.

Can you blame me though, aint like nobody ever taught me how to handle money.

Still my dumbass should have learned from the hundreds fucking times I had made the same mistake. Shit always left me looking stupid, struggling to find a way to make shit better. Well, I'm not sure if better is the right thing to say. Because the shit that came through my head, probably would have made shit a million times worse.

Man the thoughts of a broke nigga is enough to get a nigga life in Prison. I swear I'll never forget. Boy, it was times like that when I swear I used to have the most demonized thoughts running through my head. No funny shit, being broke is sometimes worse than being dead. In a world where money is everything it's the closest thing to it.

That broke shit causes you to take risk that you normally wouldn't because after all, if it don't work out the worse that can happen is that you die. And since you already feel like dying, its like fuck it. Ya feel what I'm saying?

I aint even told you the worse part yet. Dock was locked the fuck up. Yep. They finally got his ass. Had me in them streets on my dolo shit. Losing him was the main reason I was broke. It was like I couldn't think without his ass or something. With him, we at least had a chance at making some sorta profit every day.

Yeah, he was bad with money too, but he made up for it by always seeming to find a way to get some more. Even if was creeing the block, serving feigns fake drugs.

We aint like doing that because all the older real hustlers would tell us we sending the feigns away to other hoods. But when we was flat broke we aint give a damn about all that. Plus, all the older niggas knew who Dock's family was so most of them knew it won't really nothing they could do about it. But with me being alone, I was considered an outsider, it won't no telling what would happen if I would've pulled some shit like that. Especially since Demetrius and Donnell had both been sent up the road for five years a piece.

Oh yeah, before my old ass forgets, let me tell you how the fuck Dock ass had even got locked up in the first place. Shit was stupid as hell. So yeah, one day as he was walking to the store to get a couple blunts the fucking Police pulled up on him. It was school hours and his little ass strolling through the projects stood out like a sore thumb. He was basically asking for it.

Can't say I don't understand him though. We had been on the run for a while and it had gotten to a point where we won't even moving like we needed to be careful. Guess we had gotten a little too comfortable.

I heard he tried to run but apparently he won't fast enough. When news got to me. Shit fucked my head up. Being alone won't even something I had been thinking about. But shit, I had to do it. Won't no other choice.

No funny shit, a part of me wanted to join him. That bitch Chenell was stressful as hell. She always needed something. Shit won't really the same no more. Lack of money changes a lot in a relationship.

Still, I could never bring myself to walking up to no damn police station and giving them my wrists. Fuck that. Summer time was approaching and I had big plans for me and Alex. I can't even snatch, I aint have no damn idea how

I was actually going to do any of it but I damn sure knew wont no way I could do anything from behind a cage. Fuck that.

Since I'd came back to Norfolk I had been sneaking away and calling her every day. She was still telling me to turn my ass in. "Just do it. I promise I'll wait for you." I won't listening though. I was too busy thinking of ways to get paid. A nigga mind was blank as hell though.

I walked home from the dice game head hanging low. As I moped, I remember something inside me telling me to lift my head, man up, I had to be strong. When I did, I seen a pearl BMW driving down the street towards me. My first thoughts was how nice it had to feel to own one of them bitches. I knew only rapping could get me something as smooth as that.

Yeah I was still rapping, but more so just for fun. Day by day I was losing faith of it actually being a way I could get paid. I was slowly coming to terms with the fact that I probably won't gonna never see that nigga Rich again. In my head I assumed the nigga must've forgot about me or something.

"What sup little nigga," said a voice coming from the BMW.

Chenell always told me about making assumptions.

Like always my ass was wrong again. The motherfucker driving the Beamer was Rich. Ears blinging, wrist blinging, looking like a million bucks and smelling like it too. I'll never forget the fresh fragrance of some expensive ass cologne he had on hitting my nose like a Mayweather jab as I walked up to his driver side window.

I tried to speak back, but the words won't coming out. His bitch in the passenger seat had fucked my head up for a second. No funny shit, the baddest bitch I had ever seen up close and personal. The bitch was like something outta a music video or something. Brown skin, real hair hanging, skin glistening, looking good as hell.

"I said what sup nigga. Cat got your tongue or something?" asked Rich.

"Oh shit. What sup," I said after snapping outta my trance.

"I told yo little ass I was coming back," he said as he smiled. "You still spitting that hot shit?"

"Yeah sometimes."

"Sometimes? Man get in the car. I'm about to take yo young ass to the mo'fuckin studio," he said pressing the unlock button.

"Right now?" I asked.

"Yeah nigga."

"OK," I said as I opened the door carefully before plopping down on his leather seats.

"So what the fuck you been u too?" he asked as he pulled off.

"Chilling. Nothing much."

"Yeah you look like you been chilling," he said, looking through the rearview mirror. "You aint got no money in your pockets do you?"

"Naw," I said hoping he would give me some. He looked as if he had a few extra dollars to spare.

"Nigga you better get you some. Don't none of these hoes want no broke ass nigga. You don't wanna grow up to be one of them dusty ass niggas who always talking about money but don't get none. They the worse type niggas in the world. How old is you?" he asked.

"I just turned 16."

"16? And you walking? Nigga you tripping. When I was 16 I had a 300z and all types of jewelry. Fly shit. I was a God Damn motherfuckin hoe magnet. A nigga like me would have took all your little bitches back in the day," he said as he continued looking at me through the rearview. "You one of them robbing, stealing ass niggas aint you?"

"Naw," I said. "Why you say that?"

"Nigga. I'm a real street nigga. I know you is. I can tell by your whole demeanor. I aint mad at you though. The streets supposed to have niggas like yall. That's how the game go," he said before pausing. "I'll tell you one thing though. Don't run up on me with that dumb shit. Cause I'll put a hot one in your ass," he said flashing his pistol. "I don't tolerate no bullshit."

I aint know what to say so I just sat there.

"So you wrote anything since the last time I seen you?"

"Not really. I got some shit memorized though."

"Is it hot?"

"Hell yeah. Well at least I think it is," I said.

"Think? Come on man. Aint no thinking. You gotta know. Matter fact, fuck it. If it aint hot you can just write something while you in the studio. You think you can do that?"

"Yeah I can."

"Alright. I hope so. I'ma let you know now. It's going to be some heavy motherfuckers in there. Mite fuck around and see anybody. If you do good, you never know what might happen."

"Ok," I said as he turned up the music and we road in silence, bopping our heads.

Ay! I aint even gonna lie. Riding around in luxury listenting to old school RnB had a nigga feeling prestigious as hell. I stared out the window hoping somebody I knew would catch a glance of me.

After about 20 minutes we pulled up to the studio. Man it was butta ass whips every damn where. Lexus's, Hummers, everything. I hadn't seen shit like that before. First instinct was to burst through the glass and take everything in them bitches. I knew they had to have all types of fly shit on the inside; guns, money, drugs, Dock woulda had a motherfucking field day out that bitch.

I mentally remembered where the fuck we was at just in case I decided to make a surprise visit back one day.

As far as when we walked inside the studio though, its only one word that can describe the feeling. Home. Music playing, weed smoke in the air, top shelf liquor bottles scattered all around. But the best thing out of all that. Knockout was there. I don't know if you know who the fuck he is, but back then, in VA he was the shit. Naw he won't super famous or nothing. But locally he was the man.

"What sup youngin," he said to me after Rich had introduced us.

"What sup," I said, standing straight looking him in the eyes, trying to let him know I meant business.

"I'm Knockout."

"Yeah I know," I followed.

"Cool. You got something for this beat playing right now?"

I listened for a second.

"Give him some time he about to write something," said Rich as he and his girl sat on a small couch.

"I don't have that much time I'm about to dip out," said Knockout. "I thought he had something already."

"Naw I do. I do," I said looking at Rich. "I told you I had some shit memorized."

To tell the truth I was lying. Naw not about the fact that I had shit memorized. Yeah, I had plenty of shit. But what I really was about to do was get in that bitch and go off the top of the dome. I had that feeling.

Growing up I used to always listen to certain songs to get me through different situations. But shit felt way better being able to create something from my own feelings. It's like I was hosting a mini tornado in my brain or something. Thoughts would just be flying everywhere. I was just starting to figure out what it was back then but now I know that's what happens when I got some major shit to get off my chest. I start getting all jittery and anxious, bobbing my head all crazy. I'm telling you, shit gets real.

"Can I hit the blunt right quick?" I asked.

"Damn right," replied Knockout as he handed it over.

I smoked for a second as I got my mind organized. I had so much shit running through that motherfucker. With everything I had going on I probably could have rapped for days. Sometimes in life when you going through a lot, in order for you to function you tend to push shit to the back of your mind but rapping always bring everything to the forefront for me. It allowed me to express myself without having to actually speak a word to anyone about it.

The tricky part is fitting all the thoughts in my head into song format. Over the years I found myself comparing my song writing process to a puzzle. Inside of me I possesed all the pieces to a hit, I just had to find a way to make it all make sense. It aint easy but it still comes pretty natural to me.

What wasn't natural was stepping into the booth and rhyming on a beat and microphone. At least I didn't think it was. I walked in slow as hell, intimidated.

The fear aint last long though. As I stood in front of the mic I took in a deep breath, slid on my headphones, looked through a big ass glass over to Knockout and nodded my head as the beat dropped and my eyes closed. Within seconds I was letting loose. No chorus, nothing. Emotions spilled from my body onto the track.

'Sometimes I'm this,

I feel like laying a track,

Sometimes I'm that,

I feel like grabbin a mask,

Sometimes I'm here,

I love where I'm at,

Sometimes I'm there,

I wish I could go back...'.

Shit was like therapy, I aint stop spitting until my headphones went silent. Sweat dripped into my pupils as I finally opened my eyes. Removing the headphones, I looked out through the glass. Everyone was watching me.

Walking out, I was confused, as I got closer to them, they remained staring, not saying a word.

"What sup? I did something wrong?" I asked.

Then Knockout spoke. "Little Nigga we about to get you famous," he yelled as a few of his friends chimed in.

Shit reminded me of how the niggas out Wellington reacted after I'd freestyle that day after The Hustlers video shoot. I looked over to Rich, he and his girl sat in the same spot they'd been in. Refusing to break his cool, he simply nodded his head, clapping his hands softly as his girl did the same.

"Yo we gon teach you how to write some hooks and 16's and we gon get you popping foreal young'n," shouted Knockout.

"One take," somebody else shouted.

"We got us something here," added another.

I recorded two more songs that night. Those two had hooks that I had memorized before. I can't remember them right now but I'm telling you everybody loved them shits too. Knockout said he could see it in my eyes that I was going to make it. Said he could tell I had something special in me.

I think that might've been the best night of my life back then. By the time we left later that night, I was high as hell and happy then a motherfucker.

"You know you my new best friend right?" said Rich as he dropped me off at Chenell's crib.

I smiled. "Yeah I do now," I said as I exited the car before sticking my head back in. "What's your number so I can call you?" I asked as he nodded his head before jotting it down on a napkin for me.

"Hit me up tomorrow," he said, handing it over to me. "I'm about to change your life. Real shit."

I jetted in the crib and told Chenell the good news. She was so happy she aint even care that I had lost the money for the selling party. When I tell you everybody knew how important Rich was, I aint lying.

Her ass even started talking about all the expensive ass shit she wanted me to buy her when I got on. In my head I was thinking, 'You just don't know your time is limited'.

That won't the only thing on my mind though. Something ten times as important was weighting heavy on me.

"Yo I'm on the run," I said, sadly to Chenell as we stood at the foot of the bed.

"Ok. What is that supposed to mean?"

"How the fuck am I gonna be a rapper if I got the fucking police on my ass."

"Are you serious? Nigga we're gonna be rich. Rich people don't go to jail. They pay for good ass lawyers. You gonna be good," Chenell said before pushing me on to the bed. "Trust me," she said before she hopped on top of me.

"I'm really about to make it," I said to myself as I flushed the toilet later on that night. I stood naked in the mirror shaking my head in disbelief of how good life was gonna be and all the fly ass shit I was gonna cop.

Opening the door, I damn near jumped out my body. Joel, Chenell's son was standing outside. "Oh shit," I said. I wasn't expecting him to be up.

"Whoa. Your balls," he said staring directly at them. "What's wrong with them?" he asked disgusted.

"Joel what you talking about?"

"There--there so big," he said, pointing as I laughed.

"These the balls of a man," I said as he opened his underwear looking at his own. "Go on back to bed," I said, pushing him along.

"Ok," he said as he continued looking down at his little sacks.

I stepped out of the bathroom and tip toed back to the bedroom. I couldn't wake Chenell up. Her horny ass was a damn sex feign. I knew if she seen me naked, dick swinging all wild, it was definitely gonna result in another sweaty ass sex session. Don't get me wrong, I loved pussy just like every other nigga but damn sometimes a nigga needed a break. Bitch was a fucking animal.

The fresh air of the night was calling my name though. So quietly I slipped on the pants I'd had on earlier and headed out for a smoke. I had to calm my nerves a little.

After going through so much bullshit in my life, I felt as though things were finally about to change. And the fact that I was changing it by doing something that meant so much to me just made shit even better. Being in that booth was everything. It gave me a sense of purpose. Finally I had something to live for that I could call my own. Something that no one could take away from me. Something I would die for.

As I stepped outside, I lit my cigarette and told myself that it was time for me to dedicate my entire life to music. I knew no matter what I had going on, music had to come first. Even before Alex. It wasn't so much that I was putting her second, I just knew I had to put myself first in order to get where I needed to be. Ultimately putting me in position to help the both of us.

Every day I was going to have to make progress. Even if it was something as small as writing a hook, I knew I had to work to be the best. On the ride home that night, Rich had told me a story of how he started getting money. He said every day he strived to be better than the next day. And from the looks of him, his plan had worked. I was gonna apply the same shit to my music.

"I gotta make it," I said to myself as I flicked my cigarette and turned to the door to go back into the house.

"Ay my nigga, who the fuck is you?" said a voice coming from behind me.

I turned around. "Who am I? Nigga who is you?" I asked.

Before I could even fully realize what the fuck was going on dude rushed me attempting to punch me in the face. My reflexes was too fast for him though. I dodged his shit, catching him with a left hook.

No funny shit, it aint take long before I was kicking dude ass. Every swing I took connected to his face or body as he failed to get another swing in. It was easy. I was 6'3 and he was a little short ass nigga.

"Motherfucker," he screamed, as he backed away. I stood in place studying his blood covered face, trying to recognize him. I knew I'd seen him somewhere before but for the life of me I couldn't figure out from where.

Then it hit me. "Gene?" I said.

It was Chenell's baby daddy. I had recognized him from all the pictures that used to be on the wall before I had made her take them down.

"Fuck you nigga," he said as he pulled a pistol from his waist.

"Oh shit," I yelled before turning around to run. I was too late.

BOW BOW BOW

First Day Out

"Before I hand you down your sentence, Mr. Grant is there anything you would like to say to the court."

I sat timidly in a wheelchair next to my lawyer. My oversized orange jumpsuit dangled from my body as my now useless feet sat trapped inside the cold steel shackles. Slowly I turned my head to the left of me where the victims family sat. They all stared to me with the same hatred. Taking a deep breath I quickly attempted to gather my words. I knew this would be the only shot I had. I was fighting for my life. If I would have known they would ask me to speak I would have had something prepared. They played the hell outta me though. Judge probably wanted me to say something stupid so she could have even more of a reason to throw the book at my ass. Knowing that, I knew I had to come up with something good, fast.

Speaking in my most respectable voice I turned back to the judge, eyeballing her attempting to come off as sincere as possible.

"Yes Ma'am. I would like to say that I am not a bad person. Yes my crime was bad. I understand that. But I grew up tough. No Father. Basically no mother. As you can see, I'm 16 years old and she is nowhere in sight. I was forced to raise myself. There were never any positive role models around. Everything around me was negative from the movies I watched to the men my Mom bought around me. So when I was old enough to go outside I sorta found myself naturally drawn to negativity. It felt right to me. But as I've sat in my cell, thinking, reading, discovering that the way I was living was totally wrong and unacceptable I now have a new lease on life. During my time incarcerated I have been working on my God given talent. Rapping. I have connections with the industry and I'm sure I will be able to establish a career upon release. With that career I will use my gift of words to steer kids like myself away from the streets. Instead I will teach them to focus on their dreams and never stop until they make it. Please have mercy on me. I was lost but I assure you that I am found. With that being said I ask for one more chance. I will not disappoint you all because I will also be disappointing myself and I refuse to let myself down again. I deserve nothing but the best. Lastly I want to say I am sorry to the victim," I said looking back to him and his entire family as they continued stale faced staring at me. "I'm sorry for the pain I've caused you and your loved ones. I know this has to be painful just seeing my face again. Words can not express my apologies. You didn't deserve what I put you through and I hope you can somehow find it in your heart to forgive me. Again, I'm sorry," I said before turning back to face the judge.

"Are you finished?" she asked.

"Yes ma'am," I answered sincerely.

"Well in that case. After listening, I have to tell you. I come across people like you every day. You say you will change. But you never do. I have given my fair share of second chances and quite frankly I'm tired of it," she says sternly. "So with that being said. I will charge you as an adult and recommend 10 to15 years in a maximum security prison.

"10 to 15 years. Fuck," I said under my breath as I dropped my head and closed my eyes.

"Baby. Baby," I opened my eyes and Alex was standing in front of me.

Gotcha. That shit was just a dream. Well, not a dream, more like a motherfucking nightmare. Turns out I was in the hospital.

"You ok?" Alex asked as I slowly looked around at my surroundings.

I sat speechless, trying to make sense of where I was. Once it hit me I immediately began feeling trapped as my body ached and I noticed all the tubes I was connected to. "Yo you gotta get me outta here," I whispered to Alex as I thought of a quick escape. I figured they may not have figured out who I was yet and I was prepared to get the fuck out before they did.

"It's ok," she said smiling.

"No. Baby. They're going to take me away," I whispered, before trying to get out of bed. Only to realize I was in too much pain.

"No, it's ok. They said your case has been dropped for months now. The guy you guys supposedly beat up refused to cooperate."

"Foreal?" I asked, shocked.

"Yep. Me and my Mom are taking you home. They're discharging you. You passed out after getting shot."

"How many times I get hit?" I asked looking around at my arms.

"Five times."

"Five times," I shouted.

"It's ok baby. They said none of them were life threatening. You got hit twice in your arm, twice in the shoulder and once in the thigh. There all on your left side though. They're going to give you a sling but they were able to remove all the bullets. Besides saying you'd probably feel pain for a while and you might ache when it rains, they said you'd make a full recovery."

"Ache when it rains?" I asked.

"Yeah that's what they said. But I'm just happy you're alive. Don't worry I'm going to take good care of you. I promise. Plus we have a lot of catching up to do," she said, winking.

And just like that. A nigga life was right back on track. To tell the truth I don't even remember none of the pain of getting shot. No funny shit, I remember him pulling out the gun and me trying to run but I swear I don't remember shit else. Guess that's a blessing. I realized God does the weirdest things to get you out of a situation. Who would've thought me getting shot would put my life back on the right track. Well almost on the right track.

"Baby where the hell my pants at?"

"The pants you got shot in?"

"Yeah."

"They were all bloody. The guys in the ambulance cut them off. I bought some shorts for you though."

"Cut them off and put them where?" I asked.

"They through them away I guess?"

"Through them away? Ah fuck?

"What? What's wrong?"

"Nothing. Everything's cool."

I took a breath and just counted my blessings. Of course Rich's number was inside my pockets but maybe I was just going to have to do that rap shit on my own. I had no choice. On the inside I was mad as hell but at least I was about to be back in Norview.

Norfolk started off good but when I think about the bad that had occurred in less than a year; Dock, Jah and Mank going to jail, not to mention getting shot, I just had to be thankful I made it out. I knew I was gonna miss it but it was time to get back to reality. But most of all, time to get back to Alex.

"Give me a kiss baby," I said.

"I thought you'd never ask."

Dats My Life

"Hello, Welcome to McDonalds," I said trying my best to smile. "Can I take your order?" I asked.

Yep, Yep. Niggas fucked around and gave your boy a motherfucking job. Now just from me telling you my story today you should already know getting a damn job was the last thing on a nigga mind. But I was back out Norview and I had told Alex I was a changed man and it just so happened that McDonalds was hiring.

My wounds had healed up quick and it won't like I had no other shit to do. Yeah, I was back at my Mama crib. I had forgiven her for fucking my friends. I mean, when you know a person is crazy you really can't stay mad at them for too long. Plus it won't like I had some other places to go, so fuck it. But far as Weak Ass Chris and Ugly ass Chris, they knew better than to cross paths with me. Them niggas went the opposite direction whenever they seen my ass. No funny shit.

So yeah I was out that bitch dolo. Just me and Alex. Dock ass was still locked up. Found out the reason he was still in there was cause they found some crack and a gun on him the day he got arrested. Now the gun I can understand how he got caught, there was no way to stash it. But it baffled me when I heard about the crack, he always kept it stashed in the crack of his ass. Guess it probably fell out when they made him squat and cough down at the Juvenile detention home. Heard he was in that bitch wilding the whole time, fucking niggas up daily. It won't no telling when his crazy ass was getting out.

Now I aint gon lie I won't no completely changed man. Won't like I was just some bitch ass, helpful, Mickey D's ass nigga. It's just that without Dock a nigga was broke. And to tell the truth, in the beginning of working at Mcdonalds a nigga still was. I was used to that fast money, that get paid the same day money. That working shit was different. Well, until I used my street smarts to do a little finessing.

"Yes let me get--," said a girl around my age as she paused, looking up at the menu. "May I have 4 Double cheeseburgers and a Small coke?"

"Ok," I said turning around to look at my co-worker Tory. He was in the back grill making the food. He nodded to me as I turned back around. "Is that it?" I asked.

"Yep," she answered."

"OK. That will be 5.25," I said as I turned around to make her drink and throw the burgers into the bag. "Here you go," I said as she passed me the money and I passed her the food. "Oh yeah, I through an extra burger in there," I said with a smile.

"Thanks," she said as she walked away.

Turns out, without Dock, I still was a damn good criminal. I had found a way to still get a few extra dollars. I aint gon lie, initially after I got my first check for $281 I was madder than a bitch. That shit had a nigga thinking about stealing out the register and everything. But then it hit me. I had been ringing so much shit up, I knew all the prices by heart.

That along with the fact that Joseph, the manager for my shift was fat and lazy as fuck, allowed me to come up with the perfect plan. See, once Joseph knew that you knew your job and that you could manage without him, his big ass always disappeared for the entire shift into the safe room with the camera's that didn't even work. Knowing this, I hollered at Tory and gave him the game.

"Yo when Joseph fat ass go to the back. We gonna get us some money," I told him as we clocked in for work one day.

"Huh?" he asked initially.

"We're going to give the customers their food but I aint ringing shit up. Just listen out while they ordering and make it. Anytime you got spare time make sure you fix a few extras so we can always have food on deck."

"What? Bro are you sure? How is that going to work?"

"Phew, just trust me. I got this."

"Ok. I just don't understand. What are you going to do when they want their change?"

"We're only gonna do it to customers who have exact change or somewhere around it. I'll keep a few quarters dimes and pennies outside my drawer."

"Ok. But what if they want a receipt?

"They won't."

"How you know?"

"We only going to do it to all the young ass customers. Throw in a extra burger, apple pie or something and they aint gon give two fucks about a receipt."

"Yo that does seem kinda smart," replied Tory, nodding his head.

"Bro trust me. We gonna be good. I'll split all the money with you at the end of the night." I assured him.

And just like that. Niggas was on. Man no funny shit we started making a killing ASAP. Every night we was bringing home at least about $75 a piece. Ay it may not seem like a lot but you gotta remember we was only 16, plus we was still getting paid every other week. I was living good, smoking every night, taking Alex to the movies, even bought my first cell phone. Life was gravy. Only thing we had to do was make sure nobody knew what the hell we was doing. If you would've asked me back then I would've thought I'd be doing that shit forever, or at least till Dock came home and he helped me come up with another plan to get in the rap game.

But like always you already know some bullshit had to come along and fuck everything up.

"Hello, I think I left my credit card in here earlier," said an older white lady who'd came in the store earlier that evening. "Have you seen it?"

"No ma'am," I stated from behind the counter.

"Are you sure?"

"Yep. I'm afraid so."

"Ok," she said turning around.

As she walked away I remember looking down, noticing the credit card laying by my foot. Back then we had to swipe the card on our register. I don't know, I guess I must have forgotten to give it back and she'd forgotten to ask for it. I really can't remember but that's the only thing that really makes sense.

"Never mind ma'am, here it is," I said picking it up from the ground.

She walked over to retrieve it. "Thank you," she said with a smile.

Now any other time I would've kept that card and splurged but naw for some reason I attempted to do the right thing. I even kinda felt good about it. Until about an hour later when I got called back into the office.

"Hey how are you doing Skylar?" asked Joseph as I walked into the safe room.

"What sup. I'm good."

"You know you've really turned into a great worker."

"Thanks."

"We just have a small problem," he said as he leaned back in his seat damn near breaking it.

"What's that?" I asked.

"Did a lady lose her credit card earlier?"

"Yeah, I gave it back to her."

"Yeah but she seems to think you lied and said you didn't have it when you really did. She thinks you only confessed because you figured she'd call the police."

"What? What sense does that make? Why would I do that?" I exclaimed. "I aint lie about shit. I found it on the floor. If I stole it why wouldn't I just have kept it?"

"Yeah. That's what I told her. Trust me I believe you," he said before pausing. "But for right now we're going to have to suspend you. It's kinda out of my hands."

"Suspend me for what?" I shouted.

"Calm down, Calm down. We just can't have things like that going on around here. It's not permanent. In thirty days or so we'll give you a call back."

"Thirty days?"

Now most normal kids would just walk out. Head down, sad. But naw not me. How could I? After I slaved in that bitch five days a week. Came in on time. Cleaned that stinking ass bathroom at the end of every night. They gonna fire me. Me? Oh hell naw. Fuck naw. I aint gon lie I started to walk out but a nigga pride got the best of me.

Fuck that. I had to give that big back ass nigga a piece of my damn mind. He must aint know who the fuck I was. He aint know who the hell his ass had just fired. Won't no bitch in me. Hell naw. Nigga had me fucked up but he was soon to find out what the fuck time it was. Oh you can bet your last dollar on that.

"Fuck this bitch ass dumb ass wack ass fuck ass job," I shouted as I stormed out of the office.

"Calm down Skylar."

"Naw fuck you. I aint calmin shit down. Bitch. Fat no neck having bitch. Ol 5.25 getting paid bitch. I'll wipe my ass with these burgers. Always talking about you like being big. Hell naw motherfucker. Yo ass just lazy. Stinkin bitch," I said as I knocked everything in my path to the ground. Spitting on trays of fries, biting a couple of burgers, all before I stood on top of the counter shouting,". "I hope everybody know I wiped my ass with my hand before I made your burgers and that fat ass manager back there don't wash his hands after he piss," I said as I pointed over to him as customers looked at me shocked.

"Skylar. Get down from there," said Joseph, embarrassed.

"Fuck you," I said hopping down. I was about to leave until I saw a couple cookies sitting on a tray on the counter. Feeling extra petty, I stuffed them into my mouth before making my way out the door.

This was during the good ol days when you could smoke cigarettes inside restaurants. I was tempted to light one and flick some ashes on a few customers food but I decided that was too much.

Still, a nigga was mad as hell. Not so much that I had gotten fired. It just that I hated the fact that he thought he had the right to tell me what to do. It was like he controlled me. He had the power to stop me from getting money. In my head I told myself I would never work for another motherfucker again. Fuck that, from there on out I vowed that my destiny would be in my own hands. No funny shit.

I called Alex and let her know what had gone on. She told me to go home and take a shower and to come to her crib in about an hour. She had 'something special' that would make me feel better . Francis's wife was out of town and her Mom was spending the weekend over there. Yeah, yeah I know it sounds crazy but that's another story.

"Baby, it's ok. Maybe you need to just focus on your music anyway. Everything happens for a reason," said Alex as we sat on her couch after explaining how mad I was.

I thought for a second before calming down. "You right, you right. Your ass always know just what to say," I said as we kissed.

"Now come in the kitchen. I got something for you," she said as she stood up, grabbing for my hand. We walked in and her ass had chili dogs and Lemonade sitting on the damn table for me. "I know it may not be as good as your Grandma but I tried."

Now I don't know if you remember me saying this but from my childhood that was my only good memory of my Grandma. I had only told Alex one time about it and that was years ago when we were in middle school. Her remembering that was crazy. I came over thinking the 'something special' she had was gonna be some pussy and truth be told a nigga was completely fine with that. I would've taken that any day. Her shit was a scud.

But the Chili Dogs with Lemonade was on another level. No funny shit, hadn't nobody surprised me with a damn thing before that. I never got shit, not even on Christmas, shit to be honest until I met Alex I'd never even got a Christmas gift. Actually, now that I'm thinking of it, never even had a Christmas tree growing up. So, yeah this was big. Shit was completely unexpected. In a million years I never woulda guessed it. She had a nigga stuttering, I aint know what the fuck to say. "Th-- thank you," was all I could muster up.

"You're welcome," she replied.

"This the best thing anybody ever did for me," I said still staring at the food.

"Boy shut up," she said. "You aint even tasted it yet."

"Man baby you just don't understand," I said speaking slowly, from the heart. "I'm telling you. This is the best thing anybody's ever done for me. Alex I love you yo."

"I love you too baby," she said as we kissed. "Now sit down and taste it."

"Ok," I said as we both took a seat at the table.

I grabbed for the food but she hit my hand. "We gotta say grace," she said.

I smiled. "Ok. You gotta say it. I don't know how to do all that."

"Ok. Give me your hand." I placed my hand inside her palm and we both closed our eyes and bowed our heads. "Dear Lord, Thank you for giving me the strength to prepare this food. Let it be nourishing to our bodies. Thank you for keeping us safe and continue to watch over us. Also keep me and Skylar's love strong so we can eat meals together for the rest of our lives. In Jesus name we pray. Amen. "

"Amen," I said as we both opened our eyes.

Wasting no time I dug in. I can't even lie. Alex was right, the food didn't taste like my Grandma's. It was better. Or at least that's how I felt. With every bite I got more and more motivation to get my career on the right path. No funny shit. I wanted to give her the world and make her feel the same way she'd made me feel at that moment. My addiction was growing stronger and stronger and I didn't want to fight it.

All My Children

Fuck. Fuck. Fuck. Fuck. Damn, just thinking about school make a nigga mad. I hated that shit. Boring as a motherfucker. Man I pray schools aint nothing like they was back when I was growing up cause that shit was like death. But hey, who knows maybe it was just me because as I think back to the first day of school of my repeat freshman year, I remember sitting at lunch dolo, looking at all the students. Them niggas actually appeared to be having a good ass time. Laughing, joking, talking about they childish ass summers. Whole time I'm thinking of ways to let Alex know I won't coming back to that bitch.

She had told me to give it one more chance. And after everything she did for me, I listened. But that one more chance was about to end that damn day. No funny shit, I was growing nauseous just sitting in that motherfucker, I don't know if it was the smell of new book bags, sneakers and papers or what, but I hated it.

I was a street nigga, I needed to be somewhere doing something illegal. Plus I hadn't woke up at six in the morning in I don't know how long, usually that was around the time I was going to sleep. I remember sitting in every class mad as a bitch, not listening to a damn word the teacher said. Actually the first thing I remember hearing form anyone that entire day was a conversation from some kids sitting behind me at lunch.

"So you think ice is better than blade?" said one kid.

"Hell yeah I do," said another.

"Naw yall both tripping, Rico's better than both of them niggas put together," said another voice.

"Are you serious? You're the one who's trippin. Like I said, everybody knows Blade is definitely the best," said the first voice.

"Whatever. We can settle this right now. There's Marco right there," said the second kid. "We can ask him."

I looked over and some little skinny frail, happy go lucky ass boy, with a big ass book bag on his back was walking over with a swag only a mother could love. Nigga had the nerve to have glasses, braces and a jacked up hairline. In my head I'm thinking who the hell gonna take some advice from a little nigga who look like that.

Can't front though, the shit had me intrigued. I was locked in. I had to find out who the fuck was Blade, Ice and Rico. Back then I took real pride in knowing about everything going on in music. How the fuck had I missed them?

"Yo Marco, who do you think is better out of the 'Trap Squad'?" asked the first little nigga. I still hadn't turned around. I just kept my ear to them.

"Man I gotta go with Blade. That guy's sick," said Marco excitedly.

"Told you," screamed the first kid.

"Yeah, yeah but forget all of that. Wait 'til you guys here that new Surf Rider mixtape. His shit is off the chain," said Marco.

"You got it on you?" asked the second voice.

"Yep and not only that I also have the new Comrades mixtape. Check me out."

You already know I had to turn around. A nigga had to see what the hell they were about to check out.

"Look at this," he said as he dropped his backpack onto the table and pulled out a bunch of cases with what looked like blank Cd's inside of them.

Man not a second after he did that I swear damn near the whole fucking cafeteria rushed over from all over the damn place. I lie to you not, kids was going crazy, swarming that nigga like they was plucks and he was nigga on the block with the good dope. No funny shit. I'm telling you, them motherfuckers was feigning for them CD's. Outta nowhere kids started pulling money from their pocket damn near throwing it to him as he collected hand over fist.

I think I already told you about how me and Dock used to sell our stolen candy back in middle school. Actually it was a couple niggas who did, but I swear I aint never see nobody make money like that inside school.

Once the bell rung for the dismissal of lunch I had to pull up on him. I wanted in. Somehow, someway. He might've looked like Steve Urkel but I knew his little wack ass was gonna come in handy.

"Yo come here bro," I said as I posted up in a spot outside the cafeteria that I knew he had to walk past.

"What' sup," he said walking over cautiously.

"Yo who the hell is Rico and them other niggas yall was just talking about?"

"Oh, their the 'Trap Squad'. Some rappers who go here."

"They go here?" I asked. "They nice?"

"Yeah, there ok. I got better music though."

"You rap too?"

"No. I sell CD's. I actually do have a little studio at my house. I've never really tried to rap. I make beats. I haven't let anyone here them though. I'm trying to get them just right."

"You said you got a studio at the crib?" I asked as I thanked God in my head. "You allowed to have company."

"Yeah, my Moms pretty cool. You rap?"

"Yeah I do a little something."

"Aw man I didn't know that. Aren't you Coach?" he asked excitedly.

"Yeah that's me," I answered.

"I heard about you."

"What you hear?"

"Heard a lot. I'm not scared though. Actually your life could probably make for some good music. I think we could make some great stuff together. Like some of the classic hip hop duos."

"Yeah. That's exactly what I was thinking."

"Cool. Well I gotta get to class man. I'll see you around and we can set everything up," he said.

"Ok," I replied as I gave him dap. From the look in his eyes I could tell he was just happy to have a nigga like me talking to him. I knew I might be able to use that to my advantage.

As I walked off my mind started racing. Excited won't even the motherfucking word. I had found a new way to make music. I had so much shit in my head, that I had nowhere to record.

Now the next step was getting everybody in school to rock with me the same way they was rocking with Trap Squad. I knew I had to figure a way to use my reputation to get people to fuck with me. I had to make the transformation from having niggas scared of me, to making them my fans. I aint know how I was gonna actually do it. But I knew I had to. For the rest of the day my mind was on overdrive, thinking of a master plan.

I had tunnel vision, even with all the little cute ass girls walking around with they first day of school out fits on. I aint pay them bitches no mind. Yeah I saw them. But fuck them. I was a brand new Coach. I aint need them bitches nor did I want they ass.

At least that's what I kept telling myself. Man I was doing good as hell, all up until a bitch put me in a compromising position in last period. With five minutes left before dismissal, the little jank sitting in front of me passed me a note.

'Hey I'm Mia. I think you're sexy. I've had a crush on you since Middle School,' I read.

First reaction was to ball it up. Fuck her. But when I took a look at her pony tail which was all shiny and done up, I couldn't help but to fantasize about pulling that shit while hitting her from the back. I had already seen when she walked in class that she had a fatty. So me, being a dumbass, I wrote back 'Thanks', and passed it back up to her.

My heart was pounding, I knew I shouldn've did that but it was too late. Seconds later she passed me the note back.

'I'm a virgin. I don't want to be anymore. Can you take my virginity?' it read.

I tried to fight it but my hand was way too powerful. 'Ok. So when do you want to do this,' I wrote before passing her back the sheet of paper.

After writing, she smiled as she slid the note back to me.

'My Mom goes to work at 8. You can come over if you want. My number is 8570146.'

I read it and put it into my pocket. I knew I was wrong but hey what can I say.

After class I looked around for Marco but couldn't find him. I did run into Alex though. She was getting off the Vo-tech bus. Vo-tech was a vocational school. Alex went for hairdressing. She only came to regular school every other school day.

"What sup Bae," I said as we hugged.

"Hey baby. How was school?" she asked as we began walking home.

"Boring as hell," I said.

"Boring is good. You're there to get an education."

"Yeah. I guess."

"Ok now let's get to it. What sup with those thirsty females? You talk to any of them?" she asked looking me in the eyes. "Am I gonna have to beat anyone up this year?"

"Hell no. Come on baby. Why would I talk to any one of them creatures? I got the baddest jank in Norview. You gonna look good every day for the rest of your life. Everybody knows after the first week aint none of them hoes gonna look like they do now. I swear to God I aint talk to not one bitch the whole day. I swear to God," I said as I raised my right hand to the sky.

And the crazy thing is, I wasn't lying. It was true. I aint say shit to not one girl. Yeah, I may have wrote one. But never actually spoke. Big difference.

Can't say the same for after school though. I didn't want to, but later that night I called Mia. Ten minutes later I found myself in her crib smoking a blunt with her. That shit made her freaky as hell. Little bitch was all over me. In no time we was butt naked in the middle of her Mama's bed.

I don't know what the hell had gotten into me. Maybe it was the fact that I hadn't had any new pussy in a while. But I went to work on her ass. No funny shit, I damn near used every trick Chenell had taught me on her ass, I left her little young ass shaking in them sheets.

Still, when it was over, I left, I aint stick around to talk or none of that soft ass shit. I threw my clothes on, and jetted out the crib. I aint hug her, kiss her, nothing. Straight gangsta.

Pussy Nigga

It was the second day of school and I was walking out of my first period class when I heard a familiar voice yell "Yo get off of me."

I looked a little further down the hall and noticed it was a big ass crowd surrounding somebody. As I walked closer I discovered it was that nigga Marco. Wasting no time, I ran over.

"Yo what the fuck you think you doing?" I screamed as I broke through the crowd.

"Nigga--," the bully started to scream before realizing who I was. His whole demeanor changed. "Oh my bad," he said as he backed away throwing his hands into the air.

"Yeah you right. It is your bad. Leave my lil homie alone. I don't wanna have to hurt nobody. I'll shut this whole Goodman hallway down," I said stepping to his face. "No funny shit." Embarrassed, his bitch ass walked away without saying shit. I stared him down as the crowd whispered to themselves. I tried to act like I aint care about what they was saying but you know me. I was happy as hell. Hadn't lost my touch. "Come on nigga," I said to Marco as he and I began walking the other direction away from the crowd.

"Yo thanks man. He's just mad because of all the money I've been making from the 'Trap Squad' C.D.'s. He said I had to start giving him all of it for now on."

"What?"

"Yeah man I don't know who he thinks he is. I've already told him I'd give up half. But that's it."

"Man fuck him. You aint gotta give that nigga shit. Tell him I said it," I said before looking up and seeing Mia walking towards me. She was walking with some nigga, holding hands and shit.

That was cool and all but you wanna know what she said to me? Nothing. Not a damn thing. She walked right on past me like I aint even exist. Oh hell naw. After I had gave her little ass the best 30 minutes of her life. How dare she not acknowledge me? I mean I understood she was with her little boyfriend and all but she could at least gave a nigga a head nod, a wink or something. Bitch had me feeling used. Like I was just a damn piece of meat or something.

Don't get me wrong I won't heartbroken over the shit or nothing I just won't prepared for that shit. But as I thought about the fact that I had a girl, who just so happened to be in school that day. I couldn't be too mad.

"Fucking Rico," said Marco.

"Huh?" I followed.

"That was Rico walking with Mia."

"Rico?"

"Yeah. Rico. One of the other guys in 'Trap Squad'.

"Oh really," I replied, looking back.

"Yeah and that's Blade that he's giving dap too."

"That's Blade." I shouted as I turned around. "You sure?"

"Yeah."

I couldn't have wrote it any better. I looked back and all three Trap Squad members was standing at the opposite end of the hall along with Mia and you'll never guess who Blade was; the nigga who's Jordan's I stole back in middle school! Immediately an idea hit me like a ton a bricks. I had thought of the perfect way to get my name popping around school as a rapper.

I couldn't wait for school to be over. Soon as it was I walked Alex home and shot straight over to Marco's.

"Wait right here. Gotta tell my Mom you're coming in," he said.

He walked in as I sat on his porch chilling. He aint come back for like 10 minutes. Probably had to warn his mama that I was a little different than his other friends. "Ok cool," he said as finally came back, holding the door open for me.

I slowly walked into the gloomy crib. "Hey, how are ya?" asked his Mom. She was a ol weird looking ass lady. Not saying she was ugly. But just weird looking. I don't know how to describe her but she aint really look real to me. Reminded me of a robot or something. Stiff as hell, I hadn't never seen a mama like her. She had on a apron, with a little short haircut, and she smiled looking in your eyes the whole time she talked to you.

"Fine," I answered.

"You want any Kool-Aid? We got red," she said properly, still smiling.

"Naw, I'm ok, ma'am"

No funny shit. I remember being thirsty as hell but I just wanted to get the fuck away from her ass. Black mama's aint act like that. At least not the ones I knew.

Ok, so we get downstairs to his little basement studio. First of all I gotta tell you. It won't shit like the one Rich had taken me too. Probably as far from it as you can get. I don't even know if you could really even call the shit a studio. All he had was a little ass Wal-mart microphone that he'd plugged into the computer.

I couldn't complain though. I appreciated whatever the fuck I could get. It was gonna get the job done. And that's all that mattered.

"Do you already know what beat you want to rap over?" he asked as we both sat in his chairs he had in front of the computer. "I got almost every popping instrumental that's out right now."

"You got Knock's 'Shoot em Down'"

"Hell yeah of course," he said.

I nodded. See, Knock's Shoot em down is one of the top five diss songs ever. Probably number one back then. I knew that if I got off on a beat like that, it would be a classic.

As Marco cut on the beat I sat silent thinking to myself. Before long I had was ready.

"Let's do this shit," I said.

He pushed a couple buttons and said, "Alright."

The beat came on and I picked up the mic and let off.

"Fuck The Trap Squad,

More like the Wack Squad,

Pull out my 4-5th,

Now they the Track Squad"

I went at every single one of them Trap Squad nigga's. Speaking straight facts. It was easy.

When I was done, like always. Not tooting my own horn but Marco had the look everyone had when they first heard me rap.

"Yo dog, you're fucking amazing."

"You already know what time it is with me bro," I said confidently.

"Yo I didn't know you could rap like that. '*Eyeballs stained with pain... I done seem some crazy thangs.*" he said quoting a rhyme.

"Bro I told you I do this shit."

"Yo that shit was classic. But I got one question," he said.

"What?"

"Don't you go out with Alex?"

Man I was focused so hard on trying to get popping I didn't even realize what the fuck I had said. To put it in a nutshell I basically snitched on myself. But the way I saw it, I had to do what I had to do. That shit was business. Rapping was my career.

I had just bitched Ice in front of damn near the whole school, beat up Blade in 6th grade, there was no way I couldn't put the icing on the cake and say I'd fucked Rico's girl Mia.

"Fuck that shit," I said. "Play that shit one more time."

Later that night. I found out just how much of a young genius Marco was. Yeah, his beats sucked. Them shits was wack as hell, I can't even lie. But his mind was sharp. He came up with the idea to put my song in the middle of all of the mixtapes he was making. That way everyone would be forced to listen to it without even knowing. He had sold out earlier that day so he had to make a fresh batch anyway.

"Yo this song is so dope. Before long the whole school will be talking about it," he said.

That nigga was motherfucking right. The next day in school he sold his CD's and by lunch the whole damn school was buzzing about the song. Real shit. I don't know how they heard it at school. I guess from their portable CD players or some shit. But everybody had some shit to say about it. I still sat by myself at lunch but I could tell I had all the attention in that bitch. Only this time it was for all the right reasons.

Motherfuckers knew it was a new rapper in town and he won't taking no prisoners.

I'm a Dog

"Who the fuck is Mia?" Alex screamed to me as she burst through my room door.

"Huh what?" I asked, hopping up from my bed, It was times like them when I hated the fact that my Mama let her in anytime she came. What if I had a bitch over or something?

"Skylar you heard me. You fucked that bitch?" she asked as she stood inches away from me.

"Hell naw that shit was just a song."

"Just a song? You think I'm stupid or something?" she replied.

"Baby, I'm with you every night. When would I have time to just be fucking random ass bitches, think about it," I said pointing to my brain.

"I aint thinking about shit," she answered before smiling. "But ok. I got something for your ass. I'ma solve this," she said before exiting out my room.

I laid back down. Can't say I aint already know that was gonna happen. But I had thought about it. She aint have nothing on me. No proof. I was clean. It was just a fucking song. She was the one who told me I had to find a career. It won't my fault mines just happened to be rapping. I already had a speech for her and everything. Well not exactly a speech but I was gonna name her all these different rappers who were married but still made songs about fucking bitches. It's just part of the game.

Laying there had me nervous as hell though. I aint know what the fuck she was up too. I had to find out though. Fuck that. So I blew up her phone. No answer. I sat on my bed biting my finger nails till about two hours later she walked back in my room.

"Hey baby," she said, as I sat up again. I aint know what she was about to do. She was crazy, she might have come back to shoot me or something.

"What sup? Where you been?"

"Oh nowhere. Just around the corner," she said as sat next to me. "What you watching?"

"ESPN," I replied, suspiciously.

"I hate sports," she said nonchalantly. "By the way. I just beat Mia. She denied she had sex with you but I beat her ass just in case. You want to go to the movies?" she asked as she looked at me in a way she'd never done.

"OK," I replied.

I aint know how to react. You ever looked into the eyes of a crazy bitch? Well if you haven't, I have; my Mama. And at that moment Alex was looking just like her. It won't hard for me to realize that Alex had lost it. It was cool though. I was used to it.

To tell the truth I was happy as hell. Fuck Mia, I'd rather her get her ass beat then me any day. So yeah, we went to the movies like nothing ever happened. Had a good ass time too. Niggas even gave us some free snacks. Turns out one of the niggas at the concession stand had heard the diss. Had me feeling like a local celebrity foreal.

That was just a hint of what was about to happen the next day in school. Shit was different. I lie to you not, I swear them hoes was licking they lips, blowing me kisses and twisting hard as hell as they walked past me. I'm in that bitch thinking I'm in the Truman Show or something. I don't know if you've ever seen that movie but it's when this guy's whole life since the day he was born had been recorded for a TV show. And everybody knew it but him.

Yeah I knew my song was hot but the shit won't that damn hot. At first I thought maybe I was seeing shit but when I got to my first class I knew it was true. It was a note on my desk and as I looked around I saw this girl looking over to me winking.

I opened up the note.

'Mia told us what you did. Can you take my virginity too?'

Man despite the fact Alex had beat Mia's ass, she still spreaded the word that me taking her virginity was the best thing since sliced bread. After that I swear I started knocking bitches down left and right.

And the best part about it was that they all kept it a secret. Aint none of them bitches want Alex going upside they head. No funny shit, I was hitting them all, 9th thru 12th grade. Ugly bitches, cute bitches, tall bitches, small bitches. Real shit, and I was doing it anywhere, bathrooms, hall closets, garages. Them bitches was willing to do anything to experience the Coach treatment. I was the man.

And before you go on thinking I'm just some dog with no feelings, let me at least say this. Every time I cheated I felt bad as hell. I aint wanna hurt Alex, but to a young nigga my age, back then that pussy was calling my name. Every time I tried to fight it, in my head I'd hear 'Coach, Coach, come get this pussy. You know you want it'. No bullshit. And like a dummy, I'd give in every time.

But on the bright side. Every time I did it, I would start missing Alex bad as hell. And it never fails I'd always end up calling her right after. The next day I'd take her out or buy her something.

It might sound a little crazy but cheating actually kinda made my relationship a little better. It made me appreciate her, cause at the end of the day, them bitches just got a taste of my dick, Alex had control over my heart. It's a difference, at least that's how I feel.

Black Tee

"You already know what time it is," I said as I pointed a pistol to some little nigga. I was dressed in all black with a big ass hoody over my head and black bandana around my face. I had seen him walking down the street from my bedroom window and followed his ass to Manor Street, nobody was ever over there. "Get your ass on the Goddamn ground,"

"Coach--Coach is that you?" he asked from his knees.

"Nigga shut the fuck up," I followed as I reached down to run his pockets.

"Coach foreal man is that you?" he asked as I pulled out his wallet. "Aw man this is crazy. I was just listening to your song 'Robbing Season'. I aint no you really did stuff like this."

"Nigga this aint no damn Coach," I said as I took $50 from him. "You better shut your little dumb ass up before you get smoked."

"My bad bro. I'ma shut up," he said as I removed his shoes.

They were a pair of fresh red and black Charles Barkley's, they had just came out about a week prior. I was siked. I had always wanted some since I was little. That was the first time they'd been released in a minute. Foreal,

foreal, that was the main reason I even robbed the nigga. I had to have them shits.

"Alright get your bitch ass up," I said backing away. "And motherfucker this aint no damn Coach," I said as he stood to his feet as I still held the pistol towards him."

"Naw bro. I'm sorry maybe you aint Coach," he said with his hands to the sky. "But foreal bro if it is you. I love your music man. I can't wait to cop your new CD. I'ma get it either way."

"Nigga shut the fuck up," I shouted.

Now I know I was supposed to smoke that nigga. That was rule #1 in the how to rob handbook. If a nigga find out who you is then he's supposed to automatically die. Not only could he go to the police but he could retaliate and get revenge. But I aint even gon lie. The nigga was a fan. Inside I was just kinda siked he fucked with my music. No funny shit, I started to ask him what was his favorite track. Of course I aint really ask, but yeah, I wanted to.

Real shit, I couldn't wait till I aint have to rob niggas no more. At that time I really aint have no choice in my eyes. My niggas needed shit. I already told you Donnell and Demetries was in the pen so that really left no one to send Dock money for food and shit in jail. Not to mention Jah and Manks Moms were both crackheads so you know they aint have shit either. I made it my duty to make sure they was straight.

Plus I had a reputation to uphold. I was a rapper, I couldn't walk around looking all bummy and shit. Niggas in Norview took fashion real serious. In school they even had these random ass inspections called 'Jean Checks'. That's when a group of niggas stand together checking to make sure everyone's jeans were name brand. If they weren't, consider yourself lunch. Niggas was gonna eat you alive.

Of course damn near the whole school was still somewhat scared of me so they probably wouldnt've said a damn thing. But still, I had to make sure I was designer down at all times. Not to mention I had a girl I had to do for.

Rap money was slowly approaching though. I had been rapping my ass off. Recording three songs a week at Marco's crib for about three months straight.

Every week I saved two and released one for Marco to put in the middle of all of the mixtapes he was selling. Of course that whole plan was another one of his ideas.

No funny shit the more I kicked it with his ass I was starting to like him more and more. Yeah the nigga was wack as hell. Nothing like nobody I'd ever hung with before. But he was real and sometimes that's all you can ask a motherfucker to be. And on top of all that, the nigga was a fucking hustler. I woulda been dumb as hell not to keep him on the squad.

But yeah after a while I had enough tracks for my first mixtape 'Problem Child'. I can't even lie, Marco came up with that title too. The time had finally came for us to get some money together.

To tell the truth he was already making a killing off me. Shit, his Cd sells had tripled since putting my exclusives up there. I coulda extorted him and made him give me a cut. But shit, I couldn't. He was the reason I could even record. I won't dumb enough to bite the hand that fed me. That's why 'Problem Child' was so important to me. I could finally cash out on my hard work. We planned on selling them $5 apiece.

The money won't even my only motivation though. I really wanted to see how the hell niggas was gonna like it. Man, I had put my all in that shit. Made me feel accomplished. I hadn't never completed a project in my life. I had to know if my hard work was gonna pay off.

"Don't leave here until you count to 10," I said as I backed away from the nigga I was robbing still holding the pistol.

"Alright Coach, I mean, I mean."

"Nigga shut up," I said running into the night.

That Monday Morning I walked into school with my new Barkley's along with my debut mixtape. I started off with 100 CD's and by the end of the day I'd sold a thousand dollars' worth. A nigga ended up making five racks in one week. To a teenager, I was rich. You couldn't tell me shit. I even thought about giving the nigga who I robbed his $50 and his shoes back. You know I didn't though. I did kinda feel bad when he walked up to me and asked to buy the CD. I hadn't even realized the nigga was in my damn science class. But I aint feel bad once he gave me that $5.

I couldn't wait for Dock to see what I was up too. He was gonna be home in about a month. I was hoping I'd be rich by then so I could make sure he aint never have to go back.

You Know What It Is

"Knock Knock, Room service," said a voice from behind the door.

Yeah, Yeah. A nigga was moving on up. Getting room service and shit. I felt like a motherfucking boss. I remember standing up, naked as a blue bird, grabbing my white cotton robe from the side of the bed and yelling out, "One second Please" in my most distinguished voice. I was stunting. I threw on my comfortable ass white cotton bedroom slippers and walked up to the door.

"Here you go sir," said the Hotel worker as he slid me my food on a roll cart. He looked at me shocked, he aint know a young black gangster was about to open the door. I wonder what the fuck he thought I did. Probably thought I was a drug dealer or something.

"Thank you," I said before closing the door. Just like a true nigga I had forgot to tip the nigga. So I ran over to pick my Evizu jeans up off the floor, reached in my pocket, grabbed ten slugs, then ran back to the door. "Yo," I said, after discovering the nigga was still in my view. "I forgot to give you this," I followed, holding out the cash.

Boy that nigga was happy as hell to see that money. He probably was calling me all types of names before then. "Thank you," he said as he rushed back to grab the dough.

"No problem," I said closing the door before walking over to a small eating table on the corner of the little ass room we had. I took the food off the cart and set up a breakfast for two. I was moving fast as hell. Alex was in the shower and I was on my romantic shit. I wanted to surprise her.

Just as I was finishing setting up I heard the sound of the shower being cut off. I lit a little scented candle I'd bought from Super 10 earlier that week and opened the blinds. Man, as big as the motherfucking window was you'd think we woulda had some top notch pretty ass view. Hell naw, we was in New York City, that shit way too God damn congested to have room for no damn beautiful views. It woulda been nice considering how much that damn room costed. Looking out that window all we seen was a dirty ass brick wall filled with bird shit.

Only good thing about that was the fact that it allowed me and Alex to walk around naked without worrying about everyone in the city peeping us.

"Aw," said Alex grinning from ear to ear as she stepped out the bathroom, hair all wet and wavy, looking like a motherfuckin mermaid. Goddamn, I'm telling you she was beautiful as hell, water drippin all down her body. Had me wishing I was the towel or some shit. I swear man it was like she was walking in slow motion over to me. I couldn't keep my damn eyes off her. I was acting like it was my first time seeing her without clothes or something. Damn. Boy I swear every time I looked at her I found something new about her that I loved. "You're so sweet," she said when she finally made it to me. "Who taught you to be all romantic and shit?"

Of course it was Chenell but you know I kept that shit to myself.

"I do what I can," I said stepping back, admiring our food; Eggs, Pancakes, sausage, and orange juice on the side. We needed that shit. Real talk. The night before, a nigga had went balls deep. I'm telling you, that was the best dick I had ever given her. I was slanging dick all over the place. The whole damn hotel probably knew my name. Surprised they aint kick our asses out. No bullshit, we both probably lost damn near 30 pounds, we needed that food.

"I'm glad you did because I'm starving. You sure you aint take no Viagra or anything last night?" she asked as she walked away to toss her towel on the corner of the door. Her perfect frame, tempted me to continue where we'd left off the night before. I'm telling you, Alex was bad as hell.

"Viagra? Girl have you looked in the mirror lately," I said as I removed my robe. By that time I was confident that my dick won't little. Matter fact that motherfucker was big. I don't even know why I'm saying was, cause the motherfucker still is. Like that nigga Bernie Mac said, 'Shit, I'm blessed, I'm big boned, I'm heavy structured, if I pull my shit out this whole room would get dark.' You feel me. "Alex you know this shit stay on alert when you around," I said as I held it in my hands.

"Boy. Shut up," she followed blushing as we both sat down for our first naked breakfast.

Oh shit I'm telling you all this and didn't even tell you what the fuck we was even doing in New York. But yeah it was Alex's 16th birthday and with the money from the C.D.'s I decided to take her ass to out of town. The Chinese bus was only $70 a piece roundtrip from Norview. We got one of her older cousins to put the hotel in their name and shot on out there. I was feeling like a real player. I knew I had to travel like that more often.

Alex was siked too. Aint nobody in town our age do no shit like that. Had her feeling like she was a real boss's wife. We planned on fucking the whole city up. I told her she aint have to spend a dime. I was gonna pay for it all.

"So where you tryna go first?" I asked as I put a fork to my food.

"I have no idea," she said taking a sip of orange juice.

"Me either. All I know is that we gotta get the hell out of here. I can't keep smoking in that little ass bathroom. Plus I'm in the mood to smoke amongst my people."

"Your People?" Alex asked jokingly.

"Yeah b. You aint know I was from Harlem son? 125th and Broadway. I'm ill kid," I joked in my best New York accent.

Foreal foreal I did want to see if I could run into some rappers. You already know I had bought my Cd. I knew them niggas hadn't never heard a nigga like me before.

"If you don't shut your country ass up," Alex joked.

"Oh hell naw son. You wilding b. Niggas always hating on the kid," I continued in my New York accent.

"You know you're a clown right," she said.

"Fuck you b. Deadass. Word to Mother we can get it popping right now," I followed up before standing to my feet, rushing her pushing her onto the floor playfully.

"Get off of me," she screamed as we fell. We play fought until eventually my dick got too hard and I started kissing on her neck and shit. "See," Alex said, backing up from me. "You always wanna be freaky. You can't never just play around."

"It's your fault. You shouldn't be around here looking so damn good." I said, holding my dick as she stood up.

"Yeah, I guess you're right," she said as she admired herself in a body sized mirror hanging on the bathroom door. "Who could blame you?"

"See, now you understand. Now come over here to Daddy," I followed as I waved her over to me.

"Nope. We aint come here to hump all day. We came to have fun. It's my birthday," she said before sitting back down at the table. "Now eat the rest of your food so we can get the hell out of this little ass room."

"Ok. Mama," I said sarcastically.

"Mama? Yeah, right. Your Mama wish she looked this good."

"Fuck you."

After we finished our food and got dressed our first stop was supposed to be 125th St. in Harlem. That was all my idea. See, back then my favorite rappers was the 'Comrades'. Matter fact every street nigga around the country would probably say the same shit if you asked them. Them niggas was just sweet as hell. Moet, Lulla Jay, and Nat Turner was the leaders.

Moet was like God back then. Nigga had the swag, the money, the hoes and the flow, Lulla Jay, was only bout 18 or 19 back then and he was just like a Moet in training, then Nat Turner was just, he was just, a fucking gangster. Really couldn't rap but his swag made up for it. It's crazy how your idols become your rivals. We'll get to that later though.

But yeah, we was definitely going to Harlem, I was hoping to bump into one of them bad as hell. Or atleast somebody from their crew. It was damn near 100 of em. I figured if they heard me spit they wouldn't have no choice but to sign me on the spot. I just had to meet them.

It wasn't only the rappers we was interested in. We'd heard Harlem had a lot of different stores and shit that Alex wanted to go to. Not to mention the Apollo, I had to take a picture in front of that shit to show to Dock and the homies when they came home.

We was staying in Manhattan so we won't far from Harlem but like dumbasses we'd both forgotten our damn cell phones back in Va. I was always forgetting mine and I guess my forgetfulness had started rubbing off on Alex ass or something. We needed directions but Alex had been to New York the summer before, she thought she knew everything, so I just followed her. I aint care foreal. You know I aint really like following directions anyway.

I remember walking down the street staring up at all the big ass building as pointless noise corrupted my ears. Still, only thing my criminal ass could think of was how easy it probably was to pick niggas pockets. I had always heard that's what they did around there and at that moment I realized how. It was just too easy, so much shit going on.

Especially where we was at; Times Square. Man it looked exactly how it did on TV. Shit was poppin. Every race, nationality, everything was so different from back home. It was like a whole nother world or something. And to think I thought Norfolk was a big city. I aint know shit. Nigga couldn't even move without somebody bumping into me. No funny shit, it was actually kinda getting on my damn nerves. I was ready to smack a nigga.

Everybody out that bitch was rude as hell, walking fast as a motherfucker. I even heard someone say "I hate these fucking tourist, always walking so damn slow," as they speeded past us.

When I looked to see where the fuck they was going, them motherfuckers went into 'The Gap'. I'm thinking 'Bitch, why the fuck was you in a rush to get to 'The Gap''. Dumb ass motherfuckers was in a damn hurry to go nowhere.

I was pissed off, until I seen two guys I'd looked up to since a kid. My niggas Bert and fucking Ernie from Sesame Street.

"Oh shit look, Babe." I said as I pointed to our former childhood hero's. I aint even gon lie I was excited as hell, I used to love them niggas. I seen it was crowds of people waiting to take pics with them and I wanted in. It was other characters out there too. I can't even remember which ones they was. They was irrelevant. That's why nobody won't waiting to take no pics with they ass. So like everybody else, me and Alex just waited on Bert and Ernie.

"I can't wait to take this pic," said Alex. "Bert. Ernie. I haven't seen you guys in forever," shouted Alex over the loud New York atmosphere when we were finally up next.

"Hey," both Characters said as they waved to her.

"What's up fellas," I followed as they waved over to me also.

"Oh my God, we gotta get a picture," said Alex.

"Come on," Bert replied as we walked up to them.

"Can you take a picture of us?" asked Alex to some white dude who was walking past.

"Sure, why not," he said.

Alex pulled her camera from her pocket. "Don't try to steal it. I'm fast," she joked.

"I won't. Trust me," he said as Alex, Bert and Ernie smiled as I stooped down for a classic jail pose. "1.2.3. Cheese."

"Thanks," said Alex to the guy who took the picture.

"No problem." He said before handing the camera back over and walking away.

"Aw we look so cute," said Alex as she showed me the picture.

"Yeah we do," I followed.

"Nice meeting you Bert and Ernie. Thanks," said Alex as we began to make our way away from them.

"Aren't you guys forgetting something?" asked Ernie.

"Yeah," followed Bert.

"What?" I asked confused, as Alex and I both turned around.

"Sorry, but I don't feel like giving out any hugs today," Alex said laughing.

"No, our tip," replied Bert. His voice had changed from the friendly one we'd just heard to a deep anger filled one.

"Yeah. We don't do this shit for free. We aint running no damn charity around here," added Ernie.

Me and Alex looked over to each other confused as hell. "Hold on. First of all who the fuck you think you talking to nigga. Aint nobody know shit bout no fucking tip. Yall better suck the tip of this dick. We may have gave yall something if yall wouldn't have got no ol bitch ass attitude. Fuck yall. Yall aint getting a damn thing," I said.

"Fuck us? No fuck you," shouted Bert.

"Yeah. Fuck both of you bitches," followed Ernie as he and Bert took their helmets off, revealing that they were two middle aged black men.

"Bitches," Alex and I shouted at the same time.

"Hold on my nigga. Who the fuck you calling a bitch?" I asked as I pulled up my pants preparing to square up.

"Whoever the fucking shoe fits," Bert followed, stepping closer to us.

"Yeah, this is the last time anyone stiffs us for tip money. This is our fucking job, ya know."

"Fuck your Job," said Alex standing closer to me as we both walked towards them.

I was just about to swing. I aint give a damn if I grew up on them motherfuckers or not. Won't no way in hell nobody was just gon disrespect my girl right in front of my face. Bitch ass niggas was about to learn a lesson. Fuck that shit.

I was too slow though. In the blink of an eye Alex mased both them motherfukers. What's so crazy is that I aint even know her ass owned no damn pepper spray. "AHHHHHH," screamed them both.

"Let's get the fuck out of here," Alex shouted as I quickly punched both of them niggas, knocking them to the ground. Fuck that. Wont no way Alex was gonna be the only one with a story to tell.

We sprinted for about 5 blocks before we finally stopped.

"Oh my God," Alex said, bending over to catch her breath. "I can't believe we just had to beat up Bert and Ernie. I gotta tell everybody about this," she said as she laughed hysterically.

Man I can't even snatch, shit definitely was funny as a bitch. I couldn't help but to laugh too. Felt real good to do some gangster shit with Alex. Felt like Bonnie and Clyde or some shit.

"Yo we gotta get high," I said looking over to Alex as she finally caught her breath.

"No, you know I don't smoke," she replied.

"Fuck that it's your birthday. You gotta try it. Just one time. No funny shit."

Alex had never smoked with me before. She never really said nothing bad about it but it just won't her thing. And I never pressured her. This time was different though, I wanted her to have the best time possible and I knew weed would help with that. She must've been feeling the same way because with little hesitation she smiled and said, "Ok."

"Looks like we stopped in front of the perfect spot," I said as I pointed across the street to a convenience store.

I walked in, bought a backwood and rolled up on the side of the building. It was one of them rare New York side streets that not too many people walked. After I finished rolling we smoked right then and there.

Man I don't know what it was but that high was different. See, back then we was just smoking regular weed in Norview. But earlier before we had left the hotel that day, one of the workers had sold me some Sour Diesel. It was my first time trying that shit.

No bullshit we got zooted. All of a sudden shit got wild. I looked up and I coulda sworn the buildings was shaking, looking like them bitches was about to fall or something. Not only that, I was losing my balance, a nigga legs was wobbly as hell. No funny shit, I couldn't even walk a damn straight line. I knew if I was feeling like that it won't no telling how Alex was feeling.

I looked over to her, eyes low. "What ya looking at?" she asked looking exactly how I felt.

"You feel it?"

"Do I feel it? Are you crazy," she shouted. "What kinda dumb question is that? Of course I feel like it. I swear for the last five minutes I been feeling like I been floating," she said before bursting out laughing. "Hold my hand," she said as she grabbed mines.

Suddenly we both couldn't stop laughing. "Are you hungry again?"

"Hell yeah," she replied.

So for the next hour we stumbled our way down them long ass New York sidewalks. I swear for the life of us we couldn't find shit we actually wanted. McDonalds. No. Burger King. No. It was like a million choices but we was so damn high and out of our element we couldn't focus on just one place. It was like we was craving something but neither one of us could figure out just what the fuck it was.

After almost losing hope we somehow came across a bright ass flashing sign. We both looked up at the same time and I asked, "You wanna try 'Ray's Barbeque'?"

"Yeah. Why not?" she said, eyes still halfway open.

We walked in. It was different. Big as hell. Dark but still lit up like a motherfucker. Kinda resembled the inside of a nightclub or something. To tell the truth it didn't matter how the shit looked. We had walked so long that this was gonna be the place we ate at no matter what. Feet was hurting and I don't know about Alex but shit was growing blurry as a bitch to me. I needed to sit my ass down and chill.

By the time we were seated I still was still high as a kite. We flopped down in the seat, ordered, than sat in silence, zoneing out until our food arrived. Once we started eating, we was back. Guess that's all we needed. My Barbeque sandwich was on point. I was crushing that bitch, straight demolishing it. I remember looking over to Alex, her face was damn near kissing the plate as she threw back some baby back ribs.

For some odd reason something told me to look around. When I did, shit got crazy ASAP. At all the other tables, you'll never guess what the fuck I see. Now before I say this let me make this clear. I don't give a fuck about no faggots. They can live they life however the fuck they please. But back , at 17, I won't use to no shit like that. It was like fucking Homo Heaven in that bitch. And that won't even the crazy shit. The craziest part was that all they ass seemed to be staring at me. No bullshit! And not just staring; smiling and shit. Groups of em. I started feeling nervous as a bitch. I aint know what to do.

I looked over to Alex. Without saying a word she already knew exactly what I was thinking. "Yep. We somehow found our way into Club Gay," she said trying but failing to hide her amuzement.

"What the fuck," I said as I dropped my head.

"What?" she asked. "It's cool. You're with me. They know you're not gay."

"How the hell you know?" I asked. "You act like the majority of them gay niggas don't be having female best friends. Them niggas probably over there thinking you just my bestie and we over here having a fucking girl's day out or some shit." I whispered.

"Girl--, I mean boy be quiet," Alex joked in a flamboyantly gay tone.

"See, you play too got damn much. No funny shit we gotta get the fuck outta here."

"Boy shut up. Aint nothing wrong with gay guys."

"Man I aint say it was. I can handle one or two. But not a whole gang of these niggas."

"Skylar please, aint no gang of people staring at you."

"Alex yes the fuck they is. Trust me. Ima nigga. I know how other niggas think. The same way straight niggas feel when we see one girl is how their feeling about me right now. There probably making bets on who can get me first. We gotta get the fuck outta here. Let's go," I demanded.

"We didn't even finishing eating yet," she said pointing down to her food.

"Man Alex we can get a to-go box and eat on the bench across the street. I just can't do it. Come on. We gotta go."

"Ok," Alex said as she continued to laugh.

We asked the waitress for some to-go boxes and jetted across the street onto the bench where we finished them shits off.

"You ready to go to Harlem now?" I asked.

"Yep," followed Alex.

"Let's go," I said as we through our to-go boxes on the ground with the rest of the New York trash and made our way to the train.

We aint even get halfway down the block before we heard someone yelling over to us, "There they are right there officer."

We looked over and it was Bert and Ernie standing with the Police, pointing down to us. Immediately they start to chase us.

"Oh Shit," I yelled, still high. "Come on Baby,"

"Ok," Alex said as we both started to run.

Man that shit was far from my first time running from the cops, I was a pro. I was outta there, bumping people out the way and everything, straight hauling ass. No funny shit, I fucked around and ran so fast without looking back I aint know where the fuck I was by the time I stopped. I hadn't looked back once. Good news, I had lost the Police. Bad news, I had lost Alex too.

I turned around fast as hell looking in all directions trying to find her ass. She won't nowhere in sight though. I even screamed her name to the top of my lungs. "Alex." But it was so damn noisy out there, won't no way she woulda ever heard me. Remember I told you we had forgotten our phones too. This shit was all bad. Nigga started panicking. I aint know if the police had caught her or if she was out there lost too. I knew how to survive anywhere. But my baby. I didn't know about her. If I aint know where the hotel was. Wont no way she did.

All types of crazy shit was popping up in my head. By then my high was blown. Sweat was dripping down my whole damn body. I had just seen on the news that morning that they had a rapist on the loose. And I didn't even bring my damn strap. Of course that wouldn't have mattered anyway. I won't even nowhere near Alex to protect her. Yeah she had her mase. But what the fuck was that gon do. Shit was crazy. No lie. For hours I wandered trying to somehow recognize a damn street name. Shit wont working though. By the time the sun set and it got dark, I still hadn't come up with shit.

Not knowing what the fuck to do, I had to take a break. So I sat down next to some passed out bum on a bench. His eyes were closed leaving me confused. I couldn't tell if he was just taking a nap or he was dead. Considering how bad the nigga stunk I'm kinda leaning towards him being dead. After only a couple minutes I couldn't take it no more, his stench was killing me.

As I got up I for some reason placed my right hand into my pocket. That's when my dumbass realized how fucking dumb I really was. I had the hotel key the whole damn time. And not only that. The shit had the damn hotel address on it.

I shot across the street and asked a convenience store owner where to go. He was one of them foreign motherfuckers so I couldn't really understand him at first. But when I finally realized what the fuck he was saying, I found out I was only two damn blocks away from the hotel. Feeling stupid as hell I rushed over, praying the whole time. Alex had to be in there. If she won't I aint know what the fuck I was gonna do.

Darting through the hotel lobby I ran up the steps to the 7th floor. I aint have time to be waiting for no elevator door to open. Once I got up there I slid my key card in and burst through the door. "Alex," I shouted.

There she was in bed, naked, leg's cocked fingering herself. No funny shit. "I've been waiting for you Daddy."

"What happen?" I asked, relieved. "I thought I lost you baby?"

"Shh," replied as she placed her moist index finger to her lips. "Take your clothes off. Get in the shower. I'll be waiting," she said as she blew me a kiss.

With no hesitation I did exactly what she'd said. And as for the rest of the night. Let's just say a nigga got his grown man on. New York style, I even kept on my timbs.

Kick Door

Within a week of each other the whole squad was back in full effect. Yep, Jah and Mank had somehow beat their case.

"Nigga we knew we was oming-cay ome-hay," said Mank.

"Yeah nigga, a closed mouth go home every time. Everybody know Murder is the easiest charge to beat," said Jah.

I aint gon a lie I aint think they was ever coming home. Nigga was happy as hell they was though. Shit felt good. I had missed them niggas foreal. Especially Dock. You know that was like my right hand. My brother. I was glad I was surviving without him but you don't know how good it felt for him to be back by my side. No funny shit.

Man niggas had changed so much. Jah and Mank had both grown taller and bigger since they'd left. Of course Dock little ass was the same size but the change I'm talking about aint physical. Their mind state is what I'm referring too. Everybody was released with a new lease on life. My niggas had really grown to see life for what it was, realizing shit wont a joke or game. It was time to buckle up. The idiotic behavior of the past had to seize. No funny shit, they had really manned up.

Sike! You know that was a damn lie. My niggas got released and was back on the same bullshit. Even crazier foreal. It was time to get back on the money train. Yeah I was getting a little bit of rap dough but my love for Roca Wear and weed had me running through that shit like it won't nothing. I still couldn't save if my life depended on it. When they dropped, only thing I could treat them to was a couple blunts.

Oh yeah, and drive them around, I had bought a little $400 ol school cutlass from some nigga I was going to school with. His grandfather had died and had given it to him. He was one of them broke ass niggas who feined for weed, so once he seen the cash in his face he aint have no choice but to sell it. Yeah the car was old and beat up but it got me from point A to point B and to me that was all that mattered.

Plus my niggas was happy as hell one of us finally had a car of our own. We could go from Norview to Norfolk anytime we wanted and that was perfect because after being behind the G-Wall for so long, them niggas had thought about every possible lick we could hit. Together we set up the plans to put them shits in motion.

"Yo, you know we shot the monkey to that nigga 'Gene'," Jah said to me as he and Mank sat in the back while Dock and I rode in the front of my car.

"Who the fuck is Gene?" asked Dock.

"Coach knows who the fuck Gene is," replied Jah.

"Yeah I know," I said.

"Ok. Who the fuck is Gene?" asked Dock again looking over to me.

"The nigga who shot me," I said.

"Foreal?" Dock shouted. "Man I hope yall beat the dog shit outta his bitch ass."

"You damn right we did," said Mank.

"That nigga was in there screaming like a little bitch. We had blood coming out his damn scalp, no funny shit," said Jah as he and Mank gave each other fives.

"Deputy, Deputy," yelled Mank as he laughed, imitating Gene.

"Yeah bro shit was crazy as a bitch," said Jah, still laughing as we cruised through Ocean View, a neighborhood in Norfolk.

"Ay Coach, pull up right here," Jah said pointing ahead of us.

"Ok," I said.

"Yo what's up little nigga. Where the smoke at?" asked Jah as we drove up next to some young nigga probably a couple years younger than I was standing on the block.

"I got a 8th on me right now. It's some exotic shit. Got purple hairs and everything," he said.

"Bet. Let me see that shit," said Dock rolling his window down, sticking his hand out.

The little boy pulled the weed out of his pocket before handing it over to Dock.

Dock sniffed it. "Oh yeah. I like this. I like this a lot, no funny shit."

"Shit we might as well get two 8^{th's}," said Jah from the back seat. "I got some money from this bitch last night."

"How much you want for this little nigga?" asked Dock.

"$80 for both."

"Ok. Yall cool with that?" Dock asked.

"Yeah bro," Jah and I both said.

"Bet. Go get the other one for us," said Dock to the kid.

"Cool," he said running off.

"Yo did his little fat ass just leave us the eed-way?" asked Mank.

"Hell yeah he did," said Dock. "Pull off Coach. Pull off," he yelled.

I sped off as the boy screamed, waving his hands in the air as his body shrinked smaller and smaller.

"Damn I can't believe yall just had me run off on a little nigga," I said as everyone laughed hysterically.

"Fuck that lil nigga, his lil ass shouldn't have been outside so damn late. I been running off with niggas shit all year," said Dock.

"Hell yeah I can't even count the number of ag-bays I ook-tay," said Mank.

"Damn right. I got so hungry one night I went in a nigga bag while he was sitting there. His bitch ass aint do shit about it though," said Jah.

"What the fuck is a bag?" I asked.

"That's where niggas keep all they cantine in. They be having all types of snacks and shit in there," said Dock.

"Yeah, you gonna see one day when you behind the G-Wall. Aint shit nice bro. Real shit," added Jah.

"Amn-day ight-ray," said Mank.

"Fuck that. When I go, I already know Alex gonna keep me straight," I replied. "I aint gonna have to steal shit."

"You better hope she do," followed Dock.

"Shit, even if she do you still gon fuck around and lose some of it gambling and shit. I use to get hit for everything I had and just go steal it back, fuck it," said Jah.

"Yall niggas crazy," I said, laughing. "Ay yall got a blunt already?" I asked.

"Nigga you ate-lay. We already olling-ray up," said Mank as I looked in the rearview and saw he and Jah, both twisting them.

They was done in no time and we drove down the street smoking.

"Ay bro I heard you that nigga now no funny shit. I'm surprised your ass aint already famous," said Jah.

"Bro I'm just tryna get paid," I responded.

"Aint we all," added Mank.

"Bro, you our ticket," Dock said, looking over to me. "You gonna get us out the hood."

"Damn right," added Jah. "Boy, I wish I could've had your cd in the bean. I still made sure I told niggas about yo ass though."

"Hell yeah me too," said Dock. "I got tired of niggas talking about that nigga Young Trell all day."

"Yeah. Niggas was on that nigga ick-day in there," said Mank. "I can't lie though that nigga do be itting-spay."

"Fuck that nigga, he aint better than Surf Rider. That's that nigga, no funny shit, all he do is spit that real shit," said Jah.

"Yeah, he cool but yall already know aint nobody fucking with Nat Turner. He the best rapper ever no funny shit," I followed.

"Nigga, you taking it a little too far now," said Jah. "Dude nice and all but I can't say he the best rapper ever."

"Then who is?" I asked.

"Ou-yay" shouted Mank.

"You right about that," said Dock as everyone got hype. "Yo I swear when niggas really get a hold of you, you gonna change the world phew. No funny shit."

"Damn right just don't forget about us when you make it bro," added Jah.

"Nigga shut the fuck up. I aint no snake," I said.

"I aint say you was. I just know how shit can get sometimes," replied Jah.

"Man I know my nigga aint gon switch up," said Dock. "Shit, you the only nigga who put money on my books so I could eat the whole time I was in that bitch."

"Shit me too," said Jah.

"ell-hay eah-yay," added Mank

"Trust me I aint want too," I added, laughing. "I just aint want nobody beating yall ass cause yall was too frail to fight back or something."

"Shut the fuck up," said Jah as everyone laughed once again. "But naw seriously I appreciate that shit phew," said Dock.

"Yeah bro," said Jah "Hopefully we don't got to do nothing like that no more."

"Hell naw I aint trying to see no more ell-cays"

"Real shit Coach, that shit aint where it's at," said Dock looking over to me seriously. "You doing the right thing with that music shit."

"Yep and it aint like you lying in your ap-rays," said Mank.

"Yeah bro just stay positive and keep the bullshit out of your way," said Jah.

"You already know. I'm gonna make this rap shit happen no matter what. I aint gonna let nothing get in my way," I said pulling over on the side of an old house in the hood.

"Damn right. That's the kinda shit I like to hear."

"Alright. Yall niggas ready?" asked Dock as we all pulled ski masks from our back pockets.

"Hell yeah," I said as I through mine on.

"Aint nothing to it but to do it," said Jah as Mank cracked his knuckles, loudly.

"Bet," said Dock. "Come on."

We all hopped out the whip, heads on the swiffel as we followed Dock silently to the back door of the house.

"Let's do it," said Dock, as we all pulled our guns from the sides of our waists. "1, 2, 3."

BOOM. Jah kicked in the door as I shouted, "Alright all yall motherfuckers get on the motherfucking ground."

Pussy Rehab

Man going to school and keeping up with the homies was damn near impossible. To keep it real a nigga had been failing every class before they even got outta jail. Even gym, teachers always thought cause I was tall and muscular, I was a athlete or something. Fuck no. I couldn't bounce no ball, throw no ball, nothing, plus they always wanted us to change into them wack ass gym clothes. Fuck that, I won't gon have nobody running up in my locker stealing all my fresh ass shit. I won't no fool.

It got to a point where I aint even go to no classes anyway, all I did was show up around lunch. I aint care not one bit about that school shit. My only concern was making a damn name for myself as far as rapping. And after a lot of hard work, with the help of Marco, I had done that.

While I was in that bitch I had made the best of it, my CD's was consistently selling out, I was still putting out a song a week on Marco's mixtapes and had even did a mixtape with 'The Trap Squad'. It won't on no shit where we did songs together or nothing. It was more like us just battling. But it was creative as hell. Marco came up with the idea. He asked around school for people to vote on what beats we should rap on. After we tallied up the votes we chose the top ten.

Next we both rapped on each beat, leaving Marco to put them on a Cd where niggas would hear my version of the song followed by their's for the whole mixtape. I'm telling you, that nigga Marco was a young genius. Who would've thought of some shit like that?

When the tape came out, shit sold out even faster than 'Problem Child'. Think about it, by having all of the hottest rappers in town on one CD, everybody had to cop it.

All that week we was the talk of the town. No funny shit, niggas went platinum in the hood. How couldn't we though. Not only was me and Marco selling the CD's, Trap Squad was too. It's always strength in numbers. Shit worked out perfect for me cause of course I killed them on every track. It won't no debate on who was the best in town no more. Everybody knew it was me.

With all the success the tape was having I knew I had to take our shit to Norfolk. They hadn't even heard Problem Child yet. That's when I officially dropped out of school. I still worked with Marco but I had business to handle. I had to put them Norfolk niggas up on game.

Only issue was that I knew them motherfuckers won't just gon be spending $5 on no damn mixtape. Shit, some of they rent won't even $5. The best ways to get them on board was to just give them shits out for free. Won't like it was really costing me no money. A pack of 100 Cd's was $10.

Niggas out the Park appreciated gifts. Can't say I don't understand. I feel the same way no funny shit. Something about receiving something for nothing always made my dick hard. Like the saying goes, the best things in life are free.

Plus people out the Park was just day to day people. Money was scarce, a lot of motherfucker's aint have no damn job. Not saying all of them was lazy or nothing. Yeah, a lot of them was, but mostly the Park consisted of motherfuckers who was just straight up schemers and shit. They aint have time to be helping my hustle when they had they own to tend to.

But yeah, after a while, after passing my mixtape around, damn near everybody in Norfolk was fucking with me. Not to mention, if any nigga told me he rapped and wanted me on a song. I did it. Fuck it. The way I seen it, it was just a better way for my voice to be heard by more people. And trust me, I made sure I went hard every time.

I hadn't made a dollar in Norfolk but I knew I was one step closer to getting my shit in the right hands. That was big since I had lost contact with Rich. I was hoping somehow he'd run across a copy and find my ass again. Chances was looking good too. Especially since I had sorta made a hood hit that everybody was fucking with.

"Pull up, Pop out, Drop me a nigga," everyone sang.

That was a line from my song 'Drop Em' The Park niggas was going crazy over that shit. I had been out there passing out Cd's and what not. But as far as me being out there for big events or anything like that, I hadn't. That was until Lil Ricci's 18th birthday on Fourth of July. He was a nigga Dock and them had grew up with.

Ricci's party was the shit. Besides Rich everybody who was anybody in Norfolk was in attendance, even some of the City niggas. The beef had been squashed. Can't lie I still wanted a fair one with TJ. I remember him walking up to me telling me he was fucking with the music. I wanted to steal off on him. Instead I chilled and told him I appreciated it. I aint wanna fuck up the vibe of the event. It was a lot of real love out there that night.

Niggas treated me like I was really from Wellington Park or something. Good times. Good drugs. And good people. Foreal man, niggas seemed happy to see me, Jah, Mank and Dock out there together. Hugs and daps all night. Shit felt good not to be on the run. I aint have to keep looking over my shoulder or nothing.

Oh yeah I aint even mention how sweet we was looking. Yep niggas was balling harder than ever around that time. Gold Fronts, rings, fresh kicks. Besides the fact we was all living out my little hoopty and hotels, we was fresh as a bitch. Niggas aint know what the fuck we was doing but they knew we was doing something. We won't stingy though, we shared the wealth.

Matter fact we had supplied Ricci's whole cookout with brews and weed. Plus we had a party pack of ecstasy. We had been hitting lick after lick, sticking up convience stores, check cashing joints, basically anybody or anything we thought had some cash. So yeah, it was only right we showed the hood some love.

A few weeks before that we'd already through a big ass end of the school year cookout, out Norview. We was branding ourselves as hood heroes.

That's when we first came up with our name 'HB'. I don't remember how we came up with it or which one of us did but it basically meant anything that we wanted. 'Hot Brothers' when we was on some robbing shit; 'Horny Brothers' when we was chasing bitches; 'Hungry Brothers' when we needed some money or we was just actually hungry; 'Homicide Brothers when we was ready to smoke something.

At that time, I don't think I could have asked for more. Not only did I have Alex still riding with me but I had a squad who everybody loved, I was getting money, and as I looked around the cookout, everybody was partying rapping along to my shit. We had paid the DJ to keep my shit spinning along with the other hot songs. That way it would get people in the feeling that my shit was just as hot as the signed artist. Yep, yep, Marco had me on some real marketing shit. That whole night I just stood in the corner, not really talking to nobody, yeah I was smiling and conversing when need be. But foreal. I was just soaking it all in.

It was the first time I could just really appreciate shit. Life was good. Not a care in the world. Seeing how far I'd came made a nigga damn near shed a tear.

I really almost shed a tear when I saw something I didn't want to see. It was her. Yeah you already know who her is. I knew it was only a matter of time before I seen her ass.

I tried to turn away from her hoping she hadn't noticed that I'd noticed her. I knew I was wrong though. I could feel her staring at me burning a hole through my back. Tried to play it off but I was doing that nervous sweating shit again. Man I had hated her for so long. Always said I'd spit on her if I ever seen her again. But when she was in my presence, just a few feet behind me. I aint know how to feel. Cause to tell the truth, I did kinda miss her.

Come on now, how couldn't I? I mean shit, when you spend time with somebody day in and day out you naturally grow a bond with them. Plus, I aint tryna sound like a ol bitch ass nigga or nothing. But man I needed some closure. Real shit. I still had questions that needed to be answered.

Something told me she didn't know that nigga Gene was getting out of jail that night he shot me. But then again I aint know. Life had already taught me I couldn't trust a soul. No bullshit. I knew firsthand how grimy motherfuckers could be. I had done my fair share of fucked up shit. Can't even count all the times I talked to a nigga, playing cool, whole time plotting on how me and my niggas was gonna rob him. No funny shit, when you dealing with street niggas and street bitches you always gotta think the worse.

But yeah, before long I could feel her body silently inching closer to me. I thought quickly for my next move but nothing came to mind besides just straight up ignoring her, acting like she won't even there.

Man just the smell of her had bought back so many old memories though. And as she bumped up against me her skin felt so damn soft. Finally, she walked up in front of me as I closed my eyes, shaking my head. I knew that shit won't gonna end up good. Yeah, I had cheated on Alex but never with bitches I had love for. That bitch was the Devil and I knew it. Me and Alex was doing so good. I aint wanna fuck it up. So I did the right thing. I kept ignoring her, just like I knew I should do. Acted like she won't even there. Just walked away. Fuck her, with every step I took I felt better and better about myself. I knew I could do it.

Then I heard her voice. Damn.

"Where you going?" Chenell asked as I paused, looking back. My worse mistake. We made eye contact. That was all it took.

Next thing I know...

"Oh my God I missed you," said Chenell as we both fell onto the floor of her bedroom, dripping sweat. She had just reminded me of what had made me fall in love with her in the first place.

I sat silent. Trying to gather my thoughts.

"Oh so you aint miss me?" she asked.

"Nope."

"Nigga, you lying."

"How you figure that?" I asked.

"Well besides the fact you told me you love me at least ten times in the last thirty minutes. I could tell by the way you touched me. Trust me I know the difference."

"Girl hell naw."

"It's ok. You can play hard to get. But let me at least say this. I am so sorry for what happened. Ya know about Gene and shit."

"Man," I said turning from her.

"No. I'm serious," she said as she put her hand on my shoulder. "I had no idea he was getting out."

"Whatever."

"Foreal. He just popped up. Nigga I was just as surprised when I heard them gunshots as you. His ass is crazy. That's exactly why he back locked up."

"So. You aint even bother coming to see me at the hospital. You never even checked on a nigga to see if I was dead or not. "

"Bullshit," she shouted. "Bull Fucking shit," she continued, causing me to turn to face her.

"Man I know who came and seen me. And it damn sure won't you."

"Yeah I know who came too," she said with an attitude.

What?" I asked curiously.

"Yeah, I came. Flowers, card and everything. I knew you was on the run. So I wanted to make sure I saw you one last time. But when I came I saw some bitch and her mama crying and shit over you."

"That was--,"

"You don't gotta explain," she said, cutting me off. "I knew you probably had some girl back home. I aint mad."

"Man Chenell--."

"I'm just saying, would you rather me had burst in there and ruin your little teenage romance?"

I didn't say anything.

"Exactly Motherfucker. So tell me again why you mad at me?"

"Never mind I guess everything's cool."

"You damn right it is."

"Besides I got something that could change your life. So you better be cool with me."

"What?" I exclaimed. "Your pussy good and all but it aint changing nobody's life."

"Nigga you crazy. I bet you done already changed some bitches life's with the shit I don taught yo ass. Don't forget when you met me you aint know shit. But I aint even talking about sex," she said before standing to her feet.

"Where you going?" I asked as I stood up along with her as she walked over to her dresser drawer naked.

"I'm talking about this," she said as she pulled out a small piece of paper.

"Hell is that?" I asked as she walked over to me, handing it over. It read 'Rich 7430923' "Oh shit. When you get this?"

"A couple months ago. He told me to give it to you if I ever saw you again."

"Yo. This really might change my life. You won't bullshitting," I said still staring at the number amazed.

"See, that's exactly why your little young ass need me in your life," she said stepping closer to me as our body's touched.

"You right."

"I know I am," she said smiling. The same smile that made me weak to my knees.

"Thanks Chenell. I do love you," I said, looking into her eyes.

"And I love you too. But you know how I like to get thanked," she said as she grabbed my dick.

Jewelry

Beep Beep.

"That's him," I said to Alex as we stood on her front porch.

"Ok. Good luck. Gimme a kiss," she said as we pecked. "I'm so excited," she followed.

"Me too. It's the best day of my life."

"Mine too," she said as I stepped off of the porch.

I ran over to Rich's whip. This time it was a Range Rover. All black, with penut butter seats. Fresh as hell. I'd called him ASAP after Chenell gave me the number. We'd talked a few times on the phone but it was finally time to hit the booth and I couldn't wait.

"Whatsup lil nigga. You a little player aint ya," he said as we slapped fives. "How many bitches you got? Remind me of a little me. Except I was a little worse than you. I had a different bitch for every hour in a week."

"Yeah, I got a few," I replied as we drove off. "But I think I'm about to slow down on the hoes. That girl you just saw is about to be my Baby Mama."

"Aw man, don't tell me she's pregnant," Rich said disappointingly.

"Yeah, what's the problem?"

"You crazy as hell. That's the problem. You aint even got no bread yet."

"How you know what I got?" I responded.

"Nigga I aint talking about that little money you and your homeboys getting to go by Jordan's and fake ass gold chains. I'm talking real money."

"Well nigga aint that what you here for?" I rebutted.

"That was a good come back," he said looking over smiling. "You right about that. Matter fact I been listening to your new shit. That shit hot. But we gotta go to a real studio. That shit you recording is cool for the hood. But I'm gonna get you on the radio. I can tell you got better from the last time we went and that shit was hot already. I want you to re-record the track '*Pop Out*' that's my shit."

"Naw man."

"Naw? What the fuck you mean naw."

"I got some hot shit to get off my chest. I don't even want to do them old songs again. That shit is the past. I rap about what the fuck going on right now. I don seen a lot."

"Nigga you aint seen shit," he joked playfully. "Naw but I understand. Just whatever you do make sure it's hot. I got some real live millionaires in there this time. Foreal. I'ma set you up some club dates, pay a couple major D.J.'s and sit back and watch you take over the game. This time next year you gon be on a yacht, kicked back getting your dick sucked counting paper."

Rich word was law to me. Real Shit. No matter how long that nigga stayed away from the Park, niggas still spoke on him every day like he was God or something. I lie to you not. Just the nigga presence alone let you know he won't just some regular every day ass nigga. Naw. That nigga was special. He held his head a little higher than regular people, dressed better than regular people, drove a better car than regular people, nigga even talked different from regular people.

Real shit, the nigga spoke in a way that made you believe everything he said. I swear the man aint have a ounce of doubt in his voice. No funny shit, he's pretty much who I jacked my rap persona from. I figured if I copied his swag than I would have no choice but to shine. I already had the lyrics.

Back in the day you couldn't pay me to admit some shit like that. But fuck it, it's the past. Besides it worked didn't it. Shit, part of the reason I never gave too much in my interviews was because of him. Niggas in the hood only knew what he allowed them to know. That right there made him mysterious. And when shits mysterious, people always want to solve it. Makes them curious. And in a business where your job is to sell yourself. What better way to do it then to keep people guessing. To me it was genius. You think I would have the whole world fighting to interview me damn near 50 years later if I didn't.

The few things I did know about him only made me look up to him more. I hadn't never met a nigga who aint do drugs or alcohol. He said he needed to be able to think clearly at all times. I aint never wanna try that shit, I loved drugs too much for that, but I respected it.

Nigga owned a night club and a laundromat. No bullshit, I can't even remember a time when he ever even mentioned that he sold drugs. It was just something that I knew. Well at least thought I knew, I told you I really aint know shit.

What I did know, was that in his presence I needed to carry myself different. I wanted him to know I was serious about my craft. Them times I was around him, I aint even say much, just listened. Why wouldn't I? Any nigga who came from the hood and could end up where he was at was worthy of my undivided attention.

Aw man before I go any further let me talk about Alex right quick. Yep my baby was pregnant. She had just told me that day. Boy, I was happy asa bitch.

And I can't even snatch, a nigga had kinda did the shit on purpose. Actually I can't even say kinda, I definitely did it on purpose. Fuck it, I won't letting her ass go nowhere. So I did what any real nigga in my situation would've did. I trapped her.

Aint like I won't planning on being there for my seed. That was a must. After living with Chenell and her son, I knew it won't no way I wasn't gonna be in my kid's life.

I still can remember one of the first times I chilled around Chenell's son Joel. After knowing him for 15 minute that little motherfucker started thinking I was his damn Pops. Crazy ass little nigga just kept looking at me screaming, "Daddy. Daddy." And it won't like he was saying it in a cute way or nothing. Even though that wouldn't be cool either. But this nigga was looking me square in the eye basically telling me I was his Daddy. Real shit.

That aint even the wildest part. Besides the fact the nigga followed me everywhere I went and wouldn't stop staring, touching and pinching me, that motherfucker had the nerve to lick my damn face like I was some damn ice cream or some shit.

Not to mention the little nigga breath smelled like hot dumpster juice. Ay man, I aint mean to but I fucked around and smacked the hell outta that little nigga. Fuck it, it was a reflex, he was alright though, he cried for about a minute but he soon forgot and was back being my shadow.

But yeah, fuck that, right then and there I realized just how important Daddy's was to little kids. Wont no way in hell my seed was gonna act like that over some random ass nigga. Hell naw. I was gonna be the best Daddy in the world. No funny shit. I couldn't wait.

I'll get back to that story later though. I still gotta tell you what happened in the studio that night. Shit was Epic.

Alright so we got in that bitch and the first person I see is T-Rell. THE T-Rell, Grammy winning, platinum selling millionaire T-Rell. Yep, Virginia's very own. Oh yeah I had to throw that VA shit in there. It's a must I let motherfuckers know how special we is. And I aint just talking about music. I'm talking about all around the board. Even sports, don't let me get to talking about Mike Vick and Allen Iverson. I think it's' just something in the water, we the shit.

But yeah, I aint gon lie I damn near shitted on myself with T-Rell standing in my face. Dude was like a God back then. When I tell you, you couldn't listen to the radio without hearing a series of his beats I aint lying. I knew if I could just get him to fuck with me, the sky was the limit. I was nervous, excited, man I had so many emotions I can't even begin to tell you. I knew I had to impress his ass.

"What up man? I'm T-Rell," said T-Rell in a low, calm tone as we shook hands. He spoke so humbly, it was like I was the famous one or something. "I've heard all types of good things about you," he continued before pointing over to a guy sitting behind the control boards. "That's my man Leo. He's a producer I have working under me. He has some fire. Hopefully the two of you can make some magic. I can't wait to hear it."

"Cool," I said. Of course I was a little upset that he won't staying and wouldn't actually be the one producing a track for me but just hearing him say that he would take a listen, was enough for me.

"Well alright guys I'm out," he said as he made his way to the door. "And again, good luck," he said looking back at me.

"Thanks," I said before remembering I'd bought my mixtape along with me. "If you ever get a chance, give this a listen," I said walking over. "No funny shit. I think you'll fuck with it."

"Bet. I definitely will," he said as he grabbed the CD.

Now it was just me Leo and Rich. I was kinda happy it wasn't more people there, Even though I had rapped in front of strangers plenty of times, it still was just a little more comfortable to not have a million eyes looking at me.

"What do you think about this?" Leo said to me as he turned the beat on.

Soon as I heard that motherfucker my head started bobbing. Can't lie that shit was smooth as hell. "I like this shit," I said looking over to Rich who was obviously feeling it too because he wore the same facial expression as I did.

No funny shit, it was the type track that made you just want to sit back and reflect on life. The beat was full of pain, it had so much soul. It was talking to me and I was ready to talk back, I had a lot to say. It was the perfect canvas to paint my picture on. My insides started bubbling, feigning to release my feelings.

Shit like that was the exact reason I loved music, I could tell how I felt about things without feeling like I was being judged or soft.

"You need a pen or something?" asked Leo.

"Naw," I said opening my eyes. "I'm ready."

"You sure?" he asked.

"Yeah, I'm sure," I said as I opened the door to where the mic was at. As always I felt supreme comfort as I stepped in. Thankful that I was able to spit on a beat that wasn't already made famous by someone else. I'm telling you, aint no feeling in the world like creating something from nothing. It's unexplainable.

So yeah, I through on my headphones, "I'm ready," I said into the mic. Like always I didn't know what I was going to say but it didn't matter, I knew I was going to make it work.

"Ok," Leo said, as he restarted the beat.

Once again I closed my eyes and before I know it, all those feelings and thoughts I said I had inside of me exploded onto the beat.

'Ohhh lorddd ohhh lorddd,

So much pain don brought me here,

Cried enough its time to dry my tears,

Strapped up time to face my fear,s

Was taught to never be scared of shit,

Learned loaded pistols turn g's to bitch,

Swear I'll never go from g to snitch,

But im destined to go from broke to rich....'

Finally, after I guess about four or five minutes, the beat turned off. Wiping the sweat from my face I removed my headphones and walked out to Leo and Rich.

I know I've told you plenty of times how every time I rapped people stared at me in awe. But not this time. This time was different. Instead, as I trotted out I discovered Leo and Rich going crazy. Popping champagne, bowing down to me, telling me they won't worthy of breathing the same air as me.

Alright ok, maybe they aint do all that but they really was going crazy.

"Yo that shit was fucking perfect. It's a little long, but I can chop it up into three versus and use that line when you said, *'You can put a strap in his hands and tell that nigga squeeze it... But can he go to the P.O.C. and keep the shit a secret...* and just repeat it, chopped and screwed for the hook. I can see it right now. That shit was cold. No pen, no pad. You the shit bruh, I aint never seen nothing like it," Leo praised.

"You like that shit foreal?" I asked.

"Hell yeah," he followed. "You think you got some more in you? I got plenty beats."

"Damn right I do," I said excitedly before Rich butted in.

"Yo we gonna have to do that another day. I gotta little emergency I gotta deal with right quick."

And just like that we were gone. We rushed out of the Studio. Rich didn't even have time to take me all the way back out Norview so since we were already in Norfolk he said he was just gonna take me to Chenell's. I aint have a problem with it. I hadn't seen her in about a week.

Before we could make it to Chenell's. Rich got a phone call.

"Man. I'm fucking busy as hell. Why can't you handle it on your own?" he said before pausing to listen to the response. I could hear the voice of a female. "Alright I'll be ho--," he said before looking over to me. "I mean, I'll be there in a second."

We shot over to his crib. Well his 'friends' crib as he later put it. I knew it was his crib though. He just didn't really want me knowing where he lived. But I understood. He knew I was a street nigga. He couldn't trust me just yet.

We turned into 'River Lakes', it was a real nice neighborhood. I knew exactly where we were at. Me and the homies had ran up in one them houses about a month before that. Came off real decent to, they had a lot of electronics and shit that we eventually sold.

"I'll be right back," said Rich as he exited the whip. Looking at his crib I can't lie I was a little disappointed. It's not like it was some ran down shack or nothing. I told you it was a nice neighborhood. But he had the smallest crib on the block. It was cool and all but back then I guess I expected him to have some big ass mansion or something.

He aint stay long inside, he was back out in about two minutes. We rode listening to old school RnB as usual before we finally got to Chenell's crib.

"Man with the shit you just layed in there. I'ma have some shit lined up for you in no GodDamn time. I'ma hit your phone soon as I get something."

"Cool," I said hopping out the whip, feeling like the world was in the palm of my hands.

How These Hoes Be

Back in the day they had this little spot in Norview called the Red House. It literally looked like a big ass Red house. Only on the inside it was built like a little club and shit. Even had a stage.

I was in that bitch damn near every weekend. Every kid in town was. This was the beginning of the social media age. Myspace was popping and you couldn't log on that bitch without seeing Norview teen-agers talking about the shit. Even Mank and Jah use to come all the way from Norfolk to fuck with it. Actually by then Norview was like they second home. Everybody knew them niggas. It won't no way you could miss they ass with all that damn dancing they was doing. They use to have them parties lit. I'm telling you, the Red House was the shit.

Only problem was, it won't no liquor in that bitch. But with Marco serving as DJ and promoter, we snuck shit in that motherfucker every time. We used to have bitches wasted in that bitch. Throwing ass, sucking dick, boy I swear we use to have a ball in that jank.

After a while though, it was time for the Red House to upgrade a little bit. Not only were they gonna be hosting parties but the owners had decided to start bringing in performers and having little concerts and shit. And who else better to start it off than me.

They even cut me in on the deal. My first paid show. Wont much, 200 beans. I aint give a fuck though.

Anytime I got paid to do what I loved was the shit to me. At first I was happy as hell about doing it. But when it came time for me to go on stage. Shit changed a little.

"You ready for this shit bro?" asked Dock as him along with Jah, Mank and I stood in a small room behind the stage, that was serving as my dressing room.

"Bro I'm nervous," I replied leaned up against the wall.

"Nervous? Hell you mean you nervous?" Dock shot back.

"Nigga. Gangster's don't get nervous," added Jah. "Hell wrong with you?"

"Fuck yall niggas," I said still leaned up against the wall. "Yall aint never had to get on stage and perform for motherfuckers."

"Shut yo hoe ass up nigga. You performing in front of niggas and bitches you don seen your whole life, aint nobody tryna here that bullshit," blurted Dock.

"Nigga fuck you," I shot back. "I don't know the first thing I'm supposed to do on that damn stage."

"What? Man you seen other rappers perform. Just do what the fuck you seen them do," said Jah.

"Bro fuck all that. Just do what you be doing in the ood-hay," added Mank. "Plus, you just took the ex ill-pay, once that shit kick in, it's gonna do all the work for you."

I don't even know why I even had stage fright. I'm thinking it was because of how much I loved that shit. Rapping was the only thing I took serious. I cared about it so much I aint want to fuck up. Shit was killing me. I knew that was one part of the game I hadn't experienced yet. If I fucked up then maybe I won't built for it. At least that's how I was feeling. No funny shit, a nigga was tripping. I started pacing, walking in circles, just straight overthinking. I aint know what the hell to do with myself. I wanted to go home.

Yeah, I knew my niggas was right, it really wont too much difference from me rapping in the hood, it's just something about stepping on that stage was different. In the hood when I rapped it was easy, shit was always spontaneous, I aint have to sit back and think about what the hell I was gonna say or do. Or even if I was gonna forget a couple words, or if I was gonna be holding the mic right.

Soon it won't no more time for thinking.

"Yo they ready for you," said Marco as he opened the door, peeking his head through.

"Ok," I said, as I took a deep breath, faced my fears and walked out the door with my crew behind me, all of us dressed in all black.

Within seconds I was standing on stage with all eyes on me. Well at least I think they were, I was too much of a bitch to even look out at them. That was only until I walked over to Marco's DJ booth and grabbed the Mic.

No funny shit, when that shit touched my hands it's as if it gave a nigga special powers or something. I turned around looked out at everybody and shouted "Aye Marco."

"What sup Coach," said Marco into his Mic.

"You think these Motherfuckers ready for me to shut this bitch down."

"I don't know but it's only one way to find out," he said as he turned on the beat to my song 'No Funny Shit'.

Man if the booth didn't let me know that I was chasing the right dream then that night most definitely did. I lie to you not, I smoked that damn stage.

Jah and Mank was all up there dancing, hitting the Wellington Shuffle, Dock was hyping me up, rapping along to all my shit. His crazy ass even jumped in the crowd. Shit was off the damn chain. We had everybody in that jank going crazy and when it was all said and done we had shut that bitch down. I guarantee you nobody who ever performed in that motherfucker ever did it like we did it. FACTS.

"Ay I wanna thank yall for coming out and supporting me and shit," I said wiping sweat from my forehead, after performing my last song and looking out onto the crowd." I love yall Motherfuckers. No funny shit, I'ma put Norview on the map. Watch," I said as everybody cheered.

For about a minute I just stood there letting it all soak in. Shit felt good. I had all my niggas and my whole city behind me. That's when I realized I hadn't seen Alex or any of her friends.

As Marco turned back on the music and everybody got back to dancing and shit, I started looking around. Something aint seem right. She had told me she was gonna make sure she got a up close and personal view.

Looking through the crowd I aint see her ass nowhere. Hopping off the stage, I searched high and low. Still, I aint see her. I even busted in on the girls bathroom "Alex you in here?" I yelled. "Any of yall bitches seen Alex?" I asked.

Nobody had, so I stepped outside and called her. I aint get no answer though. I was about to call one more time but then the phone rang. The caller I.D. said her name.

"Yo baby where the hell you at?" I answered.

"Sky this isn't Alex. This is her Mom. Alex has gotten beat up. We're in the hospital."

"The Hospital?" I shouted. "She ok?"

"She's alive." She replied.

"I'm on my way up there right now."

"I'm not sure--." Alex's mom started to say but I had already hung up the phone and shot back in the party to find the homies.

"Yo Dock gimme the car keys," I demanded. My car had broken down so we were now all riding in Dock's new Lincoln LS.

"For what? Where you going?" he asked.

"Bro just let me get the fucking keys."

"Nigga who the fuck is you yelling at?"

"Dog just give me the damn keys," I shouted. "Alex is in the fucking hospital."

"Oh shit what sup. What's wrong?"

"Nigga I don't know. Just let me get the keys."

"Fuck that bro we going with you," said Jah as Dock handed me the keys and we all dipped out.

I sped to the hospital, mind racing a hundred miles a minute until finally we made it. After finding out what room she was in, I hopped in the elevator as the homies chilled in the little waiting area.

Heart beating out my chest, I burst into her room. Her Mama and her friend Tierra were the only other people in there besides Alex. Man it give me the chills even thinking about that night. Her pretty face all beat and bruised.

I can still picture all three of them looking over to me. Everybody with a different version of hatred in they eyes, before Alex spoke. "The baby's dead," she said softly as tears slid down her scarred face.

"Huh what?" I asked stopping in my tracks feeling as if my heart had just been ripped from my motherfucking chest.

"Chenell did it," she said angrily.

Hearing them words come from my baby took everything outta me. I fell to my knees, weeping like a sick child. I was stuck, couldn't move. My life at that moment wasn't real to me. It couldn't be true. How? Where? When? I had so many fucking questions but I wouldn't even get a chance to ask.

"Get out! Get out! I hate you," screamed Alex.

"But--," I attempted to speak, still on my knees.

"Get out," she screamed again as her mother and Tierra stared over to me as I stood to my feet and turned around.

"What's going on?" asked Jah as I shot past the waiting room as they all followed me to the car asking questions. I ignored all them niggas. I was heated. I couldn't even speak.

I knew everything was all my damn fault. The week before that I had told Chenell that we had to stop fucking around because Alex was pregnant. She acted like she was cool with the shit. I guess it was all an act. The bitch was crazy. But I was ready to get crazy right along with her ass.

"I'll be back in 5 minutes," I said to the homies as I exited the whip in front of Chenell's crib.

We had just drove back to Norview and all I'd told them was that my baby had died. They had no idea why I'd came to Chenell's crib.

Knowing Chenell never locked her door I walked straight in and up the stairs. It was three in the morning, she was sleep but my presence must've woke her up or something.

"The hell you doin in here?" she asked as I stood stiff at the foot of her bed struggling to fight back tears. "Don't tell me you crying cause I beat up your little weak ass girlfriend."

"Bitch you killed my baby," I shouted as I hopped onto the bed, colliding my open hand with her face before choking life from her as she screamed.

Up until then I had never put my hands on a woman but I felt like I had too. Shit was personal. The only chance I had at a real family and that bitch had ruined it for me.

No funny shit, I hadn't thought about shit but my baby since I found out. Still had months to go but I already had baby clothes and everything. I was ready. Even had a name, 'King Sky' if it was a boy. I didn't try to think of a girl name. I was gonna let Alex do it.

Half of whatever I was making from rap I had decided to save for the baby. Me and Alex was gonna get a crib, I was gonna get a new whip. Boy I even thought about marrying her.

I knew with Chenell pulling that stunt all that was probably over. I had did plenty of shit to Alex that she forgave but that was different. I aint know if I stood a chance.

"I hate you," I screamed as Chenell seemed to be seconds away from her last breath before her son ran in the room.

"Mommy," he said as I quickly turned around as he shot over to the bed to defend his Mother on some 'Baby Boy' shit. Real talk, I still aint give a fuck. Fuck his Mama. It was eye for eye. She deserved everything I was giving to her.

Still something made me let up. I guess I won't as heartless as I thought. I removed my hands, through her son up off my back and silently walked out of the house. Slamming the door behind me.

Lawnmower Man

"Fuck," I said under my breath after reading an article in the paper.

Boy oh Boy, when it rains, it motherfucking pours. I don't know who made that saying up but they damn sure knew what the fuck they was talking about. Growing up I always thought about killing myself. Before I met Dock it seemed like I would never be happy. I looked to my future and saw darkness. I couldn't figure out why if it was a God he would make my life so damn hard. I figured it would be better if I just won't even on the earth at all. If it wasn't better going where ever the fuck I'd end up after I died, I still figured it couldn't be any worse than what I was already going through.

As I got older and Dock had introduced me to the wonderful world of drugs, I never really had them feelings no more. That was until the day I found out Rich had gotten his ass locked up.

Man my life seemed like it was crashing down. I aint know how the hell I was supposed to get in contact with T-Rell or Leo, it won't like the studio I'd recorded in was their own personal one. With the loss of Rich I felt like I'd lost everything. Yeah, I still had mixtapes and songs popping around town but it was only so far that shit could take me.

I needed that nigga. Word was the Feds had snatched him up. Niggas said he might not never be coming home. He aint have no bond, nothing. Shit was just all wrong. On top of that. Jah and Mank was locked once again.

This particular time had me worried though. We had all did a little sting. Same shit as we always did. Nothing too special. Only this time shit got real. While we had everybody tied up at gun point, some kid had slipped underneath the bed without us knowing and called the police.

Them motherfuckers pulled up soon as we was leaving, we aint even have enough time to get back in the whip, we had to dip out on foot. On top of that we aint even come off with nothing but a few ounces of weed and $800.

The next day the police came and snatched up Jah and Mank. I knew they wouldn't snitch but shit was still stressful considering I aint know how they had figured out it was them who'd been involved. Man I was petrified, thinking they could be coming for me and Dock next.

Life was fucked up, and I aint even have Alex there to comfort me.

"Man that nigga Rich in jail bro. The Feds got him," I said turning to look at Dock. We were sitting on my Moms front Porch.

"So. Fuck that nigga, you don't need that nigga. Your music popping out here in these streets," said Dock.

"Dog it's only so far I can get selling little mixtapes in the hood"

"Nigga you thinking like a chump."

"Bro it take money to make money. Rich always used to say we gotta pay these DJ's to even listen to us. We aint getting that kinda money. Can't keep robbing all these niggas bro. Ever since Jah and Mank got snatched up, niggas been catching on to us."

"Man fuck these niggas they better catch on to these nuts."

"See man," I said shaking my head. "You always joking. I'm serious though."

"Alright. I hear you. But it is one nigga who aint catching on to us."

"Who?" I asked.

"Yo boy Rich."

"Rich? Nigga what the hell is you talking about?" I asked.

"Didn't you tell me last month Rich had showed you his crib?"

"Yeah."

"You think he don't got hella shit in that jank? That nigga was loaded. I bet we can make a killing. You just said the Feds got him. Dude aint getting out bro. We might as well get everything we can before the pigs get a hold of it. I bet his ass got some money hidden in that motherfucker too," Dock said convincingly.

"Break in Rich's crib? Hell naw. Nigga you trippin."

"I'm trippin? Nigga don't you wanna make it. We can sell everything he got. Get sweet ass whips instead of these little hoop rides and really stunt. We gon look so butta niggas aint gon have no choice but to want to listen to your music. Shit probably inspire you to spit some ol flossed out shit. Gotta be honest, niggas feel your shit but sometimes niggas just wanna party."

I sat speechless.

"Bro we got to," Dock urged. "Nigga we getting older. We gonna have kids soon. We can't have them niggas growing up like we did bro. I don't even want them to have to even think about robbing shit," he said as he looked over to me as I looked away. "Bro what's the address we can do that shit now. Aint no sense in waiting. I'm ready."

I prided myself on being loyal. At least to the niggas who did right by me. Foreal I couldn't even believe Dock was suggesting that shit. He was the main one who taught me all that loyalty stuff. Rich hadn't did a damn thing to me but help out. And to keep it all real, I always kinda wished dude was my Dad. You know I had never had one. Technically he won't even old enough but it was always a feeling of having one that I couldn't shake.

But shit on the other hand. If he won't getting out it really wont no sense in letting the feds take all his shit. Feel me? Think about it. Would you rather have the fucking dirty ass Police take your shit or your homeboy.

Didn't take me long to make up my mind. I told myself when I got on I would send him money and shit. It was gonna be the best for the both of us.

Within a few hours we had went and got dressed in all black and pulled up on his crib. He lived on the corner, it was perfect because we could get out of the car, hop his gate and we'd be in his back yard.

"You ready bro?" Dock asked before we exited the whip.

"Yep."

"Bet. Let's go change our lives."

Breaking in cribs had become nothing to us. We had did the shit a million times. We followed all the proper protocol. Before going in we even cut all the wires in case they had some sorta security system.

Next, Dock picked the back door lock. He was a master at that shit. Which was perfect because we aint have to kick no door in or nothing. Within minutes we was in there.

When it came down to the inside of Rich's crib, it was exactly how you would expect him to live. Fucking Immaculate. Bossed up. The whole crib just screamed out money. He obviously had paid an interior decorator to do that shit or somethin. Shit was sick, nigga even had big ass chandilers hanging from the ceiling.

"Yo. We can strip this whole house and probably make a million dollars," Dock said looking around.

"Hell yeah," I followed.

"Ay I'ma stay down here. You go upstairs and see what you can find."

"Ok," I said.

As I crept through the dark house my conscience started getting the best of me. Even though I knew the feds was gonna come and take all that shit anyway. I still felt like a fuck nigga for even creeping round Rich's crib without him being there. I knew without a doubt he'd kill me for pulling some shit like that.

Can't snatch though, the moment I saw his gold Rolex sitting on a table next to the steps all that soft ass shit went out the window. No funny shit, everything was instantly worth it. I grabbed that bitch, through it in my pocket, made my way up the steps and opened the door to the first room that I saw.

"AHHHHH" I heard as someone screamed.

Man how the fuck had I forgot Rich had a fucking girlfriend. The same bad ass bitch who was with him the first time he took me to the booth. "Get the fuck out of here," she screamed as she rolled out of bed, grabbing her pistol from the bed rest as I quickly grabbed mine too.

Next thing I know we both standing 15 feet away from each other pointing guns. I stood, still trying to come up with my next move. As I stared through the holes in my ski mask I realized she had no idea who I was. I wanted to just turn around, grab Dock and get the fuck outta there.

She aint give me alotta time to think though. Without saying a word she pulled the trigger. Thank God the bitch was on safety. "Shit," she shouted as she took her eyes off me for a split second to remove it.

That left me with just enough time to either run out or fire at her. I didn't wanna shoot her but I didn't wanna risk her killing me as I turned around.

With little time to think I knew what I had to do.

BANG BANG.

She fell dead to the floor. Two shots, one to the head one to the shoulder.

"Bitch," yelled Dock.

After hearing the commotion from downstairs, he had snuck back upstairs and laid her as down.

As I stared at her body, Dock looked over to me, "Bro you don't need that shit on your conscience," he said before running right past her dead body to search through the drawers before looking over to me. "Yo I gotta big ass surprise for you when you get downstairs. Boy we about to be on," he shouted, without an ounce of remorse as I followed his lead, searching through Rich's shit.

Antisocial

Money, Cars, Clothes, Hoes. Man I swear to God a young nigga was balling harder than ever. Straight stunting. Living life to the motherfucking fullest.

Chill though, before you get to thinking I'm just some heartless, conscienless monkey, let me at least say I felt bad as hell about what had happened to Rich's bitch. I regret the shit happened to this day. But hey I aint God I can't change the past. Its outta my control. May sound harsh but all I could do was move forward and try my best to keep the shit off my brain.

With that being said, man I got deeper into the drugs than I ever been. I use to get high just to have fun. But shit had changed. I was addicted to the feeling of not being myself. Shit had gotten so bad that I didn't even really care what the drug was. I was popping pills, smoking, drinking, and even sniffing coke. I quit the coke though, whenever I was on it, my dick wouldn't get hard. But yeah I still got high as a motherfucker off damn near everything else.

Oh shit, what am I doing? I didn't even tell you what Dock had found in the crib. You ready? Brace yourself because you aint gonna believe it.

$100,000! No funny shit. So much damn money I threw up from the smell, trying to count it. And guess where he found it? Burried under the tile beneath the kitchen sink. See, I know what you thinking, why would anyone hide money under the kitchen sink. And what the fuck would make Dock even check there in the first place.

Ok, let me explain, so jail is sorta like college for criminals and shit. So one day me and the homies was talking and Jah told us about some King pin nigga he'd gotten close to while he was locked. He said he gave him a whole lotta game and one of the pieces he penned was that if you ever acquire alotta dirty money, hide it under the tile beneath the sink in the kitchen. Police never check there.

I guess this was a common thing amongst hustlers cause when Dock checked underneath Rich's sink, there it was. Hundred Racks. It was like finding some buried treasure or something.

And I aint even tell you about all the jewelry we found. Besides the Rolex, we came up on gold and diamond necklaces, blinged out rings. Real deal shit too, none of that middle of the mall fugazy stuff.

When we first got a hold of everything we told each other we was gon play it cool and not wear any of it. It was gonna bring too much attention to us. Only problem was, we said that shit when we was sober. Once we got high, we both said fuck that shit. We stepped off in the club flexed up shining like a bitch.

Man we use to be in V.I.P. so much you would've thought we lived in that jank. No funny shit. Damn near every night we was in somebody spot taking pics flashing big ass stacks of money.

And yeah I know at first we said we was gonna be paying the DJ.'s to play my shit. But fuck that. After seeing us stunt so hard and hearing that the music was actually dope, they had no choice but to fuck with us. They was practically begging us to get new tracks. I had bought Marco some official studio equipment, so my music was sounding A1. We was on.

I had this song called '*Lotta Drugs*'. I killed them with that one. It was over with. Niggas was going crazy. I made being a damn drug fein sound cool asa bitch. I sent Drug Dealers profits through the motherfucking roof.

And speaking of drugs, we had our hand in that shit too. See, that's why I loved Dock. I think by now I don told you a million times how I couldn't handle money. So you should already know I was acting a fool, blowing the shit faster than I'd ever done before. Actually me and Dock both was. Only difference between us was that he was wise enough to invest.

Right after we got the lick for the 100 g's Dock made sure we racked up on Coke, Weed, and pills. And since we already knew all the movers and shakers in the city, we fronted that shit out to every real nigga we knew was doing they thing.

I aint gon lie, I felt good being a drug connect, no bullshit aint nothing like smoking a blunt riding out on a beautiful day to pick up some money from a worker. Hustling is an adrenaline rush like no other, shit is addictive. If you aint careful your whole life can be consumed by it. No funny shit.

The most I ever had to do was bag up the product up or cook up the coke. I liked cooking up. Felt accomplished after I learned. To me it's kinda a mandatory skill every street nigga should possess whether you sell crack or not.

I can remember getting so into it that me and Dock would have competitions on who whipped it up the best. The further you stretched it the more money you could make. Dock was good but real shit I became a beast at that shit.

Can't snatch though, being around all that shit used to have me paranoid as hell. Before then I aint even really know what the fuck a kilo of cocaine was. I had heard of it, but seeing it first hand was an experience.

Docks Plug used to come through our trap and drop them bitches on the table. All of them wrapped up in Vaseline, straight drop, smelling like straight amoneia. They say they wrapped them like that so police dogs couldn't smell them or some shit. I don't know, but I do know all them motherfuckers used to be stamped, sometimes, it had a letter, sometimes a car symbol and one time I can even remember it being the Chicago Bulls logo. I aint never figure out why the fuck they used to stamp them. I was usualy too busy peeking out the window. I always felt like the feds was about to run up in our shit at any minute.

They didn't though. I'm glad. We had enough shit in that crib to get us thrown under the jail. Ak's, shot guns, pistols, hidden all over the place, not to mention we used to get Heroin in.

We aint never have a whole kilo of that. That shit was too damn expensive. Probally like 80 or 100 thousand or some shit. I don't know. But I do know we used to have some top knotch shit. Sometimes our shit would even be pink. Niggas had'nt never seen no shit like that. Before long motherfuckers who was scoring from us was calling us the 'Pink Panthers'. I liked that shit.

But yeah other than that we aint have to touch a damn thing. Not one time did I sell a drug to a user. I skipped all the bullshit and went straight up to Plug status. And niggas always payed on time. Always. Our names held weight. With all the shootouts and robberies we'd been involved with in the past niggas knew not to play with us. Niggas was lucky, my trigger finger was still itching, I can't even snatch I was ready to catch a body.

So yeah I guess all in all after the Rich situation, everything was going great. I just knew I was on my way to the top and to tell the truth I aint even give a damn how long it took. I was living good for te time being.

Well as good as life could be without Alex. She hadn't talked to me in months. Her ass real live hated a niggas guts. Shit still hadn't really sunken in with me. I couldn't accept it. Fuck that. The thought of losing her forever had never even really crossed my mind. After all, this was the same girl who could finish my sentence.

I remember one night I got so high at a tattoo party that I told them motherfuckers to tattoo her name on my neck. The next day when I sobered up I didn't even remember doing the shit. Still, hoping for the best I decided to go to her crib when I knew Francis and her Mama won't home, I hadn't tried to contact her in a while. I was gonna show her what I did and hopefully she was gonna give me another shot.

Knock Knock. "Alex open the door. I know you're in there. Just come talk to me. It's Sky. Don't do me like that. I'll stay out here all night. I don't care. I just need you to talk to me. I love you man," I screamed from her porch. I had been out there for about an hour. "Come on Alex. Open the damn door." I continued as I heard footsteps coming towards the door.

The moment I'd been waiting for was finally there. I was sure she was about to curse me out but I was prepared, standing strong, hoping the sight of my face would give her a change of heart.

As the door knob turned I braced myself, grinning from ear to ear until the door was finally opened. That's when I saw her. By now I don't even have to tell you how beautiful she looked. All the scars from her fight with Chenell was now nonexistent. She was flawless. Looking better than ever.

"Hey baby," I said looking into her eyes.

Completely ignoring me, she looked past me as if I was invisible as she made her way to the street causing me to look back. And what do ya know, I'll be damned if she won't walking towards a damn cop car that had just pulled up.

"Yo Alex what the hell going on?" I asked as two cops hopped out.

"How you doing officers?" I overheard Alex say before her and the officers talked quietly.

Now any other time I would have ran. But since I didn't have any drugs or my gun on me. I stood there. I had to find out what was going on. Then finally after talking for about five minutes and signing some paper, Alex shook the cop's hands and walked back towards the house.

"Alex what the hell going on?" I asked as she ignored me before casually walking back into the crib.

"Hey Coach," said one of the officers as I looked back. "Come here. I got something for you to sign," said the officer as I slowly walked over.

"Yo what sup? I aint even do shit. What the hell going on?"

"Well Coach, you don't mind if I call you Coach do ya?" he asked as I shook my head. Why the hell would I mind? Every police officer in town called me that. Even though I had never officially been locked up it still was a known fact that I was a problem and they harassed me every chance they could. "Alright well Coach, Alexandra made it clear that she didn't want you to go to jail but she does want you to sorta stay away."

"What? She told yall that?" I asked.

"Yep," said the officer. "She actually filed a restraining order out against you, stating you can't be within 100 ft. from her for a period of 30 days."

"Are you serious?"

"Afraid so. So if you don't mind. I'd like you to sign this paper," he said as his partner walked over to me with a pen.

"Man this some bullshit."

"It's ok. Happens to the best of us. Just move on, its plenty fish in the sea," he said as I signed and walked off.

Yo never in a million years would I think she would call the boys on a nigga. What if I would have had a warrant out for my arrest or something? She aint give a damn. I couldn't believe that shit.

Still as crazy as it sound, I still aint lose hope. Yeah I felt like it was gonna take a little more time but fuck that she won't going nowhere, especially with me having her name on my damn neck.

I went straight to Marco's spot. I had to let some shit off my chest. I wrote a song called '*My Baby*'. You already know what it was about. In my head that was the closest way I could talk to her. I just hoped she would hear it one day.

Life had to go on though. So I made sure I made up for it with bitches. Plenty of them.

Mama

"Yo you gotta drive I'm fucked up," said Dock as we approached his new all black Lexus LS430, I had the same one in blue.

We was leaving club 'Badabings'. The hottest club in Norview. You already know we was drunk as a bitch. "I'm not driving," I replied. "Nigga I can't even walk."

"Nigga you walking right now," said Dock drunkenly.

"Man you know what I mean."

"Both of yall can shut up," said Deena. She was this bad ass bitch Dock had been kicking it with. I was fucking her friend Tisha. That hoe was finer than a motherfucker too. Phat asses, big titties, and both they ass indulged in just as many drugs as we did. We went out with them all the time. "I'll drive," she said.

"No bitch. I think I should drive. You drunk more Henny then me," added Tisha.

"So bitch. You act like I aint pop that ecstasy pill. You already know that shit make me concentrate good as hell."

"You right bitch, you right."

"I know I am. Now Dock give me the keys," she said as Dock and I both leaned on the back of the whip, nodding off.

"Here," he said as he handed them over and we all walked to our doors. Dock and Deena in the front and Tisha and I in the back.

"Yo where the fuck we about to go at anyway?" I asked as I flopped down in my seat.

"Yeah, where is we going?" asked Deena to Dock.

"Shit, I don't know. What time is it?" he asked.

"1:45," added Tisha.

"Oh shit, it's early as hell," I said.

"Hell yeah," said Dock. "Yall tryna go to Lil Steve selling party?"

"Shit, I don't care, I just aint tryna go to the crib," I replied.

"Hold on. Didn't somebody just get killed at his selling party last weekend?" asked Tisha.

"So," Dock and I both said looking over to her.

"What yall mean so?" she asked.

"You must don't know who the fuck we is."

"Naw maybe we don't," said Deena. "Explain."

"Aint nobody gonna do shit to us." Said Dock.

"Damn right. Niggas know what time it is with us," I added.

"Boy boo. Niggas don't know shit," said Tisha.

"Yeah right. You know better than that," said Dock.

"Yeah. So what's up? Is we going to the selling party or not?" I asked.

"Girl what you think?" asked Deena, looking back at Tisha.

"What the hell you asking her for?" asked Dock.

"Because that's my stick girl and I aint gonna have her nowhere where she feels unsafe."

"Deena if you don't drive this motherfucker," he said before pulling his big ass desert eagle from beneath his seat. "I got all the safety we need. You starting to make me mad," he said as he gripped the pistol.

"How the hell I'm making you mad?"

"I feel like you taking my gangsta as a joke. You gonna make me pop me a nigga to show your ass I aint no game."

"Boy shut up you always taking shit too serious. Ok, I guess we can go to the little selling party."

"Bet," I said.

"But if any of them hating ass bitches pop some shit, I'm gon need you to shoot they ass. We just got our nails done," said Deena looking down at her hands. "I aint got time to be fighting no hoes."

"Baby you know I got you," said Dock as he leaned in for a kiss.

"I know Daddy."

"Man if you don't get me the hell outta this damn parking lot. I aint got time to watch yall niggas breakup to make up and shit. I need me another damn drink," I said.

"Yes, I was just thinking the same thing," said Tisha.

"Man fuck both of yall. Yall some haters," Dock said as Deena backs out the parking lot.

I don't really remember saying too much for a while. I don't know if them niggas was talking or not. I was too zoned out. The next thing I can remember is them damn red and blue lights flashing behind us.

"Oh my fucking God. Do yall see them niggas?" asked Tisha, looking back.

"What's going on?" asked Dock making sure to look straight ahead.

"It's the Police," I said.

"Aw fuck," said Dock.

"Yo we good, just be calm and try not to act too drunk. They don't have probable cause to search the whip. You got your license don't you Deena?" I asked.

"No," she said slowly.

"No," Dock and I both blurted.

"Why the fuck you volunteer to drive if you aint got no license?" Dock screamed.

"I didn't think about it. I was just tryna do yall a favor," she said as she began pulling over.

"Yo what the fuck you doing?" Dock yelled, panicking.

"Pulling over. What the fuck you think," she yelled back.

"Bitch! You fucking tripping. Do you know what the fuck I got in this motherfucker?"

See that's when shit got tricky. Cause I aint know what the hell that nigga had in that bitch either. I knew we both had guns on us. That's what I was afraid of. But a gun in VA won't shit. Yeah they was gonna take us downtown and book us but we was gonna make bail and be out the next day. I won't really tripping about that. But when I seen Dock pull a big ass ziplock bag from the glove compartment that's when I knew shit was real.

"Yo what the fuck is that?" I asked as Dena pulled over and Dock clumsily attempted to stash the open bag into his underwear as tiny ecstasy pills slipped out onto the floor.

"Oh shit," said Dock as he looked down at the pills that had fell between his seat.

"Yo why the fuck you got all that shit?" I asked as Dock tried to slip his finger through the crack to retrieve them.

"Oh shit they coming, they coming," said Dena.

"Chill chill," Dock said as he finally got a hold of them, tossing the pills into his mouth.

"How you guys doing?" asked the officer as we all nodded our heads trying to remain calm.

"Ok, officer," said Deena. "Just trying to make it home."

"You aware that your back tail light is out?" he asked.

"No sir I didn't know."

"Ma'am have you been drinking?" he asked as he shined his light into the car. "Hey fellas, Coach and Dock. Now that I see who you're with, I already know the answer to the question. Come on everyone step outside of the car."

"For what officer?" asked Deena.

"You'll find out soon, just step out the car with your hands up," he said.

"Fuck," I whispered as we all stepped out hands to the sky as the officers back up arrived and immediately began to pat us down, quickly throwing cuff on us all.

Motherfucking police had completely blew my high. Had a nigga all worried and shit. Dock was on probation but luckily the car wasn't in his name so I could just say the guns were mine so he would never have to be taken down. You already know he woulda did the same shit for me.

After about 15 minutes they'd finally finished talking trash and taking our names and shit. "Alright go sit on the curb," the officer said as we all sat next to each other.

"Yo, whatever they find I'll take the wrap. I got a clean record," I whispered before looking over to Dock. "Yo you hear me?" I asked after he didn't speak.

"Coach," he whispered, struggling to speak.

"Yo," I whispered back.

"Don't let me die."

"What?" I said looking over.

"Ahhh," yelled Deena. "Help. Help," she screamed.

"Help," Tisha also screamed.

I was speechless. Man I aint know what to do. That nigga Dock was shaking, twitching and foaming at the mouth. I couldn't even move. I'd never seen nobody have a seizure right in my face like that.

Man for the remainder of the night I didn't say another word. Neither did Dock. Before the ambulance even came I could already tell he was gone. I felt something inside of me die, leaving a void that's still empty to this day.

And if you wondering what the hell happened. Man, you know my boy was only bout 5'4. When he dropped them ex pills on the floor and had to throw them in his mouth, it was too many for his body to handle.

It's crazy, I'd watched him take lives but never thought I'd watch him take his own.

The worse day ever. I ended up in jail and my nigga died. I had just turned 18 and week before.

Worst Enemy

I never really knew what pain was until I went to jail. I thought I did. Always figured growing up the way I had was the worse. But after enduring the pain of unexpectedly losing the one person I had that truly had my back, right before my eyes, was some shit I wouldn't wish on my worst enemy.

I cried for two days straight. Day after day I felt as if I was sinking deeper and deeper into a sickening depression. I was stuck. Empty. I had been fully prepared to die in a cell with Dock but for him to die without me hurt. I just couldn't believe it was real. Like how? Why? To this day I still aint came to terms with it.

I always knew I was going to jail but I would have never thought I would have went under the circumstances that I did. Life had beat me up and turned me into someone I couldn't recognize. Someone I hated. I was angry, confused, ready to murder some shit, with no one in my corner, or any drugs to numb the pain.

Crazy thing is, I had a bail. Only $5000. Won't like I had it though. I was dumb as hell. All the money to my name was either fronted out through drugs, to the hustlers in Norfolk and Norview or either I had it on me the night I went in. Aint no telling what the Police did with that shit.

And you'd think with everyone buying my music and supporting me and shit, someone would help. But naw. Can't really blame them though, to tell the truth I didn't even reach out to anybody and ask. Never even opened none of the many letters I'd received. Maybe I should have. I don't know. But I felt like either way, in jail or the streets, I aint feel like facing life. I had reached a point where I didn't' give a fuck about shit anymore. Fuck rap, fuck everything. I had a chip on my shoulder big as the moon.

I went in straight savage mode. Feelings and consequences won't nothing I could comprehend. Fear was in the air whenever I stepped foot anywhere inside of the jail. I was the big youngin, I ran shit, silently. It won't no secret I had robbed damn near half the jail. But what the fuck was they gonna do about it? Everybody knew I was a loose cannon that could explode at any second. They aint want no problems.

When the deputy screamed 'Trays gentleman Trays' at chow time niggas knew to be extra careful. Depending on what mood I was in, I might just take your shit.

I couldn't help it though. Nightmares of Dock burning in hell haunted me nightly. Slowly I started to lose my mind and control of myself.

If I was hungry I stole, mad I fought, I didn't giva a fuck. I do remember this one ol head who tried to save me though. He sat me down and had a talk with me. I can't really remember word for word. But it went a little something like this.

"Ya know, it's crazy how we hurt our families when we keep it real to the streets. Man, boy does the Devil Dance. I know exactly how you feel. You want to live the right way, it's just hard. I know what you been going through youngin, I can see it in your eyes. You hurt. But you gotta remember life aint over. At least not yet. Me on the other hand, I'm done, I just got sentenced to 30 years. But it's still light at the end of your tunnel. You just gotta make sure you tighten up once you get released. See, in this life you can run outta chances. Youngin, do your math and count all your blessings," he preached.

I listened, I knew he was just trying to school me, cause he had learned his lesson. Still later that week when he got his cantine, even though he used to share with me, I took all his food. When he found out he tried to talk it out. I punched his old ass in the face. We fought hard asa bitch. Ol head was pretty strong. Naw he aint whip my ass or nothing but it was a good ass fight. But all that was irrelevant foreal. We both ended up in the hole.

During that time God was sorta on my bad side. It's like the Devil was in my ear over powering his voice causing me to blame God for all my problems. Now that I look at it, it doesn't really make any sense what I was doing. I was cursing him, telling him that I knew he didn't exist, so in actuality what I was doing was basically talking to myself. I guess deep down I sorta hoped I was wrong about him being unreal. Probably one of the main reasons I asked his 'Unreal' ass "How dare you force me to be in the streets. Only thing that shit ever bought me was pain. Nigga if you really real, give me a sign. Give me a sign that this life aint no bullshit."

And like clockwork, the next day I got a sign.

Dear Sky,

I wanted to write you sooner. I just didn't know what to say. Can't lie a part of me wanted you to suffer. But it seemed like the more I tried to, the more I thought about you. I saw you in my dreams, everything reminded me of you. I can't imagine how you're feeling. Yes I know you hurt me by your actions. But I honestly know you didn't mean to. I know you love me. You're just stupid and no matter how bad I told myself I wanted to, I just can't leave you in there by yourself. I know how much Dock meant to you. And I also know how much our baby would have meant. I cry every time I think about how you must feel. I know you're tough. I know you're ok in there but I know you're hurt. I wish I could break you out of that place. You'll get through this. I know you will. Oh yeah, can you believe they've been playing your song on the radio! Everybody loves you. I know you're going to make it out and take over. I just know it.

But anyway. I love you. Can't wait for you to get back. And I would like for us to start over. If that's ok. I hate life without you.

P.S. As you can see my address is different. Francis kicked me out of the house once he found out that I had gotten pregnant by you. I'm staying at Tierra's.

Love Alex xoxo

For the first time in I don't know how long, I could finally think. My head was clear. I stopped looking at myself as the victim and realized that maybe I deserved the shit that was going on in my life. Ya know, when you a street nigga sometimes you do so much dirt that you forget some of the wrong you'd done over the years. Only thing is, Karma never does.

Once again I knew I had a purpose in life. Right then and there I began beating on my cell with my hands, rapping aloud.

'What's the use of joy, when pain follows so close..

What's the use of love, when I can't trust a hoe ...

What's the use of friends, when they act like a foe ...

What's the use of grind if I never touch gold...

I'm askin God questions that only he knows...

Sometimes I feel my soul's been re-poed...

I pray for strength to get me through ...

But I never see change ...

So what's the use...

what's the use ... '

By the end of the song. I had grown men crying.

And just when I was coming back to believing and trusting in God. He gave me even more of a reason to believe. The next day I made bond. And with that bond I got an even closer bond to him. Not saying I never veered away but I always knew if I did what I was supposed to do which was touch people with my music, in return he would always make a way for me.

Still, I aint know who the fuck had bonded me out until I walked outside. After taking a whiff of the air I'd missed for 6 months I heard a strangely familiar voice coming from the left of me.

I looked over, I couldn't believe what I was seeing, it was one of my favorite rappers 'Surf Rider' sitting in a Benz Truck. "What sup big dog you ready to get this money?" he said.

Outro

"Nana sit down," said Sharly. "Hold on one second Coach."

AMERICAN RAP STAR 2 COMING SOON!

If you enjoyed American Rap Star make sure you spread the word.

If you purchased on Amazon or Kindle please leave a review.

If you're in Prison please request to get this book and my other books 'American Maniac, 'American Boy' and 'Us Vs. Them' in the building!

Thank you for the support. If you need to contact me call 757-708-4890

Facebook: Kevin Brown
Instagram: __KevinBrown
or email
Americanboybook@aol.com

Thank You!

Made in the USA
Columbia, SC
21 April 2018